The Hero Laughs While Walking the Path of VENGEANCE a Second Time

5 The Selfish Village Girl

NERO KIZUKA

Illustration by **SINSORA**

YEN ON

NEW YORK

The Hero Laughs While Walking the Path of VENGEANCE a Second Time

5

NERO KIZUKA

TRANSLATION BY JAKE HUMPHREY • COVER ART BY SINSORA

NIDOME NO YUSHA WA FUKUSYU NO MICHI O WARAI AYUMU Vol. 5
KYOEIBITARI NO MURABITO
©Kizuka Nero 2018
First published in Japan in 2018 by KADOKAWA CORPORATION, Tokyo.
English translation rights arranged with KADOKAWA CORPORATION, Tokyo, through TUTTLE-MORI AGENCY, INC., Tokyo.

Yen On
150 W 30th Street, 19th Floor
New York, NY 10001

Visit us at yenpress.com • facebook.com/yenpress • twitter.com/yenpress
yenpress.tumblr.com • instagram.com/yenpress

First Yen On Edition: April 2023
Edited by Yen On Editorial: Maya Deutsch
Designed by Yen Press Design: Eddy Mingki, Wendy Chan

Yen On is an imprint of Yen Press, LLC.
The Yen On name and logo are trademarks of Yen Press, LLC.

Library of Congress Cataloging-in-Publication Data
Names: Kizuka, Nero, author. | Sinsora, illustrator. | Humphrey, Jake, translator.
Title: The hero laughs while walking the path of vengeance a second time /
Nero Kizuka ; illustration by Sinsora ; translation by Jake Humphrey.
Other titles: Nidome no yusha wa fukushuu no michi wo warai ayumu. English
Description: First Yen On edition. | New York, NY : Yen On, 2021.
Identifiers: LCCN 2021038196 | ISBN 9781975323707 (v. 1 ; trade paperback) |
ISBN 9781975323721 (v. 2 ; trade paperback) | ISBN 9781975323745 (v. 3 ; trade paperback) |
ISBN 9781975323769 (v. 4 ; trade paperback) | ISBN 9781975323783 (v. 5 ; trade paperback)
Subjects: LCGFT: Fantasy fiction. | Light novels.
Classification: LCC PL872.5.I97 N5313 2021 | DDC 895.63/6—dc23
LC record available at https://lccn.loc.gov/2021038196

ISBNs: 978-1-9753-2378-3 (paperback)
978-1-9753-2379-0 (ebook)

10 9 8 7 6 5 4 3 2 1

LSC-C

Printed in the United States of America

The Hero Laughs
While Walking the Path of
VENGEANCE
a Second
Time

5

"I promise to lead a happy life."

LUCIA

"You can never bring back what we've lost."

KAITO UKEI

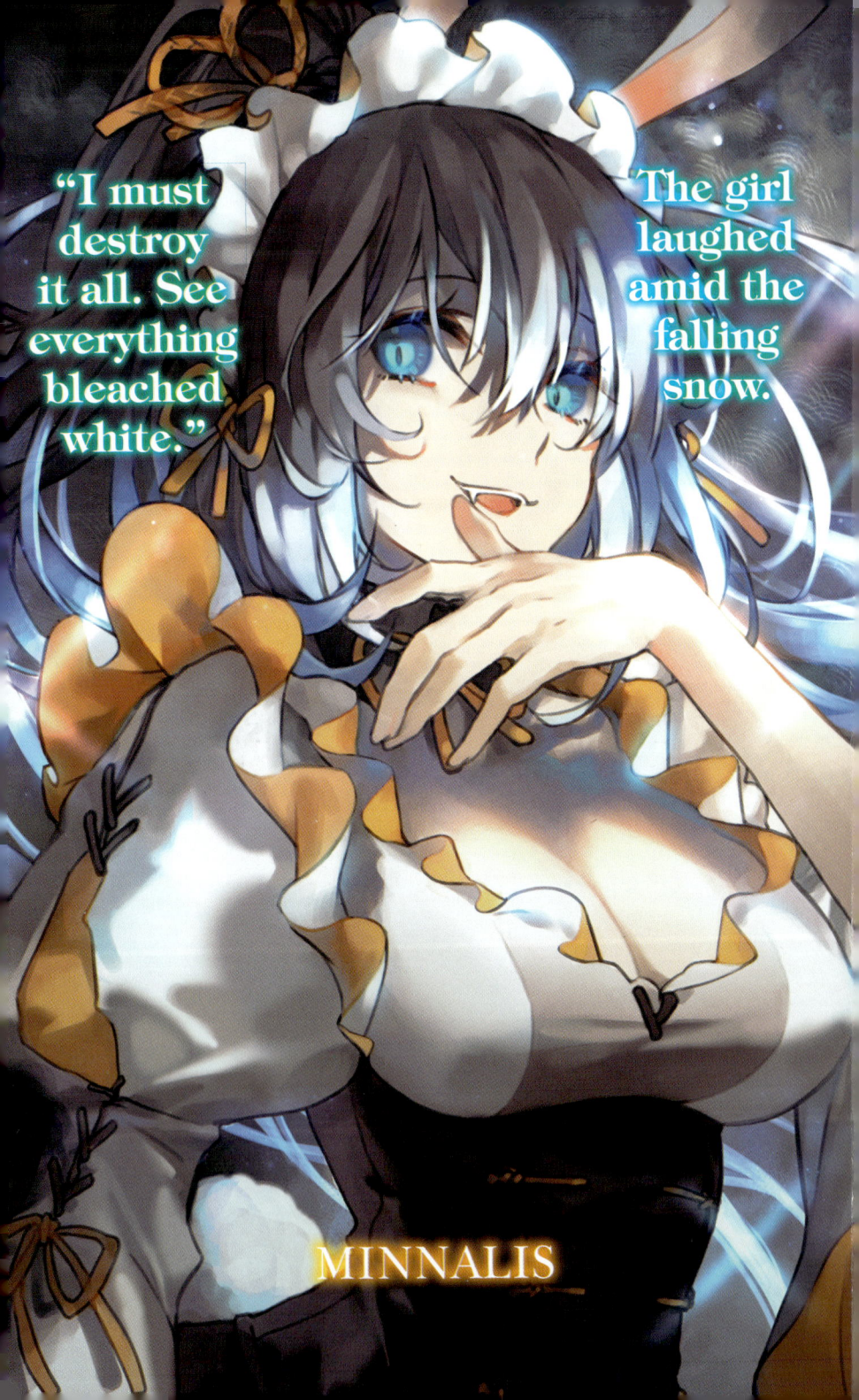

"I must destroy it all. See everything bleached white."

The girl laughed amid the falling snow.

MINNALIS

5 The Selfish Village Girl

The Hero Laughs While Walking the Path of VENGEANCE a Second Time

NERO KIZUKA

CONTENTS

"You need to be destroyed, don't you?"

"I will find my
happiness,
I swear!"

PROLOGUE

The world I lived in was like a fairy tale, a blanket of snow that seemed to stretch on forever, twinkling oh-so beautifully in the sunlight.

There I lived out my life, a merry lie. And long did I remain blind to that lie.

Until the day those walls appeared.

They knocked me back, and I sat dumbstruck on the floor, struggling to comprehend. I turned and looked behind me…

…and found only a world of dirt and muck.

Before I could flinch, I was struck with a snowball packed full of mud and pebbles. And there I spotted her, looking down at me from her hiding place. It was then that I realized.

My boundless world was far smaller than I'd thought.

*   *   *

My beautiful world was far uglier than I'd thought.

Beneath that thin blanket of snow was a swamp of sneering smiles, filled with people who threw stones at me long before I could even get close.

That's all it was. That's all that village ever was.

To a rabbit like me.

CHAPTER 1
The Egg Hatches, and the Hero Gives a Troubled Sigh

From our room in the Dartras inn, I heard the church bells toll noon. It had been two nights, and Master still had not woken up.

After what had happened with Grond, Master had trusted us to take care of him, so Shuria and I were taking turns watching him.

"…Master."

I stroked his cheek as he lay silently in the bed. The wounds on his face were healed, but they had left scars.

"…"

He was looking much healthier now than he had been when all this started. The first night was the worst, and I had doubted if his pain would ever end. Now it was almost like he could spring to life at any moment, yet the only sounds were that of his quiet breathing.

"It's going to be okay," I told myself. "Everything's going to be all right." But my heart felt as though it was tearing its way out of my chest. I hated feeling like this. It was just like when my mother had died. I knew Master's life was in no danger, yet I couldn't help but be reminded of her as I looked at him. Her gaunt jaw, her thinning arms, her slackening skin. The smile with which she had drawn her last breath.

I couldn't do anything for her. And I couldn't do anything for him, either. I hated feeling so powerless.

"...Nmgh."

"Master?!"

Just then, Master's eyes slowly fluttered open. Two feelings crossed my mind at that moment: First, a relief so powerful I felt I would cry, and second, a desire that dwarfed any and all I had previously harbored.

I needed to become worthy of standing by his side.

No, I didn't need to. I wanted to.

I wanted to spend the rest of my vengeance with him.

"Master?!"

"...Heh. You should see the look on your face."

When I came to, I saw Minnalis's face above mine. She appeared concerned, like I was going to die. It was an expression I'd seen many times before.

"How are you, son? Do you think you can hold down an apple?"

"Here, I made porridge. It's hot, so don't burn your tongue."

"I went out and bought you some pudding, dear brother. I'll feed it to you so you don't get it all over yourself like a pig."

Whenever I got a cold, my father, mother, and little sister Mai would take turns taking care of me, making the same face that Minnalis was making now. I grinned and sat up.

"I'm so glad you're awake," she said. "Is there anything you need? Does it still hurt?"

"I'm fine, don't worry," I reassured her. "Though I suppose you will anyway. How many days have I been out?"

"Today's the third. The midday bells just rang."

"I see... I am starving, actually. Do you think you could make me a stew? Something I don't have to chew, with lots of meat and vegetables."

"Of course, Master! I'll begin immediately!!"

"Thanks a lot, I...oh."

Minnalis left the room so quickly she nearly tripped over her own feet. I didn't even think she heard me. Given her dedication to a good lunch, I suspected she'd be gone for some time.

"Ghh... Damn, that hurts..."

I slowly laid down in bed again. I felt incredibly heavy, as though my whole body had been replaced with lead and my joints had rusted up like a neglected tin doll's. They cried out in protest each time I tried to move.

Having someone else's mana worm its way through your body was never a good sensation.

"I didn't think this curse would follow me through the reset."

It was a curse the priestess had placed upon me. Or to put it in their terms, a covenant. It activated whenever I used and dismissed one of the "Sword of Sin" soul blades, and it allowed the priestess to discern my approximate location, while filling my body with foreign mana. That mana would then be rejected, like a blood transfusion of the wrong type, causing a state of paralysis much like the one I was in now. Not even healing magic could do anything about it. The only thing I could do was wait for the foreign mana to leave my system.

Needless to say, both of these effects were highly inconvenient.

The damage caused by mana rejection wasn't anything I couldn't handle, especially at the peak of my first life, but the Sword of Sin series of soul blades also came with their own costs. As such, they were only to be used in the most dire of circumstances. Between the risk of handing my location over to the enemy while immobilized from mana consumption, the curse's effects, and the soul blade's own costs, you can see why I'd considered the Swords of Sin to be effectively forbidden when I'd been on the run during my previous life.

"...Perhaps it's time I started thinking about grinding some levels?"

I was still only level 1, as the only thing I'd spent my experience points on was unlocking soul blades. But I would need higher stats if I was going to be able to deal with this curse. Its effects had almost completely subsided, yet even now I felt so exhausted that I was finding it hard to stay awake.

"No," I said, shaking my head. "I can't waste my experience points like that. At least not until I kill *her*."

The effects of the curse weren't lethal in themselves. And the only one scouring the land for me at present was the princess. Above all else, I had my partners in crime to protect me.

"...It's fine. If this pain can buy her despair, then it's a small price to pay."

Laugh at my suffering if you must, but know that each drop of blood is the coin with which I purchase your heads.

The time was not yet right. Sooner or later, I would need to raise my level, but that would have to wait. If this was the worst I had to endure, then I could push through. It would be the height of folly to throw away everything I'd worked for in pursuit of my vengeance so far.

My one concern was the possibility of the priestess learning my whereabouts. At this point in time, she wouldn't know who I was. Besides, there was still unrest within the Church. Even if she did her research and found out about me, they wouldn't just let their precious figurehead up and leave.

That's all far off in the future, though. Right now, I have to focus on cleaning up around these parts.

Perhaps this was just my way of trying to make amends for all that I'd done the first time around. But still, I needed to do it. Minnalis and Shuria should have gotten started while I was asleep.

"Three days, huh? It's going to be rough, but let's get some food in me and then see what the deal is out there."

My soul blades and skills were still sealed. Nothing would happen if I tried to conjure my trusty weapons. When I attempted to focus my mana, it felt unresponsive, like pushing water with a knife edge. The foreign mana coursing through my veins caused me constant irritation, too.

Nevertheless, I was awake, and I could still act. That was the most important thing.

"...And I can't just force those two to clean up after my mess."

The next day, I visited the slums on the outskirts of town. I headed to a building at the heart of the district, beyond even the territory of those Lemonade dealers.

I didn't come here to drink tea, though. I was here to strike a deal.

"...Ah, I see. That's pretty much in line with our expectations, then."

Before me sat the boss of these slums. An unremarkable man, with an unremarkable face. He listened to his officer's report, then turned to me.

"We've finished assessing the goods," he said. "We'll split it fifty-fifty, like we agreed. Here's your half."

With a loud jingle, the man dropped a pouch of silver coins on the desk. It was half the money he expected to make from selling Grond's former assets. Their part of the deal had been smuggling me onto Grond's convoy; killing him had been mine.

"..."

"Hey, don't look at me like that. I know what you're thinkin', but I ain't about to screw over a friend of Diufain's. You know what they'd do to me if I tried?" The man sighed and shrugged. "Take a look inside if you want. It's all there. Every last coin."

After a short pause, I replied, "Well, not like it would even matter. I wasn't in it for the money, anyway."

Any profit I made from the whole affair was a neat bonus, a tidy little bow on my otherwise perfectly wrapped vengeance. Still, it never hurts to have more cash.

After I took the money, however, I grabbed the man by the collar and pulled him close.

"Grh!!"

"Hey, hands off!!"

I ignored the lapdog's defensive barking and whispered in the man's ear.

"This silver means nothing to me, understand? The bag could be full of rocks for all I care. But renege on our *other* deal…"

My words were slow, deliberate, like a curse.

"…and you'll be next. Got that?"

"Don't you worry," replied the man, with nary a batted eye, nor bead of sweat. "I don't go messin' with monsters."

He's a tough customer. I guess that's what it takes to lead the slums.

My threats did little to sway the man, but so long as he kept to our agreement, then it was all the same to me.

"I'll hold you to that," I said. Then I finally let go of him and left.

"Gosh, what lovely weather. I bet the children's clothes will be dry in no time."

I hung up the laundry to dry on the clothesline, basking in the sun's warmth. After picking up the last item, I stared at the empty wicker basket.

"..."

Today marked two months since my husband's passing. I was slowly getting used to a life without him, a life that once I could never have imagined.

"Working hard as usual, I see, Miss Myun!"

"Oh, Euphon!"

A woman called out to me. She was the head of a trading company from whom I often purchased daily necessities. The two of us had been friends ever since we were girls, and she had even helped build the schoolhouse alongside my husband. She'd been one of the orphanage's staunchest allies ever since.

"I just caught myself craving your cooking," she said. "Here, I brought some pretty nice stuff, so why don't we cut a deal?"

She giggled and shook a basket containing food items at me.

"Should you really be taking time off work?" I cautioned her. "I heard there's been some kind of trouble recently, hasn't there?"

Rumors of money disappearing from merchant coffers had not managed to escape my ears. Based on how Euphon had been acting lately, I figured it had happened to her, too. It seemed like she'd been working hard to cover the loss.

"Oh, that," she replied. "Yeah, I don't really get how, but it sorted itself out." She scratched her cheek, almost looking a little embarrassed. "I guess you heard the story, right? All the money from you-know-who suddenly vanished?"

"...Yeah."

When she reminded me of that man and his company, I felt a little knot in the pit of my stomach. They had pestered me into giving up my husband's sword, the Leafstone Blade, even resorting to threats and intimidation. My husband had been adamant about hanging on to the sword, and it was the only thing I had left to remember him by after he died. Selling it was the worst decision of my life, but I'd had no choice. It was the only way to keep the orphanage afloat.

Even now, I felt those old wounds reopen whenever I heard that company's name. In fact, I couldn't even find it in myself to be happy when I learned that the Grond Company had gone bankrupt.

"Well, you didn't hear this from me," said Euphon, "but the truth is…every last coin came back."

"What?"

"I know, right? I just went into the vault one day and found that it was back, with a little extra on top, too. I talked to the other companies, and they all said the same thing happened to them."

"Wow. How strange."

"That's not how I would put it. *Concerning*, more like. What's it say about my security if the thief can just come and go as they please?"

Euphon gave a deep sigh and shrugged in exasperation.

"Anyway, that's the sitch. Hey, at least it means I can swing by here a little more often. I'll be inside. I'm itching to soothe my weary bones with some of your fine cooking."

And with that, she headed into the building, not even waiting for my answer.

"Oh, Euphon…" I sighed. "I told you that you don't have to do that."

I picked up the empty basket. I knew her job wasn't so easy that she could "swing by" whenever she felt like it. I was truly blessed to have such a great friend.

"…The kids should be back soon. I'd better make them a meal to remember."

""""Miss Myun!!""""

As if on cue, I heard several voices calling me from a distance. I turned to see the children waving eagerly to me. It was almost noon, so they had come back from their playtime.

"Miss Myun! Look at this! I made you a present—it's a shiny mudball!"

"Stop it, Kelly," said Shenfa. "Girls don't want to see that!"

"Whaddaya mean?" replied the boy, pouting. "Can't you see how shiny it is?"

In his hands was a brilliantly smooth sphere of mud, gleaming like metal in the sun.

"She's right, Kelly!" came a voice from behind him. "Miss Myun is a lady, she doesn't wanna see your mudballs! This is why I can't stand boys!"

It was Toria. She was very quickly maturing into a young lady and was past the age where she could engage with the boys in their silly games. Girls will be girls, after all.

Toria ran up to me, one hand behind her back, the other pulling frantically at the hem of my dress. "Miss Myun!" she said. "Bend down, bend down!"

"Hmm? What is it?" I replied.

"Quickly, quickly!"

"Oh, okay…"

I did as she said, and Toria gave a lovely smile before placing something atop my head.

"Eh-he-he! I got you a present, Miss Myun!"

"Wow, look at Miss Myun! She looks just like a princess!"

"Whoa! You're so pretty!"

"Huh? What's…what's this?"

I took it off my head to take a look at it. It was a beautiful crown of flowers Toria had made. Handwoven, with yellow and white petals, and as precious as any princess's tiara.

11

"It's wonderful," I said. "It looks just like the real thing."

"Heh-hem. I made it myself!"

"Me too, me too! I helped!" said Shenfa.

"But you shouldn't take it off, it's supposed to go on your head! Here, bend over again and I'll put it back on for you."

"Oh, very well, if you insist..."

I kneeled on the ground, and Toria replaced the crown on my head.

The two girls giggled and told me how pretty it looked. Meanwhile, Kelly grumbled off to the side.

"Hmph. My mudball is pretty, too. Look at how shiny it is! I thought girls liked shiny things?"

"Gosh, Kelly. You don't get it at *all*. Girls don't want just *anything* shiny—they want jewelry, not mudballs!"

"Whaaat? That can't be right. Tell her, Shenfa!"

"Well," said Toria, "I heard from the receptionist lady that diamonds are a girl's best friend! That's why my present is much better than your stupid old ball of dirt! Right, Shenfa?"

"Huh?! Oh, er... um..."

Shenfa was lost for words as the other two children each vied for her support.

"Now, now, kids. Can't you see you're bothering the poor girl? Let's all just settle down, shall we?"

I kneeled down and took the sparkling ball of mud out of Kelly's hands.

"I love both your gifts. The tiara and this shiny mudball. Thank you so much, all of you."

The three children all looked at one another for a moment. Then, they turned their eyes back on me.

""""You really mean it?! Does that mean you're not sad anymore?"""""

"Huh?"

I wasn't quite sure what they meant. It was Toria who spoke up next.

"The thing is, I saw you crying last night, Miss Myun. That's why we all talked about the best way of cheering you up. So...um...we decided to make you something that would make you happy again... Did it work?"

The children peered at me with upturned eyes. I embraced the three of them, ready to cry.

"...Yes! Yes, you've made me very happy...!"

""""Yay!! It worked!"""""

I felt their tiny warmth in my arms, reminding me that I hadn't yet lost everything. *This* was what remained of my husband. *This* was what I needed to protect.

"But children, I've never seen you make these before. Who taught you how to do it?"

"The man with black hair did!!"

"And there was, there was a bunny lady and a girl with silver hair there, too!"

"I bet they're in a threesome! That's what the receptionist lady said happens when a guy likes two girls!"

"...Did she now?"

Perhaps I ought to reconsider letting Toria visit the Adventurer's Guild. I had hoped she would pick up some experience for when she got old enough to find a job, but this wasn't exactly the kind of experience I'd had in mind...

"Did you remember to thank them?" I asked.

""""Yes, Miss Myun!"""" came their bright and eager replies.

"But when Toria said thank you to the black-haired man, she made him cry," said Shenfa.

"Yeah," agreed Kelly. "I thought adventurers were supposed to be tough guys, but he was a real softie."

"Oh, really?" I asked. Toria nodded in agreement.

"But he was smiling as he cried. I told him he was weird, and he said 'Yeah, I am.' I think he was just making fun of me 'cause he thought I was a kid. Can't he tell I'm all grown up already?"

Toria folded her arms and scrunched up her face.

All kinds of people ended up as adventurers. That man must have been carrying some deep trauma if Toria's expression of gratitude had moved him to tears.

Just then, I heard Euphon calling out to me from inside the orphanage.

"H-hey, Myun! Get over here, quick!" she cried. She must have gotten sick of waiting for me to start cooking. The children all heard her voice, and their little faces lit up with glee.

"Oh, Euphon's here!"

"Yay, that means lunch is going to be extra yummy today!!"

Euphon frequently came to visit, and when she did she brought quality ingredients for me to cook with. That meant that not only were the children used to her presence, but they also very much looked forward to it. The children also worked part-time picking apples in one of the orchards Euphon's company owned, and they were allowed to play there in return. The other kids were probably still there.

"Can you three go and call the others over? I'll get started on lunch."

""""Yes!""""

The three children gave an enthusiastic response and ran off toward the orchard. Then I went inside to prepare everyone a delicious meal.

"What took you so long?" asked Euphon as I entered. For some reason, she was standing in a corner of the kitchen, having spread out all the ingredients she had brought for me on the kitchen table.

It was all of high quality, stuff that I could never afford to eat on a daily basis.

"You don't have to be so impatient. I'm making your lunch, just sit tight."

"That's not it, look!!"

I couldn't for the life of me tell what Euphon was so excited about. "What is it?" I asked.

"Can't you see it?! Aargh!!"

She came over and grabbed me by the arm, pulling me into the corner of the room.

"Look!" she cried. "What on earth is this?!"

"Hmm? I don't know what you..."

I glanced where Euphon was pointing and saw a wooden box. It was filled to the brim with money. But it wasn't the coins that caught my eye.

"Where did you get all this cash from? You could open a shop with this! And this sword, what's with the...? Hey, Myun?"

By now her voice sounded distant and faded. I couldn't take my eyes off it.

"That sword... It's..."

Lying atop the pile of gold coins was a single blade inside a dark green scabbard engraved with ochre trimmings. The grip looked like a tree trunk, and even the hilt was made of twisted raw wood. It was unmistakable. It was the sword with which I had been protected many times, the memento of my late husband, the Leafstone Blade.

"Ahhh...ahhh...aaaaahhh!"

I couldn't contain my elation. Before I knew what I was doing, I grabbed the sword and hugged it, crying. Even though I promised myself I would never shed a tear again.

It felt impossibly warm and comforting, almost as if my husband were hugging me back.

It was a dark, moonless night. In the depths of the forest, we sat around a crackling bonfire eating supper, a vegetable stir-fry that Minnalis had made for us. Shuria, however, was particularly concerned by the presence of an eggplant-looking vegetable in her dinner, and I caught her in the midst of sneaking it into the mouth of her pussycat doll.

"...Shuria, make sure you eat all your veggies," I said.

"Eep!" the girl squealed, and the doll echoed her cry of fright with its characteristic "Khii-hii-hii!" noise.

She had done well to hide her behavior from Minnalis, but unfortunately for her, I could see everything from where I was sitting. The bunny girl turned around and looked at her with a smile that barely concealed her displeasure.

"Oh, Shuria. Again?"

"B-but it's all gooey and I don't like it!!" protested Shuria, shaking her head furiously. "That is no vegetable, it is the fruit of the devil!"

Shuria had never encountered this eggplant-like vegetable prior to meeting us, and it seemed she was unable to stomach the texture. It wasn't like I couldn't sympathize with her plight, but...anyway, that was not relevant right now.

"How many times have I told you?" chided Minnalis. "You mustn't waste food. It doesn't matter whether you like it or not..."

"Then does that mean Kaito has to eat bugs?"

"Minnalis," I said, stepping in. "Everyone has one or two things they don't like. It's not going to kill her if she avoids a few vegetables, right?"

"Master... Don't you start, too. You think I don't see what you're up to?"

My flawless attempt at smoothing things over nonetheless earned me a sharp rebuke from Minnalis. If her gaze had been any icier, my meal would have gone cold.

"You mustn't waste food," she reiterated. "That goes for the both of you. Come on, Shuria, why don't you eat it with the meat? You like that, don't you?"

Minnalis wrapped the not-eggplant up in a strip of meat and offered it to the girl. Shuria gave it a sour look but opened her mouth.

"Ugh... *Om.*"

"Good girl. What a good girl you are," said Minnalis, stroking her head.

"Please stop that... You're making it hard to eat!" Shuria complained. Still, she didn't seem *entirely* put off.

Seeing her like that made me recall something.

Oh yeah, this is how I got the orphanage kids to eat things they didn't like, too.

My sister had always been a fussy eater, which had given me plenty of practice.

I hope they have a good life this time. They deserve that much, at least.

It had been two weeks since we put the town of Dartras behind us. We'd returned all the stolen money to its original owners, plus a little extra for the trouble. The remainder went to the orphanage, along with a little something I'd picked up along the way. Lastly, I'd left the slum bosses with a warning: Mess with the orphanage, and I'd see to it they paid the price.

That was all I could realistically do. From here on out, I could only pray things would be okay.

As much as I'd like to say their safety was my top priority, I think we can all agree that it wasn't. If I really wanted what was best for the children, I would stay in Dartras and watch over them forever, but that wasn't on the table. I had my vengeance to complete.

It's better to do something than nothing.

I wouldn't forget them. But I had to keep moving on. There was no other option. My enemies were still many, and I needed to crush every last one of them into a thick paste.

My mind swam with the possibilities, and before I knew it, my plate was empty.

"Urgh. My mouth still feels funny. That *was* the fruit of the devil, I am sure of it!"

Suddenly, there came a cool gust of wind that rustled the dry grass.

"Eep! That's chilly!" yelped Shuria, clutching the hems of her cloak, which was imbued with the skill "Retain Heat." Minnalis had grown up in a cold region, and I was accustomed by now to the most extreme environments this world had to offer. Shuria, by comparison, had only ever known the balmy climate of Elmia and its surrounding villages. While her clothes, like Minnalis's, already came with a stack of Retain Heat, a second one was handy for cold temperatures like these. It seemed like it would snow at any moment.

"It does tend to get cold this far west," I noted. "But don't worry—tomorrow we'll be arriving in Karvanheim, the city of magic. They have a great big barrier there that stretches out over the whole city to keep the inside nice and pleasant. You just need to hold out until we get there."

After crossing the imperial border to the north of the kingdom, we'd set our sights on Karvanheim, the realm of sorcery. Sharing a name with its capital, Karvanheim was a small nation founded some time ago by a group of wizards displaced by war, and it was located in what was now the intersection of the three great nations. Though only about five percent the size of its neighbors, it had made a name for itself as the frontier of magical engineering.

Karvanheim was founded around the same time as the empire, but unlike its territory-grabbing neighbor, the country had opted to focus on bolstering its defenses. To that end, the wizards of Karvanheim had developed a series of barriers: one that covered each city, and a larger one that stretched across the entire nation. This large barrier prevented wizards below a certain level of ability from casting magic of any kind, while the smaller barriers protected the cities from physical and magical bombardment. Thus, the territories of Karvanheim were cheap to defend and costly for foreign powers to invade. This was how it had survived all this time stuck in the middle of the kingdom, the empire, and the beast lands.

Karvanheim had also adopted a policy of neutrality and nonaggression, focusing its efforts not into war, but in advancing magical comprehension. Preeminent spellcasters from all across the world came there to train and hone their skills. *Our* agenda, meanwhile, consisted of getting into one of the nation's magical academies to gain access to a dungeon nearby.

"I've prepared some small ricolle fruits, so let's have them for dessert," Minnalis suggested. "They're supposed to prevent disease when you cook them."

"Oh!" exclaimed Shuria. "I'll have two!"

"All right. But don't come crying to me if you get a bellyache."

Minnalis sighed and took out four small fruits the size of tangerines. She really did spoil that girl sometimes. She placed the fruits on the same skewers we'd used for supper and held them over the flame. While they cooked, we listened to the crackle of the bonfire.

"Right then," I said at last. "Let's go over the plan one more time.

First, we register as students of the academy. We're only going to be here for a short time, just enough to take a few courses. Many adventurers stop here to learn magic, so we won't stand out at all."

I looked around at the faces of my companions. "After that," I continued, "I want you two to take the exam that'll get you into the advanced class, where they teach the founding theory of magic."

The advanced course was only open to those with a certain level of magical ability, and it was there you learned to become a true mage. The basic class taught you how to use magic, but the advanced class expounded on the theory behind it.

"Meanwhile," I went on, "I'll be running the dungeon solo, squeezing every last experience point I can out of it while also reclaiming my old equipment. I'll probably be down there for three weeks or so, in which time I want you two to continue taking classes as usual."

"Master! You mean you're leaving us behind? How cruel! Boo-hoo-hoo!"

"I don't want to go! Please don't leave me all alone! Boo-hoo-hoo!"

"…Guys, I already told you all this," I said, straight-faced. "And what's with those perfectly synchronized crocodile tears? Did you both plan this?"

"We are doing a silent protest."

"It's our secret, secret rebellion!"

"There's nothing silent or secret about it," I said with a sigh.

"…But Master, you're asking us to take lessons from a country that once scorned you," Minnalis explained.

"I know it's important, but that doesn't mean I have to like it," added Shuria.

I sighed again, and the two turned away from me, pouting.

As was probably evident in my exposition just now, Karvanheim was a country that placed a weighty importance on magic. And as I seem to recall explaining at some point, my own magical affinities were big fat zeroes across the board. I had taught myself to manipulate mana, but weaving a single spell was beyond me. Of course, this wasn't too big a problem thanks to my soul blades, but the land of Karvanheim had little love for someone like me, who couldn't even cast the most basic of spells. They'd respected me as the hero the first time around, of course, or at least they'd pretended to, but that was about it.

"There's no use arguing about it," I explained. "I know next to nothing about casting magic, so there's only so much I can teach you. If we want Minnalis's Magic skills to become Sorceries, or to stop relying on Shuria's Puppet Possession, then I'm afraid you'll both have to go to school."

This was the crux of the problem. I could come up with all sorts of novel ways of exploiting spell craft by drawing upon my knowledge of science, but it was useless without a solid grounding in the magical theory of this world. And they'd never let *me* into the advanced class, because I couldn't cast a single spell.

But Minnalis was a different story—she had high magical affinities, which she'd been relying on in lieu of a proper magical understanding so far. Shuria also had high Misc. Affinity, so while she probably wouldn't be allowed to learn any holy magic, as that was a closely guarded secret of the Church, she would at least be able to pick up some curses or hexes.

"Once we enter the city," I declared, "I'm banning all use of your intrinsic abilities."

""Whaaat?""

"Don't give me that. You guys go through mana like a drunk in a wine cellar, and it has pretty much the same effect. With a little bit of theory under your belt, perhaps you can learn to cast spells more efficiently."

The two girls shared a guilty glance.

"Do you even *know* how hammered you get?" I asked.

MP drunkenness diminished your inhibitions, strengthening your primal instincts. It was similar to alcohol, including how it affected people differently. In my case, MP drunkenness was like pulling an all-nighter; it either made me super excited or put me on the verge of passing out, rambling incoherently.

With Minnalis and Shuria, it was like their, shall we say, *private* emotions came to the fore. I wish they would spare a thought for me, who had to deal with it all the time.

"Well..."

"Kind of..."

The two looked down at their feet. "B-but," Minnalis began, "You're also to blame, Master! You're always coming up with these complex ways of killing people, adding more and more steps that require us to use more and more mana to keep up! I haven't gotten a chance to know my limits yet..."

"And it was you who told us practice makes perfect, Kaito! That's why we use our skills all the time. It's not our fault!"

"W-well, I guess so..."

Now it was my turn to look at my feet. I couldn't quite refute either of their points.

"A-anyway! Our upcoming foes will be the strongest yet! Not to mention that monsters are growing more powerful by the day. Soon, there'll come a time when you won't be able to rely on your intrinsic abilities anymore! That's why you need to learn the basics of magic! And that's final!"

My declaration was punctuated by the perfectly synchronized sizzling of the bonfire. The fruit juices were just starting to come out, dripping onto the flames.

"Ah, I wonder if that means they're done?" I asked.

"*Hmph*. Don't think you can change the subject that easily, Master. But you're right. We mustn't let them cook any further."

"This one's mine! ♪" sang Shuria, zooming over to the largest fruit and securing it for herself.

"Shuria, settle down! They still need to cool!"

"No they don— Ah! Ow! The juice burned my mouth…"

"Oh Shuria, I told you to be careful…"

Minnalis gave a sigh of resignation and handed her some ice-cold water, cooled with magic.

"Owww…" Shuria whined. "My tongue still hurts. Hmm, but it feels kind of nice, too…"

She put her hand to her cheek and gave an oddly relaxed smile. Whenever she wasn't pursuing her revenge, the girl reverted to her hedonistic tendencies. Anyone who didn't know any better might look at her and think she was daydreaming about her Prince Charming, but I knew the disappointing truth.

Oh well, different strokes, I suppose. It's not exactly my fault… is it?

"Oh, I almost forgot. We must remember to feed the Kuu egg," I said, reaching into my bag and pulling out something that looked like a fish tank. The four sides were made of glass, surrounding a pale egg lying atop a bed of dried grass. This was in fact the Wall Eater I'd picked up while leaving the capital. I had been feeding it with mana-infused meat ever since, hoping it would come in handy one day, and it had grown larger over time. A few days ago, however, it had suddenly transformed into an egg, and because Minnalis had taken to caring for the worm and calling it "Kuu," the resulting specimen was dubbed the "Kuu egg."

I placed the cage on the ground and the egg within began to rattle. Even in this form, Kuu wanted to be fed, but since it lacked a mouth, the only way we could give it the mana it so desired was to pick it up in our arms and allow it to suck the magical energy out of us. After it had eaten-slash-drunk enough, the egg would shake, as if to tell us it was full, and stop.

This appeared to be the egg's version of a meal, so we allowed it to feed this way three times a day.

"All-righty! It's my turn!" said Shuria, standing up with great enthusiasm and stuffing the other ricolle fruit into her mouth. "Owowow!"

Burning her tongue a second time, she walked over to the container.

This was our regular routine. First, Shuria would impart her mana to the egg.

"I've got lots and lots of yummy mana for you today!"

She removed the lid and lifted the egg into her arms like she was nursing a baby. However...

"...It doesn't look like Kuu wants to feed off you," Minnalis noted.

"Yeah," I agreed. "Your mana's just spilling everywhere."

"Awww!"

Once again, it looked like the egg wasn't interested in Shuria's mana. Even when it had been a worm, Kuu would never eat the meat she prepared. Perhaps it just didn't like her taste, if there was such a thing.

"Oooh... What's wrong with me? Why do you hate my mana so much?" Shuria cried.

"It's okay, come here," said Minnalis reassuring her. "At least you tried."

Rattle. Rattle.

"Yes, all right, no need to beg."

I picked up the egg, and it began to shake as if excited. Now I just had to let it feed off me until satisfied, as I always did.

...Or so I thought.

Crk!

""""...What?""""

A single crack appeared in the shell of the egg.

Crk! Crk!

"Uh... W-wait, what's happening? What do I do?!"

Panicking, I looked around for guidance as the egg continued to hatch.

"C-calm down, Master. Let's just put it back in the box for now," said Minnalis.

"Carefully! Don't let it get damaged!" added Shuria.

"O-okay."

Calmed a little by their helpful words, I did as they suggested. Just then...

Crkkk!!

""""Ah!""""

With a superb crack, the eggshell split completely in two.

"...Ahhh, squee?"

""""Squee?"""" we repeated.

What emerged from the egg was a human figure about twelve centimeters tall. She reminded me of one of the anime figurines my friend Suehiko had showed me back on Earth.

"Squee! Squee... Sunny!"

"It's changed again...," I remarked.

Her size aside, the hatchling had a few peculiarities. She looked like an ordinary girl, which was odd enough, but her hair was tinted green, and she bore a striking resemblance to a much younger Minnalis.

However, her arms were coated in reptilian scales from shoulder to wrist, and from her back sprouted a pair of birdlike wings. Plus, she sported a tail that was long and thin, but fluffy at the end, kind of like a lion's. And to cap it all off, when I stole a glimpse of the palms of her hands, I noticed what looked like paw pads. Atop her head was something that looked like an eggshell, but it wasn't part of the egg she'd just hatched out of; she also had two rabbitlike ears that seemed to be growing through holes in the shell.

Frankly, it was all a bit overwhelming. The girl looked like she'd been designed via an internet poll.

"Squee…squee! Outside! Mom-ma! Dad-da! Sis-sa! Squee!" she said, pointing to each of us in turn. Then Kuu looked around and discovered the straw bedding in which she lay. With no small amount of enjoyment, she began tossing it into the air around her.

"Squee! Bushy-bushy! Fluffy-fluffy! Squee! ♪"

"You've turned into something really quite cute this time, Kuu," said Minnalis.

"Oh my, how adorable! She's like a pretty little doll!" said Shuria.

Suddenly, Kuu's attention seemed to shift from the straw to Minnalis. "Squee! ♪ Squee, squee! Mom-ma! Mom-ma!" she cried, stretching her arms out toward her.

"Oh? Is that me?" asked Minnalis. She reached into the cage and Kuu clambered into her arms. This still didn't seem to be enough for Kuu, so Minnalis put her face close, and she nuzzled happily against her cheek.

"Mom-ma! Mom-ma! Squee! ♪"

"A-aha… Oh dear, I feel…quite strange. Is this what motherhood is like?"

Minnalis was like putty in the child's hands, or perhaps she was trying to tell me something. She had been practicing her facial expressions ever since I'd pointed out her overuse of the "Iron Mask"

skill. Consequently, it had now been upgraded to its advanced form, "Manipulative Mask."

"Me too, me too!" Shuria pleaded.

"Squee? Sis-sa! Sis-sa!"

Minnalis handed Kuu off to Shuria before something inside her snapped. There, Kuu playfully batted at Shuria's hand before spreading her wings and flying off.

"Wah! Where's she going?!"

Kuu flew above Shuria's head and patted her hair with her paws.

"You, little sis-sa. Me, big sis-sa!" she said.

After patting Shuria all over, Kuu threw up her arms and puffed out her chest. Then she began pulling at Shuria's hair.

"Ow! I don't know what's happening, but I think she's making fun of me!"

Despite her protests, Shuria looked oddly happy... *That's just her delight at the frolicking of an innocent child, right? It has nothing to do with the hair pulling, right? I want to believe. Please let me believe.*

After apparently getting her fill of batting at Shuria's head, Kuu at last turned to me.

"Squee! Dad-da!!"

"Whoa."

Kuu sprang from Shuria's head and into my arms.

"Dad-da?"

The way she cocked her head while looking at me was so cute that I could understand why the other two reacted the way they did. As I continued to stare at her, however, I recalled a deeply unpleasant experience of mine.

She looks like a fairy... But then again, she doesn't have much in common with them besides her size. Not to mention fairies don't hatch from eggs.

Still, she couldn't help but bring to mind those twisted flies. All fairies were children of the fairy queen, and they were born from fruit that fell from the Great Fairy Tree at the center of their village. Sooner or later, I was going to have to lay waste to that village with my own hands, but it didn't seem like Kuu was one of them.

However, the moment of hesitation it took me to reach that conclusion proved too much for Kuu.

"Dad-da...hates Kuu? Squee...squee! Squeeeeee!!"

"Hold on, time out!" I yelled over her crying. "You mean me? I don't hate you! I don't hate you at all! Here, are you hungry? Have some mana! It's all yours!"

"Squee...squee. R-really? Dad-da...not hate Kuu? Give me mana?"

"Really really. Dad-da doesn't lie. Here."

"Dad-da! Dad-da!!"

I channeled mana into my palm, and Kuu quickly stopped weeping and became all smiles again. Then she began sucking my thumb, drawing the mana out of my body. It was similar to the way she fed as a worm, only now I could feel her tiny teeth scraping against my skin.

"*Phew.* That seemed to have calmed her down," I said.

"You mustn't tease the poor girl, Master."

"Exactly! The only one you're allowed to tease is me!"

Just then, Minnalis whispered something to me.

"...Master, there are sixteen of them."

"Correct," I replied. "A little slow, but in terms of accuracy you're quickly approaching my level."

"Urgh, the only thing I can tell is that they're all around us," Shuria moaned.

"Squee?"

Kuu tilted her head inquisitively and glanced at me. Just then...

""""*Screee!!*""""

Five plant-type creatures known as Monster Plantes jumped out of the bushes. They looked like huge walking Venus flytraps and could spit acid strong enough to melt through armor. No amount of hacking away at their vine-like appendages could slay them, as their lost limbs quickly regrow. The only way to put them down for good was to destroy their core, but this took the form of a single appendage surrounded on either side by the sacs that stored the monster's acid. One wrong swing and you'd tear through the sac and ruin your sword, so it was highly recommended to go against this monster with magic rather than melee weapons. That being said, if you were skilled enough with the blade, there was no reason why you couldn't cut out the core appendage and leave the acid sacs intact. These creatures were the perfect target to hone our combat skills against.

"The two of you take half each," I said. "No projectiles. Try to defeat them using only your swords."

""Okay.""

"Now, Minnalis, if you lose more than two swords, and Shuria, if you lose more than four…"

Just as I started to come up with some sort of penalty for failure, Kuu began screaming in my ear.

"Squeeee!! No! No!!"

The next instant, she leaped out of my hands in terror and flew toward the two girls.

"Wh-what?"

"Hweh? Eep!"

Minnalis tried to catch her, but Kuu slipped through her fingers. Literally, like she was made of air.

""""What?"""""

While we were struggling to comprehend the sight, Kuu flew right into Minnalis's ample bosom, disappearing into the rabbit girl's body.

"Uh? Huh? Er... Kuu? Kuu?!" she said, looking around in all directions.

"Minnalis, calm down," I said. "Do you feel anything?"

"Are you okay, Minnalis?" asked Shuria.

"Uh, I...think so?"

She answered our worried questions with something that sounded like a question itself. However, something about her had clearly changed. Her light amber eyes had turned a deep blue, and the pupils were vertical slits, like a dragon's. Even the tips of her hair had gone pale, and they seemed to glow in the night.

I immediately turned my "Appraise" skill upon my partner in crime saw that her Condition read, "???? Assimilation (Subject: Kuu)." Next to all her stats was a bonus of "(+???)," and at the end of her skill list were the unfamiliar entries: "Protection of ??? (Granted)," "Awakened Ability (Granted)," and "Maniacal Scarcalling (Granted)."

Every one of those skills, plus the "Assimilation" condition, was completely new to me. The status board wouldn't even show me who or what was providing this "Protection." Plus, I couldn't read any of the effects of these skills and had nothing to go off but their names to figure out what they did. The information was completely illegible, like a sequence of corrupted text. The only other time I had seen anything like this was when I'd tried to Appraise Leticia or Metelia.

"A-are you sure you're okay?" asked Shuria.

"Not quite...," Minnalis replied. "...But I can hear Kuu's voice. Plus, I feel... Oh... Ooh-hoo-hoo. Master, I hope you don't mind if I take care of *all* these monsters."

"...Will you...be okay?"

Since I couldn't read Minnalis's stats, she was the only one who could test her abilities further. Perhaps she could access a more detailed description via the status board, or perhaps she couldn't. Either way, if we wanted to try them out, now was the time.

"I will be fine. It's just, I feel my beastfolk instincts strengthening. With my prey standing right before me, I just can't... Oh, I just can't hold back!!"

Suddenly, a ferocious grin spread across Minnalis's face and she charged into the fray, moving so quickly that I couldn't keep my eyes on her. By the time a dying monster released a spray of acid in her direction, she was already on to the next one.

...She's fast. It's like the assimilation has turned her into a wild beast, improving her combat stats by sharpening her instincts.

Some beastfolk had the ability to transform, taking on a more bestial appearance while making themselves more ferocious in combat. That didn't seem to be what Minnalis was doing, though, as her transformation hadn't been that dramatic, and she wasn't at a high enough level to use that skill yet. However, the effect it had on her combat abilities was very similar.

"*Scree?!*" "*Skeee!!*" "*Skrkk?!*"

"Tee-hee-hee! Ah-ha-ha-ha!"

Furthermore, one downside of beastfolk transformation was that it rendered the user incapable of using magic, but Minnalis appeared to have incurred no such penalty. She was coating her sword in ice to protect it against the acid of the Monster Plantes despite the fact that she seemed to be operating purely on instinct. She wasn't using any of the sword techniques I had taught her, however, and was instead swinging wildly.

"Wow, what's happened to you, Minnalis?" asked Shuria. "You're shining!"

As Minnalis moved, her silver hair fluttered behind her, making for a magnificent sight.

After cutting down seven of the beasts, she took a step back.

"Tee-hee!" she giggled. "The rest I shall deal with in one go."

A vicious smile crept across her face, and Minnalis eyed the remaining creatures with scorn.

"I wonder whether it was the Protection or the Awakened Ability that raised her stats," I muttered aloud. "In any case, the only thing left to try is…"

"Millions of feelers, millions of teeth, millions of years have you lain underneath.

Ravage, rape, waste, and spoil. Answer the call and erupt from the soil.

Summon Antotyde"

The mana emanating from Minnalis as she spoke her chant felt like none I had ever sensed from her before. It was like something crawling down my spine.

Then all of a sudden, a deep, dark hole, shrouded in a black mist, silently appeared in the ground at the center of the Monster Plantes. There was an indescribable chittering, before a swarm of black ant-like creatures climbed out of the hole and attacked.

""""Cheeeeeeeeee?!""""

"What the hell…?"

The ants *devoured* the plant creatures. There was no other word for it. Like a black wave, they swept over their foes, drowning out their dying cries with the clacking of their innumerable teeth.

The chaos lasted mere moments—ten seconds at most. Then the ants disappeared the way they came, and the hole itself vanished. All that was left of the plant creatures were the stains of their bodily fluids. The insects had stripped the plot clean—not only of the monsters' bodies but also the grass that had been growing there. The only sign that a fight had taken place were the bodies of the Monster Plantes that Minnalis had dispatched initially with her own sword.

Suddenly, my partner in crime wobbled on her feet.

"M-Minnalis?!"

Perhaps I shouldn't have let her use it after all!

Like with my soul blades, strong abilities often exacted weighty tolls from their users. That power was far beyond anything Minnalis should have been able to handle, so it was possible the cost would be too much for her bear. However…

"Heh-heh-heh."

"Wh-whoa?!"

As I went to catch Minnalis, she pulled me down to the ground with her.

"Hah-hah! Ha-ha-ha-ha-ha!!"

It was a disagreeably tepid laugh, like a lukewarm bath.

This isn't her usual MP drunkenness, is it?

Her skin felt feverishly hot, and her heart and lungs were pumping dangerously fast.

"*Haah, haah*, Master. I feel so hot…and thirsty…"

"Stay calm," I reassured her. "Try breathing slowly. *Ngh!* Shuria, don't just stand there, help get her off me!"

The transformation had heightened Minnalis's strength even more than I expected, and it was difficult to push her away from where I was laying. But instead of helping me, Shuria was simply peering through her fingers, red-faced.

"Hawawa… That's lewd! That's lewd!"

"Grh… You're no help…"

I wanted somebody to explain to me how a girl so obsessed with sadomasochism could turn into such a trembling maiden. Though, having said that, she wasn't exactly shy about staring…

"Grh… Get off me already!"

Minnalis clung even tighter to me and gave the back of my neck a lick, her coarse tongue sending my spine atingle. At the same time, she stroked my cheek with so soft a touch it was almost imperceptible.

"I'm sorry, Master, but I can't help it... I just can't!!"

She whispered excitedly into my ear, and I felt a little pain at the back of my neck. She had dug her teeth into me, drawing blood.

"Wh—?! What the...?!"

"*Haah...haah...* Master... It's delicious..."

As I lay there, too surprised to move even a muscle, I could hear Minnalis licking the wound. I felt weak, like my will to resist was being sapped away.

"M-Minnalis!" Shuria cried. "You've gone too far!"

It seemed even she was disturbed by Minnalis's behavior, and she finally ran over to try and pull her off. But she wasn't strong enough.

"L-let go, Minnalis!!" I shouted.

"Mgh?! Gh... Uggh..."

I wrapped my fingers around her neck, tightening my grip. At last, she passed out and fell to her side, at which point Kuu emerged from her body, sleeping atop Minnalis's stomach as though nothing had happened.

"Squee. Squee..."

I took a quick look at my own status board to confirm the damage.

"I thought so. *Vampirism.* Dammit, just another thing I need to worry about."

I lifted up Minnalis's unconscious body and heaved a heavy sigh.

"Um, you're bleeding. That means you need an HP potion!" said Shuria, flustered.

"Ah, no. Get me an MP potion, please. The wound will heal on its own. And grab me an all-purpose antidote, if you don't mind."

"O-okay!"

I laid Minnalis down gently in my lap and downed the contents of the two bottles Shuria brought me. After the antidote weakened the effects of the Vampirism, I commanded the mana in my body to eradicate it completely.

That should be the end of that…

Vampirism, as the name suggested, was a curse that would transform the victim into a vampire if it got into their blood, forcing them to serve their master. The issue was, I had previously believed that only true vampires (as opposed to a thrall) could bestow the condition, and Minnalis clearly didn't fall under that category.

"That asshole was just talking crap, I guess. What a real piece of work."

That egotistical bastard had claimed he was the only true vampire left so he didn't need to reveal how to deal with the curse. Good thing I'd squeezed it out of him. If I ever see him again, he'll get what's coming to him, mark my words.

"A-are you going to be okay, Kaito?"

"Yeah, I'll be fine. Minnalis will, too. For now, at least."

I checked her status board; apart from the large drop in MP, I couldn't see anything else wrong with her. My Appraise skill did nothing against Kuu as usual, but she appeared to be sleeping peacefully enough. A cold breeze would sweep over her every now and then, causing her to shiver and snuggle into Minnalis's clothing, which was now starting to come loose…

"Mmm…"

She turned in her sleep, as if discomforted by the chilly air against her exposed skin.

"Anyway," I said, as if to distract myself from the tempting sight. "They'll catch a cold if they just lie there. Let's fetch them a blanket."

However, just as I went into my bag to retrieve one…

"Whoa!"

Out of nowhere, a magically strengthened arrow came flying toward me. I barely reacted in time to instinctively sweep the projectile out of the air.

"Goddammit, what is it this time?!"

I turned in the direction the arrow had come. From within the bushes came the high-pitched voice of a girl.

"What are you doing to Minnalis?!" she cried. "Step away from her!"

Stepping out into the light was a girl with short blond hair who seemed a little older than me. There was anger in her gaze, and she drew her bow tightly, ready to fire another shot.

"Why is it I can never seem to catch a break?" I sighed. "I sit down for one second and everything starts happening at once."

It had always been like this, for as long as I could remember. When it rains, it pours.

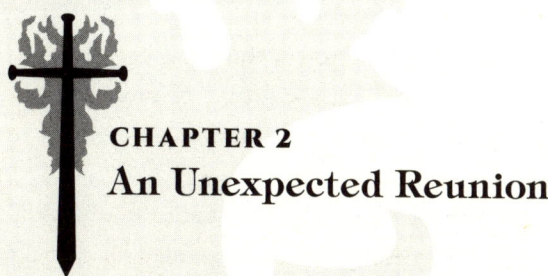

CHAPTER 2
An Unexpected Reunion

"Brr, it's freezing around these parts."

I had stopped for the night in a thick forest of needle-leaved trees. I awoke to sunlight filtering into the carriage, and I lazily got up and crawled outside. In a world without technology, the rising sun was my alarm clock.

As the cold morning air chilled me to the bone, I peered into a pail of water and saw my face. A pretty face, with short blond hair, a far cry from how I had looked in my previous life. The only features that still remained were my narrow, slanted eyes, and my incorrigible stubborn streak.

"Oh, man, I feel like I'm ready to die."

Those had been my last words. After long hours working overtime without pay, I'd trudged home and slumped fully clothed onto the bed, only to pass away from stress that very night.

However, I was only able to recall those bitter memories of my past life due to an accident that had occurred when I was five years of age. I was born "Leone Bohrt" to adventurer parents in a village where monsters and bandits seldom roamed. They had both trained me in combat for my own safety. It was during one such training session that I'd suffered a blow to the head that caused my memories to return.

With my Japanese sensibilities restored, there was no way I was going to set out on the violent and antisocial path of an adventurer. Since I had always harbored a fondness for traveling, I decided to become a merchant.

I apprenticed myself to a friendly trader and studied until I could strike out on my own. Now, after a long and taxing journey, I had finally made a name for myself.

I was born with an intrinsic ability, "Radiant Eyes," that allowed me to see the emotions of any conscious being as colors. This skill had been a great boon along the path to entrepreneurship, but I couldn't have done it without the aid of my close friends.

Admittedly, part of the reason I'd become so well-known was due to my not-so-welcome reputation as "Leone, the Mad Bow." It was true that I'd been known to defeat any monsters, bandits, and demons that came my way. And it was also true that I tended to get a little rowdy when intoxicated, but that was a matter of my constitution, not a moral failing. I could hardly be held accountable for that, could I? Besides, I'd never gotten caught up in drunken brawls in my previous life. It's just that rough and violent types are everywhere in this world, so I needed to get rough and violent in return.

Then, at long last, the demon lord was defeated, ending the war between humans and demons. All of a sudden, the streets were awash with rumors that the hero had been possessed by the demon lord, or that he had always been evil and sought to take his place upon her dark throne. The whole thing smelled a little fishy to me, but I couldn't say I knew the hero very well, and all the great nations seemed to agree on the matter, so who was I to say otherwise?

In any case, with the demon lord defeated, things began settling down, so I only had to worry about defeating the odd monster pack or bandit gang that appeared on the road. About half a year later, the demons stopped being a problem, and I saw more and more smiles on people's faces in every town I passed through.

I thought I was to enjoy a reigning peace at last, but it seemed that life had another shock in store for me. For during one of my journeys, after I went to sleep in my carriage as always, I awoke in a bed of an inn in some faraway town. Still half asleep, I had gone to wash my face with water, only to see the reflection of a girl four years younger.

I headed out into the town to figure out what was happening, but after much research, I could arrive at only one conclusion.

"Don't tell me…I've traveled back in time?"

The concept of reincarnation had been a tough pill to swallow, and here I was faced with yet another impossibility. I spent a few days wondering if I really had traveled back in time, or if it had just been one especially long dream. However, I soon stopped worrying about it. Learning how it happened was not going to help me. It was more important to work out what I was going to do about it.

I knew what was going to transpire in the future. I could save lives that had previously been lost. I tried to remember everything I could about the four years that had been snatched from me and began preparing for the coming conflict. I focused on raising my level, something I had never worried about before, and used my knowledge of the future coupled with my intrinsic ability to make a killing in the marketplace.

Everything was going perfectly. The only wrinkle was that I seemed to have somehow picked up the moniker "Leone the Mad Bow" once again. And not only that…

How come I haven't heard anything about the hero yet? I don't remember a magical storm happening in Dartras, either. Is this what they call the butterfly effect?

Pondering this, I splashed my face with water.

41

"*Phew*. Well, no matter. Whatever comes, I'm ready for it."

"What are you ready for, Captain?" asked Dan, a young man with red hair. We'd grown up in the same village, and he had been my bodyguard on my very first voyage.

"Oh, nothing," I replied. "Just thinking about where to go from here."

"You mean…you're having second thoughts about Karvanheim?"

Dan could be so insensitive at times, but he was keenly aware of my feelings at the moment. Right next to Karvanheim was a village. Something awful had happened there, so I had been avoiding it ever since.

"No, we're still going. We can stay away from that village without avoiding the entire country."

I hadn't told my associates about my little time leap, so it was understandable they were concerned for my well-being, but to me it felt like it had happened eight years ago. It wasn't like I'd gotten over it completely, but it had been long enough that I didn't feel the need to go to great lengths to stay away.

"If only I'd traveled just a little farther back in time, I could have stopped it…"

My mind was filled with visions of the girl who always smiled when I visited. What was the point in going back in time four measly years? I wish I'd been taken back to the moment I was reincarnated. At least then, I might have been able to help that girl and her mother.

"I won't try to tell you to forget about it," Dan said, "but it's not your burden to bear. What happened there was not your fault."

"…Thank you."

"Besides, I'm sure you'll meet her again someday. Come on, when has my gut ever been wrong?"

Dan chuckled and tapped the longsword at his belt. "Oh, you," I said. I was grateful for his reassuring presence at times like this.

However, just as we were talking, a teasing voice came out of the bushes.

"Ooh, look at Mr. Dan, the grown-up, helping Leone with her feelings. I remember you when you had snot dripping from your nose."

"Oh, don't let them know we were here!" came a second. "It's more fun to watch and make fun of them later!"

""Ah, you two!"" we both cried.

From out of her hiding place came a plump, attractive woman by the name of Spinne, running her stout fingers through her frizzy, deep magenta hair. She was grinning at us like she'd just found a new favorite plaything. Beside her was a somewhat short gentleman known as Zanck. He had dark hair tied up in a pale green bandanna, and he wore a short sword at both hips.

Like Dan, both of them were long-standing friends of mine from before I'd started the trader's life.

"You're such a schemer, Zanck," said Spinne. "That's what I like about you."

"And I like your mean wit," Zanck replied. Then, in response to my hastily fired arrow, he knocked it out of the air with his blade. "Whoa, that was close."

"Leone's getting violent again!" squealed Spinne.

"Shut up," I said, shooting them a cold glance. "You two started it!"

"That's why they call her the Mad Bow…" Dan muttered.

"Grr! What did you just say?!" I said, turning and shooting another arrow in his direction. However, Dan easily parried the shot with his blade.

"That's enough, Leone," he said. "Those arrows don't come cheap, you know."

How could he stay so calm when they had been making fun of him as well?

43

"Urgh, whatever," I said. "Let's just have breakfast, and then we can set out for Karvanheim. We're already running late because of all the monster attacks along the way."

"Hey, do we really have to go to school? I'm not great with magic...," Dan grumbled.

"That's exactly why you're going," I said. "You can't just swing a sword at every enemy you come across."

Leaving it at that, I got up to make breakfast. But just as I did, Dan came over and patted me softly on the head.

"We'll find *Minnalis*. I just know it."

"...Come on, Dan. Stop trying to act all cool."

"The thanks I get for trying to be nice..."

I looked up and saw a bright, clear sky. Today was going to be a good day.

That night, I sat by our crackling bonfire, happily munching on a strip of dried meat we'd heated over the flame. Back when I'd first arrived, eating rations like this had made me feel dizzy, but from my point of view, I suppose humans could get over anything after what had been nearly thirty years now.

"*Phew*, we've made good progress today," I said. "And we didn't run into any monsters, either."

"Damn, I really wanted to get my revenge on those Monster Plantes, too," said Dan.

"Even if they did show up," I replied, "I'd ask Spinne to deal with them, not you."

"Huh?!"

"Why do you sound so surprised?" asked Zanck. "Have you been keeping count of just how many swords you've ruined since we left town? They're cheap, but it's still a waste."

"He's right, you know," said Spinne in agreement. "Besides, you don't want to be fighting those Monster Plantes with swords in the first place. It's only because Leone's too nice that she's let you get away with it for so long."

Still, Dan protested. "B-but I think I'm close to figuring something out!" he said.

"And I won't let you," I shot back. "You've been through twenty-five swords this month, so I'm docking twenty silver pieces from your pay."

"What?!" said Dan, flabbergasted. "You're deducting from my pay?!"

"Well, who else is going to cover it?" I replied. "Blades aren't free. Just be glad I only charged you for twenty."

It wasn't like I doubted his words. Give it another six months, and Dan really would be skilled enough with the blade to take on a Monster Plante. However...

"Money doesn't grow on trees, you know! I'm withholding your next bonus until you learn some physical buffing spells!"

"Seriously? Man, oh, man..."

"Look at it this way," I said. "I'm giving you another chance. There are lots of strong varieties of Monster Plante around Karvanheim, so work hard on your magic, okay?"

"Yeah, but Zanck's way better than me, I bet he's gonna...," Dan began, but then he stiffened abruptly. "Leone, I hear fighting," he said. "Quite close, too. Spinne, can you find out how many there are?"

"I'm already on it," she replied. "One, two... I count sixteen monsters and three people."

"That settles it. Let's go! Early bird gets the worm," I said, rising to my feet and grabbing my trusty bow. "I figured this would happen sooner or later. If we want to help them, we'd better be quick."

"I guess if we just stay here, the fight's gonna come to us anyway," mused Dan.

Everyone else grabbed their weapons, and we all started heading in the direction of the disturbance.

"W-wow, I can sense the monsters disappearing one after the other," said Dan. "There might not be any left for us."

"That's good!" I said. "If they're strong adventurers, then that's a brilliant opportunity for trade!"

And thinking about the future, making powerful friends was never a bad thing. If I could manage that while growing my business, they would be two birds with one stone.

"They're just up ahead," he said.

"Wow. Seems like the battle really is over."

By the time we neared our destination, we could no longer hear the sounds of combat.

"Let's try calling out to them. They might be willing to trade some of the materials—"

Just then, I saw it. Standing in the clearing up ahead was a boy and two girls.

And the black-haired boy was choking out one of the girls. A girl who I recognized. All the blood went to my head, and I immediately drew my bow. Before I realized what I was doing, I stepped out and fired at the boy.

She was the girl I'd been searching for all this time. The girl who'd been forsaken by her village for the mere crime of being a beastfolk. At last, at long last, I had found her.

"What are you doing to Minnalis?" I shouted. "Step away from her!"

Okay, let's see. That woman just asked me "What are you doing to Minnalis?"

Is she a friend of hers, perhaps? I can't exactly ask Minnalis to confirm.

As a result of my tough love, the rabbit girl was out cold, and in no state to answer questions.

"Tch. What a mess," I grumbled.

The blond girl stared at me with such animosity, that I suspected she might shoot at any moment. I doubted she'd let me explain myself, and if she really was a friend of Minnalis's, I couldn't risk hurting her.

I'd asked Minnalis about her village before, but she didn't know its precise location, as she had been taken from it in chains. In fact, she had never even ventured farther than the nearby forest during her childhood, so knew nothing about the surrounding landscape. All I had to go on was that it snowed there in winter and was home to a bunch of human supremacists, which didn't exactly narrow down the options.

If this girl knew Minnalis, then perhaps she would be an important lead in exacting her vengeance.

Which leaves me with two choices: overpower her, or run away?

Tempting as the overpower option was, I couldn't see it being much help here. From the precision of the arrow she'd just fired, I could tell she was a seasoned fighter. Plus, there were three others of her caliber hiding in the bushes. I'd have to go all out if I decided to go up against them. No keeping any of them alive for questioning. Besides, with Minnalis out of the picture, it would just be me and Shuria, and I couldn't guarantee that one of us wouldn't get hurt.

I can't fight if there's a chance this lady will die. She might be someone Minnalis cares about.

I didn't recognize the girl from Minnalis's memories. That meant that she wasn't one of her sworn enemies. I needed to know how my partner in crime felt about her before I went any further. I had gone out of my way to save people I cared about, like the weapon-shop owner in the capital and the kids at the orphanage. It was only fair that I extended Minnalis that same courtesy—if she so wished, of course.

Which means the only thing I can do is scram. There's nothing I need to find out from these guys, so there's no reason for me to risk it and stay. In which case, my first move should be...

"Hey, hold it, what are you doing?!"

"Tch. Figures. Can't get a read on her."

Just like with Nonorick, the girl repelled my Appraise attempt. Not through a skill, but by manipulating her mana. It looked like I was just going to have to consider her another obstacle from here on out.

"Shuria, we're leaving."

"Aye-aye, Kaito! Kitty!!"

"Hee-hee-hee!!"

"Wha—?! Kh?!"

I tossed one of my throwing knives, and Kitty threw its silverware. Of course, I didn't forget to pepper the people in the bushes with projectiles, too.

"Whoooah?! That was close!"

"How did he know we were here?!"

"*Magical Barrier!!* Hey, wait! Grr!!"

While they dealt with my assault, I scooped up Minnalis in my arms and made a strategic retreat. However, this group of adventurers weren't so easily shaken off.

"Hold it right there!" yelled the short-haired blond, easily side-stepping my throwing knife and channeling mana into her bow. "*Hardfang Arrow: Sudden Shot!*"

Her projectile came for my arm, perhaps to ensure that I'd drop

Minnalis, but I quickly formed a soul blade and deflected it. The arrow was surprisingly heavy.

"Grr, she can use some pretty advanced magic. Just how do you know this girl?"

Minnalis, of course, could not answer me.

Since my knives were just getting deflected, I picked up a decent-size rock and hurled it at my pursuers.

"Take this!"

However, a red-haired man suddenly leaped out of the bushes and blocked the stone with his broadsword.

"Now it's our turn!"

"Wind Cutter!"

Two more people jumped out of the trees and attacked me. One, a lightly armored fighter with dark hair who tossed throwing knives at me, and the other, a magenta-haired spellcaster woman casting Wind magic.

"Kitty, Teddy!"

A clash of blades, and the pussycat doll parried the knives with his cutlery. Meanwhile, Shuria's teddy bear doll devoured the sickle-shaped blade of wind and absorbed it.

"Heh, both of them are pretty skilled," remarked the man.

"Indeed. We might have bitten off more than we can chew."

That's my line, I wanted to say, but now wasn't the time. The blond girl nocked five arrows to her bow at once and cried, *"Fleet-shot: Hail of Arrows!"* After she fired them, they split up in midair and became an innumerable swarm.

"Rgh! Shuria, channel your mana into Miss Metal and give us an umbrella!"

"Yes, sir, Mr. Kaito, sir!"

I darted over to Shuria's side, tucking Minnalis underneath one arm and drawing the Suction Blade with the other. Meanwhile, Shuria commanded her metallic servant to fend off the rain of arrows.

Though it was hard to see the projectiles in the darkness of the night, each and every one felt tougher than it should've as it collided with the shield.

"Kii-kii-kii…!!"

"Ugh, why are these arrows so heavy?!" Shuria yelled over the noise. Despite her protests, Shuria was still managing to keep the arrows at bay by channeling her mana into Miss Metal.

"All right, now everything's in place."

I stuck the Suction Blade into the ground.

"Sand, settle on the earth," I chanted, and a yellow light spread forth from the blade, causing a white dust to form just above the earth's surface. Of course, when those powerful arrows rained down, the force threw that dust into the air.

"Dammit, he's using a smokescreen!"

"I'll clear it away, give me a second!"

The spellcaster woman began casting a spell, but before she could finish, she spotted two shadows heading out of the dust cloud and into the forest.

"They're getting away! *Wind Cutter!!*"

Her spell, however, hit only some tree trunks before vanishing.

"Grr! After them!"

The blond girl led the charge, and the four of them disappeared into the forest, leaving only the thick cloud of dust behind.

"…They're gone. Let's get out of here. Try to keep your mana hidden."

"Aye-aye."

Before putting that silent glade behind me, I turned and looked in the direction Shuria had sent her doll servants, before nodding at Sir Squeaks.

"*Squeak! Squeak-squeak! Squeak!*"

I'm counting on you, Sir Squeaks.

The mouse took off to tail the four adventurers, while Shuria and I got as far away as possible. As I ran through the forest, Minnalis in tow, I devoted an eye and an ear to observing them through Sir Squeaks's senses.

"*...How did we fall for such a simple trick?*"

"*They really pulled one over on us, huh, Leone?*"

The archer girl, who was apparently called Leone, gave a sigh as she examined the wooden dolls on the ground before her. They were decoys that had been hiding in the trees until Shuria had ordered them to run, and they were completely lifeless now that what little mana she had imbued them with had faded.

"*Spinne, Zanck, can you track them down?*"

The spellcaster lady, Spinne, and the lightly armored fighter, Zanck, both shook their heads.

"*...Not with only these two dolls to go on.*"

"*I've focused as hard as I can, but I don't sense a trace of them.*"

"*...All right, looks like we're far away enough, then,*" I remarked.

Given they were unable to detect us, I stopped walking. Minnalis needed to rest, and I had some questions to ask her once she woke up.

"*Phew, that was tiring,*" said Shuria.

"I'll leave Minnalis to you."

"Okey dokey."

I sat down against a tree and took out a water canteen made of a bamboo-like wood. After quenching my parched throat, I focused once more on the information I was receiving from Sir Squeaks.

"*Rrrrghhh!! After I finally found Minnalis again, too!*"

"*Calm down. At least we know they're nearby,*" said the red-haired man, placing his hand on Leone's shoulder. "*And you know she's alive—isn't that something?*"

"Dan..."

From the way she talked about her, it seemed like Leone cared about Minnalis a lot. Perhaps that was why she had fallen for my cheap trick; the sight of me strangling her had made her so angry she couldn't think straight.

"I doubt Minnalis forged any lasting friendships while she was enslaved, but this girl doesn't look like a villager, either. Hmm...I just can't figure it out. How are you and Minnalis related...?"

Shuria spread out a thick cloth on the ground and laid Minnalis down on it before covering her with a blanket and lighting a campfire. I stared at Minnalis's sleeping form as my mind raced with possibilities, then turned my attention to Leone again.

"I've been looking, but I can't find any trace of them," said Dan. *"Look, Leone, I've been thinking. Didn't it look like that guy was fighting to protect Minnalis? And I know he was strangling her, but she was on top, remember? I'm just saying, maybe it's worth hearing him out."*

"But..."

"And you could have skewered Minnalis with your Hail of Arrows if you weren't careful. I know you were just agitated, but maybe you ought to cool off for a bit?"

"Besides," added Spinne, *"if Minnalis was sold into slavery and that guy purchased her legally, then we can't just attack him, no matter how he treats her. The law isn't going to be on our side for this one."*

" ... "

"Let's head back to where we first spotted them. We might be able to pick up some clues there. We'd better think about what to do if we run into them again, too."

Zanck turned back, and the other two followed him down the path. Only Leone stayed there, muttering something to herself.

"I couldn't afford to go easy on him..."

The only ones who heard this were Sir Squeaks, hiding behind the dolls, and me.

"Hmm? How does she know that?"

Did she have some sort of intrinsic ability that gauged my strength?

I didn't need to wonder, because soon, I heard the answer straight from the horse's mouth.

"*...An array of magical swords. Dark hair and eyes, and that face... There's no mistaking it, that was...*"

"Wh!! What the—?!"

I was so shocked by what she said next, that I crushed the canteen in my hand to pieces. The water burst all over me and the ground.

"Kaito? What's the matter?" came Shuria's voice.

"...That's...impossible. How does she know? How does she know?!"

This wasn't right. There was no way she could say that. No way she could know the words. Had I misheard her? No, it was quiet, but I was certain of what I'd heard.

...She called me *"The ex-hero who came from Japan."*

The cold morning air froze my cheeks. It was an unpleasant feeling, and it roused me earlier than usual.

"Ah, good morning, Kaito," said Shuria as I walked over.

"Oh, hi. Good morning," I replied.

Neither Kuu nor Minnalis had woken up since then. Shuria and I had spent the night taking turns looking after them within the safety of our monster-repelling item. Well, I say "looking after," but that didn't entail much, because as far as I could tell, there was nothing wrong with them. All there was to do, really, was to maintain the fire so it didn't get too cold and to keep an eye on them in case something suddenly happened.

The sky overhead was still dim. The sun had only just begun to rise.

"I'm gonna go wash my face," I told Shuria. "Once I get back, you can take a little nap, and we'll think about our next steps when the sun's up."

I left and walked to a nearby spring. The water within was so clear I could see right to the bottom. I splashed some on my face, and the icy cold chilled me to my bones.

"..."

Leone hadn't said anything else after that, just turned back and rejoined her companions. I had listened in on a little more of their conversation via Sir Squeaks, but the only new bit of information I gleaned was that the four of them were traveling merchants, not adventurers. They planned to continue on to Karvanheim, then use the city as a base while they searched the surrounding area for us.

If they were merchants, then it was possible they were members of the group I'd heard about from Minnalis who often came to her village. I'd need to ask her to be sure, though.

However, right now there was something far more pressing on my mind. Leone had called me the "ex-hero who came from Japan." *Japan.*

"It doesn't make sense. What could this mean?"

I had mentioned my homeland in passing several times during my first life, but this time around I had spoken its name only while in the company of Minnalis and Shuria. How could Leone have heard of Japan?

"And what did she mean by *ex-hero?*"

For the sake of argument, let's say she knew I was the hero.

Perhaps she had some sort of intrinsic ability that let her read the titles on my status board. It was unlikely, but not impossible. But how could that possibly tell her I wasn't the hero anymore?

"Could Alicia have sent her?"

As soon as the thought came to mind, another possibility formed. One that made my spine tingle with fright.

"...Could they have summoned someone else?"

I felt my blood turn to ice before I even finished putting the thought to words. My heart felt like it was tied in knots and pushing up through my throat.

"No, it can't be... It doesn't add up!!"

I shook my head vigorously. I was almost certain now that Leone was a friend of Minnalis's, since I'd gone to the slave market to meet her for the first time only a few hours after my summoning. If Leone knew Minnalis, it had to have been from before then.

"Dammit, just who is she?!"

There wasn't enough information. I couldn't arrive at a satisfactory answer without learning more.

Sooner or later, I was going to have to deal with her, and for that there was only one thing I could do: wait for Minnalis to wake up so I could find out more about this girl.

What I needed to think about right now was...

"Why the hell didn't I destroy the summoning circle while I had the chance...?"

I should have taken the opportunity as soon as the clock started ticking on this second life of mine. I had been so elated by the thought of getting another chance that the idea never crossed my mind. But why hadn't I just stopped to think for a moment? I could have prevented anyone else from going through the tragedy that had befallen me. And it wouldn't have been difficult, right?

Words slipped from my mouth as soon as I realized my mistake.

"Argh, dammit. I messed up again."

My heart fell cold and still, like the very waters of the spring before me. I felt nothing. Only the uncanny sensation that time had stopped for me and nobody else. However, very soon I felt a raging woe blazing its way out of me.

"Graaaaaaaargh!!"

My innards churned, as though every drop of blood in my body had been replaced with boiling acid.

Why had I left the summoning circle intact?

...It was because I felt I could use it to go home. It was the closest thing I had to a way back.

"Dammit! Dammit! Dammiiit!!"

Even though I knew my friends and family were all gone. Even though I knew that seeing it again would only bring despair.

"It's all my fault. I want to go back! Of course I do!!"

My fists struck the cold, hard dirt. I hadn't seen the barren, lifeless world I'd left behind. That was why deep down, I still harbored the aspiration that I could go back, and it would be like nothing ever happened. And as faint as that hope was, it still clung to me like a specter. I could never escape it.

"Of course I want to go back...even if there's nothing left."

That hope had guided my hand without me ever realizing it. And perhaps it was of no consequence. Perhaps the kingdom lacked the resources to perform a second summoning, but that wasn't the point.

I had wavered. I'd let hope lead me astray when it had mattered most.

"When am I ever going to learn...?"

My voice was choked with tears. It was like I'd internalized nothing. Like all my four years of hardship had gone to waste. Just one drop of that tantalizing nectar could cause the world to come crashing down. I knew that; I'd seen it happen time and time again. Hope blinded me, and my little insecurities ran away with me. That was what caused me to make the same mistakes over and over again, and that was exactly why I was in this situation now.

"Come on, Kaito, keep it together. Who gives a damn about Earth...?"

My mistakes were irrevocable. This time, just like all others. There was no way I could walk all the way back to the kingdom now, and even if I did, they surely would have blocked off the secret passage leading to the summoning chamber.

"I made a choice. I gave up everything else I had for one shot at vengeance."

I swore I wouldn't forget. I swore I'd never make the same errors. All so that I could accomplish what in that moment I decided was most important to me.

Yet still I'd harbored doubts. Yet still I'd longed for my old world. But now that I'd said it aloud, now that I'd forced myself to accept it, the truth was clear.

The possibility of returning to my world was too far off in the future to even think about yet.

"I'll drag them all down to my level. Each and every one."

I squeezed my hair, wringing out the water.

I couldn't even picture what returning to Earth would look like. My mind just went, *You must be joking.* The question of how it might be done was one for much later, after I finished with my more pressing business.

I wasn't done with this world yet. There were still more to kill. So many more. So long before I could even think about doing anything else.

Until then, I had no need for hope.

"There's no time to stand still, no time to look back."

I wasn't finished. Not even close.

All I needed was this blazing lump of coal so hot it seared my own flesh.

"...I can't go back to camp looking like this."

I kneeled back over the spring and washed my face once more.

By the time I returned to camp, my two-hour shift on night watch was coming to its end. Just as I was about to wake up Shuria, I heard a noise from Minnalis.

"Mm... Rh..."

She slowly lifted herself half-up and cast a sleepy glance around.

"Morning," I said. "Sweet dreams?"

"Master...?"

Minnalis rubbed her eyes, and her gaze focused.

"What did I do...?"

"What do you remember?"

"...We defeated the Monster Plantes... Then...I felt so thirsty...I—Oh, Master, what did I do to you?"

"How are you feeling now? Any pain or uneasiness I should know about?"

"It's not me we should be worried about, Master—it's you!"

"Calm down, Minnalis. I'm fine, see?"

I wrapped my arm around her and stroked her softly on the head. Minnalis ran her finger over my neck, but there was no longer any bite mark to be found. The touch of her soft finger tickled a little, but I put up with it. Then after she seemed satisfied, I patted her reassuringly on the back and let her go.

"You're the one who started acting strange," I explained. "We need to make sure you're okay. I still don't fully understand what happened. Is there any information on your status board?"

Minnalis examined herself carefully. "I...don't think there's anything wrong with me anymore, Master. I don't feel as thirsty as I did back— Eeek!"

She suddenly jumped and let out a startled cry.

"What is it?!" I shouted.

"Oh, er... There's something in my— Eek! My clothes! Get it out!!"

Just then, I saw a small lump worming its way around in Minnalis's clothing.

"Oh yeah, Kuu was sleeping in there, wasn't she?"

"Huh? It's Kuu?"

"Pwee! Can't breathe. Squee!"

"Eep! That tickles!"

"Pwah! Ah! Dad-da! Mom-ma! Can breathe now!"

Kuu suddenly emerged from Minnalis's breast and squealed in delight.

"Okay," I said. "Well, it seems you're all clear for the time being. Do you remember anything from when you were possessed by Kuu?"

"Yes. A great power roiled deep down within me, and I felt as hot as I do when I'm getting my revenge. It was like it would come bursting out of me if I didn't do anything." Minnalis recounted each experience as it came to mind. "And when I cast that spell at the end, it was like it used up all the energy inside me. I was so hungry...the only thing I could see was red and white... The red of y-your blood, Master..."

She flushed scarlet at the thought and nibbled on her finger, hanging her head in shame. She kept stealing glances at me, and I couldn't help feeling that she looked more bashful than guilty. Was that really the right way to react?

"What about you, Kuu? What do you remember?"

"Hmm? I dunno. Warm! Nice and warm!" said Kuu. Then she began squealing and giggling with delight.

"If I asked you to go inside Minnalis again, could you do it?" I asked her.

"Hmm? Maybe?" the girl replied, clambering up Minnalis's hair onto her head.

"I see... To be honest, I don't know what you are, or what exactly happened. It looked like vampirism to me, but I get the feeling it's not that simple. For now, I don't want you going inside Minnalis without permission, okay?"

"Okay!"

I wasn't completely convinced that Kuu had understood my request, but it was as good an answer as I was going to get. Best not to dwell on it any further.

"All right," I said. "Then, the next order of business is what happened *after* Minnalis passed out."

"What happened...after?" replied Minnalis, casting an uncertain glance at me. I proceeded to tell her about the girl named Leone we'd met.

When I was finished recounting, Minnalis nodded deeply. "From your description, she sounds like one of the traveling merchants who used to visit our village."

"Thought so. That means she couldn't have been summoned here after me. It must have been some time before."

If she was from Japan like me, she certainly didn't look it. Perhaps she was half Japanese or something.

Either way, whoever summoned her must have done so some time ago and kept it secret all this time. It raised many questions, such as who would do that, or why they would let her roam free, but I couldn't dismiss the possibility.

"Our only choice is to ask her ourselves. We need to find out what she knows about her summoning and about Minnalis's village."

"...In that case, let's trap her and rough her up a little."

"No, we don't have to resort to torture this time. You two don't enjoy it, do you?"

The sadistic grin that flashed across Minnalis's face for just a moment didn't escape me.

"Master, you can't afford to be soft on her just because she's from your world! We need accurate information at all costs!! I'm glad you're being considerate of my feelings, but we can't show mercy to anyone who gets in the path of our vengeance!"

Minnalis's eyes were filled with a cold, unwavering determination.

"That's not what I mean," I replied. "In Karvanheim, they sell magic items that can enforce contracts. If we use one of those, we can get the information we require in a safe, legal manner, without going through the time and effort of torturing them. Besides, word might get out if we kill Leone. Considering we plan on staying in town for a while, this is our best bet."

"But..."

"Besides, if she really is a hero like me, she might have all sorts of powers we don't know about. If possible, we want to avoid turning things into a fight, at least until after we've learned what we need. You know just as well as I do that ignorance is the worst fate of all."

That was how we had all ended up here.

"...That's true, but..."

"And luckily for us, she seems to have a soft spot for you, Minnalis. We might be able to turn that to our advantage...and save the torture for when we actually need it."

There was a chance, however unlikely, that this Leone girl and her party were related to the princess somehow. In that case, I'd have to destroy them all, regardless of how sad that made Minnalis.

"Right then, let's get moving," I said. "Come on, Shuria, wake up."

"Mmrgh. But I'm still sleepy..."

Far be it from me to impose upon another's valuable sleepytime, but today we were in a hurry.

"Sorry about this. Any other day I'd let you off, but... Kuu, Sir Squeaks, get her up."

"Wha? Wheee!"

"Squeak!"

The two little ones eagerly started licking Shuria's face.

"Hwah?! Stop it! That tickles!!"

Shuria peered up at me, her face covered in drool. I gave her a stern look.

"Go wash your disgusting face, you pointy-eared brat. You're snoozing on our valuable time."

"Oh, what a mean way to wake me up, and to follow it up with such abuse! Ooh-hoo-hoo..."

Her words didn't match her facial expression in the slightest. Nothing new for her, though.

"We'll set off as soon as we can," I said. "I much prefer to take the lead. Makes it that much easier to lay our traps."

We needed to make contact with Leone's caravan as quickly as possible, preferably in a public place. The inspection point at the entrance to the city would be ideal.

"Wha...wha...wha...?"

"Oh hey, took you long enough."

We met in front of the walls of Karvanheim. They were painted a distinctive sky blue color and bestowed with many unique enchantments that other cities lacked access to. From the top of the walls, stretching in a dome across the entire city, was Karvanheim's signature barrier.

The line to enter the gates extended far down the road, and shortly after we set up at the tail end, Leone and her caravan turned up to join us. She scowled and put a hand on her bow when she saw me.

"*Krh.*"

"Whoa, there. Don't do anything stupid, now."

In all honesty, I needn't have said anything. Leone's companions saw what she was doing and quickly moved to stop her.

"Let's not make a fuss here, Leone."

"He's right, calm down."

"...I know."

At the urging of her companions, Leone fell silent. Still, it would be better for me if she *did* make a fuss, so I decided to toy with her a little.

"That's right," I said. "How will you explain yourself to all these people if you attack me now? Like it or not..."

"Eek!" "Hyah?!"

"...These two are mine."

Modeling my behavior off of that egotistical slaver who haunted my memories, I wrapped my arms as sleazily as I could around Minnalis and Shuria and pulled them both close. Then I lifted up Minnalis's hair, revealing the Slave Brand on her neck.

"You...you bastard!"

"As you can see, she belongs to me. If you want to buy her...?"

"Mgh!!"

I pulled Minnalis even closer, showing her off.

"...Then let's cut a deal. Otherwise, I could always call the guards."

I turned ever so slightly in the direction of the line. I could sense members of the checkpoint security were looking our way. Even the guards were starting to suspect a fight was brewing. One of their duties was to put such conflicts down.

"…You're disgusting."

Leone stared at me with pure loathing.

"Ha-ha. Thank you. I take that as a compliment. Well then, let's return to queueing nicely, shall we?"

I turned my back on her and resumed waiting in line, feeling her prickly gaze on my back.

"*That was too easy*," whispered Shuria through our psychic link. "*What a pushover!*"

"*She hasn't changed a bit*," added Minnalis. "*None of them have.*" It was hard to say whether she looked relieved or disappointed.

We had agreed on this pretense beforehand, of course, along with using Soulspeak when we wanted to chat among ourselves. We needed to make these guys think I was some sort of freak who forced my two slave girls to submit to my every whim. That way, Leone would be inclined to do everything in her power to free Minnalis from my grasp.

"*She's so honest, it makes me sick.*"

Perhaps if everyone in the world were like her, I would still be the hero even now.

…Actually, probably not. Because no matter what I did, no matter what I chose, I could never remain on the path of the hero forever. Not after I'd learned the truth.

"*Man, I really hope she lets me do this the easy way.*"

It was a dog-eat-dog world; I knew that. But I wanted to reward Leone for being nice, even if we could never see eye to eye.

At long last, nearly an hour later, we finally reached the end of the line.

"Very well. You may enter," said the border guard, waving me through.

"Thank you kindly."

I stepped through a green, semitransparent membrane, and my two companions did likewise.

"Hooh! It suddenly got really warm!" squeaked Shuria.

"Looks like the barrier really does maintain a pleasant climate," remarked Minnalis. "I bet we don't even need to wear our traveling cloaks."

In stark contrast to the biting chill we had endured to get here, the city of Karvanheim was as balmy as a spring day. Despite its reputation as a city of magical marvels, the streets looked relatively normal. The only difference was that here there was a strikingly high proportion of magic users out and about.

"So what's first on the agenda, Master?"

"First, we need to buy a *Richmond's Contract*. We'll need one before doing any business in this city."

Richmond, the founder of Karvanheim, was said to have been the most powerful sorcerer of all time, and he'd created many magical inventions, including the Richmond's Contract. This magic item could only be activated if two parties agreed to the terms written therein, and it forced both participants to abide by its stipulations after signing. I had never seen it in action, but I had heard its compelling power outweighed even that of the Slave Brand. Supposedly, you could only break the spell through employing secret dispelling magic known only to the Church.

"Seriously?" "Whoa…" "Big spender…"

I heard the voices of Leone's party behind me. Presumably, they knew just how much the contract cost. It was the ultimate authority in any business dealing, and naturally, it had a price to match.

"…Is it expensive, Master?" "Is it?" my comrades asked me.

"They go for about ten gold pieces each."

"". . ."""

Their eyes went wide. Ten gold pieces was approximately equivalent to one million yen. It was a significant sum, but that was what people were willing to pay for an object so powerful.

While the cost wasn't outside our budget, it would stretch our purse strings a little, and I still had Minnalis's and Shuria's tuition fees to consider.

"*M-Master?*" Minnalis whispered. "*Can we really afford to buy that?*"

"*Yeah. We need it,*" I murmured back.

Still, that said, purchasing one via the normal channels would surely draw attention. I planned to obtain one through other means. So Minnalis, please stop checking inside our money pouch like that.

"*Does that mean we're sleeping in a cheap inn tonight?*" Don't say that, Shuria, we're not that poor. And don't think I don't see you smiling at the thought of it.

"Oh, this is the place. Right here."

I retraced the avenues of my memories, finally arriving before a worn-out antiques store.

"Hey, what's all this about? I thought you were going to buy a Richmond's Contract?"

The man called Dan spoke for Leone's party.

"I am. We can get one here."

I entered the store without giving him a straight answer. Inside, the place was a jumble of mismatched artifacts and arcane goods.

"Hee-hee. Welcome, welcome."

At the counter was a shady looking old man. However, he was in fact...a shady old man. No one of any importance as far as I was concerned. Just a shady old dude who sold shady old goods at shady old prices. Precisely the kind of guy I liked.

"What do you seek today, my friends?" he asked.

"Nothing, just browsing... Oh, this looks good."

I stopped in front of a pile of books and picked one up, dusting off the cover before looking back at the proprietor.

"Ah, you have a keen eye, traveler. That's..."

"We can skip the sales pitch. I'll take it. How's two large silvers sound?" I asked, dropping the coins on the counter.

"Eh?"

"Not enough? You drive a hard bargain. Let's make it three. I don't want to go any further, but I guess if you twist my arm..."

"N-no! That's quite enough!"

I dropped another coin onto the pile, and the shopkeeper greedily scooped them all up and put them away.

"Well, that's all. I'll be leaving now."

"What? You mean you just came to purchase that book?" asked Spinne with a confused look.

"Yes, that's right."

Leone's group stared at me, struggling to comprehend my puzzling behavior. It was only Leone herself who understood. She cast me a guarded look.

"...Let's go somewhere else," I suggested. "This is going to take a while."

It was getting on in the afternoon, so I decided to take us all to a cheap eatery that still had plenty of customers even this late in the day.

"So let's hear it. What kind of deal did you have in mind?" asked Spinne.

We sat across a long, rectangular table at the far end of the restaurant. As we wanted to impress upon Leone that Minnalis and Shuria were my slaves, the two girls stood beside me, making every effort to look as though I was forcing them to do so. Minnalis's maid outfit and Shuria's short kimono both went very far in establishing that I was a sicko dressing up my two slave girls for my own pleasure, though I wasn't quite sure how I felt about that.

"Yes, let's get on with it," I said. "I'm starting to feel a little peckish myself."

I took out the book I had just purchased and carefully slipped off the binding.

"Huh?!" "You're joking." "My, my…"

Hidden beneath that folio was parchment as warm as silk. A blank Richmond's Contract.

But while her three companions looked shocked, Leone herself only mustered an even deeper frown.

"There's three things I want from you," I explained. "First, I want you to share some information with me. Second, I want you to swear never to take action that would be to our detriment. And finally, I want to forbid you from attempting to cancel this contract."

"What kind of information are you after?"

"I just want you to answer some of my questions truthfully. What I offer in return is the removal of Minnalis's Slave Brand, as well as the choice for her to do whatever she wishes with her life from that point on."

"That's not good enough," Leone shot back. "If we're forbidden from interfering with you, then you should be forced to keep your hands off us, as well."

"Hmm, I suppose that's only fair."

The girl was a merchant through and through. Not one to let a loophole go unnoticed. After all, if I suddenly decided to kill them, banning "acting to my detriment" would effectively prohibit them from defending themselves.

"In that case, I'll add a clause preventing me from harming you without due cause. How does that sound?"

Leone stared at me cautiously. "And you're okay with this?" she asked.

To be perfectly honest, so long as they swallowed the clause about not acting to my detriment, I couldn't care less what they stipulated in return. By definition, nothing they could write would be of any consequence to me. In fact, the actions they would be forced to take to avoid being a detriment would in themselves become a marvelous smokescreen.

Though, having said that, it was hard to imagine any loophole in the conditions Leone had asked for. It was almost too fair.

"I am," I replied, and I wrote it down on the contract. "Now I just need you all to sign here."

"...We'll all have a read of it first, if you don't mind."

Never letting her guard down for a moment, Leone scanned over what I had written, then passed the contract to her party members. Each of them scrutinized the conditions before signing their name. When they sent it back to me, there were five names at the bottom, including mine.

"Well then," I said. "The contract is finalized."

I tore the sheet of parchment in half lengthwise, and white flames engulfed it from the bottom up. In mere seconds, the paper was gone, and the white fire split into five wisps, each darting into one of the five cosigners.

""""Rgh!"""""

That instant, I heard a booming voice inside my head.

"You must release Minnalis immediately. Do it now."

"Yes, all right, geez. You don't have to shout."

The command rattled my skull, drowning out the ability to even think about anything else.

"Show me your neck, Minnalis," I asked.

"Y-yes, Master."

Minnalis lifted up her hair, revealing her Brand. I channeled mana into the Master's Mark on the back of my hand until it glowed with a deep blue light, then placed it to her neck. The two marks began sizzling like iron quenched in water; in a matter of moments, Minnalis's Brand disappeared without a trace, and the voice inside my head vanished along with it.

"Well, that's the unpleasant business out of the way," I said. "Let's order something to eat. Come on, you two, sit down already."

"Yes, Kaito! I want lots and lots of meat!"

"Oh, I feel lonely... Like something I took for granted is missing."

"""" ...."""

Minnalis and Shuria eagerly took their seats at either side of me, while Leone's party just stared slack-jawed at their complete change in personality.

That's what I like to see. It makes all the trickery worthwhile.

"Ah, waiter? Could we have three of the chef's special meat dish, please? Oh, is that what you want, Master?"

"Huh?" I replied. "Oh, uhh, sure, why not?"

Honestly, I would have preferred the fish, but I wasn't going to make a big deal of it. However, Minnalis sensed my uncertainty. Her rabbit ears pricked up.

"Oh, Master. Why do you lie when there's no need? ...Sorry, waiter, could we turn one of those meat dishes into a fish special instead?"

"It's so obvious when you're lying, Kaito."

"Hold on, why is this turning into *Let's all make fun of Kaito?*" I protested.

We proceeded with our usual banter for a good long while before Leone finally mustered up the will to speak.

"E-erm, Minnalis?"

"Ah, my apologies," she replied. "It's been so long, and I still haven't given you all a proper greeting. It's nice to see you again, Leone, Dan, Zanck, Spinne. I'm very glad to see you're all well." She punctuated her greeting with a smile.

"Uh…uh… H-hold on a moment. I thought you were being held against your will…?"

"I'm sorry for tricking you," said Minnalis, bowing her head in shame. "But I'm afraid it had to be done."

"Actually, *I'm* not even a slave at all!" chirped Shuria.

"…Hmm." Spinne cast us an appraising eye. "Perhaps our dear Minnalis was a slave to *love*?"

"*Pfffft!!*"

"Oh, you," said Minnalis bashfully. "Slave to love…don't tease me!"

Shuria's ears perked up. "Hmm? Slave to love? What a beautiful sound…"

Mercifully, the waiter brought us our food at that precise moment. Trying to shake off the awkwardness, I dug into my meal.

"Ahhh, I see how it is. Never thought I'd see the day our Minnalis pulled one over on us!"

"I know," she replied. "And to be caught in a love triangle as well, it's like a dream come true!"

Hey, I thought we were trying not to acknowledge that! God, grant me the obliviousness of those thickheaded harem protagonists!

"I—I can't believe it," said Leone, clutching her head. "I must be a complete sucker…"

"Don't beat yourself up about it," I reassured her. "Look, I'll pay for the food tonight, my treat."

"*Sigh.* Fine. Waiter! Four of the most expensive items on the menu, please!"

She seemed desperate to get back at me in any way she could.

"Aaargh! I can't believe it! Look at this guy! A pretty girl dressed in what I can only describe as fetish wear on each arm! I thought for sure he was a complete sicko!"

"…Geez, why don't you tell me how you really feel?"

"Oh, shut up! It's not like you've got room to argue! Anyone who sees you on the street would think the same!"

"Ugh."

My attempt to defend myself had only landed me in more hot water. I shouldn't have poked the bushes. This was why I hadn't wanted the conversation to go in this direction.

"Right, well. You wanted answers, right? Ask your questions," said Leone, by now thoroughly fed up with me.

"Well, first…," I replied. "Which of the inns in this town has the softest beds?"

"Huh?"

"Oh, my."

"What a guy."

"Don't be subtle about it, will ya? You're gonna make us blush."

Leone stared blankly for a moment before standing up out of her chair and leaning across the table, red-faced and shouting.

"H-how could you ask me that?! I knew it! You're nothing but a pervert! Degenerate! Sex-obsessed fre— Owwww!"

I poked her in the forehead. "Get your mind out of the gutter," I replied "You're far more obsessed with sex than me if that's all you can think about. And you just spit all over me, gross."

Then, quietly, so only she could hear me, I added,

"I'll ask my real questions after lunch. You don't want to talk about Japan while the others are around, do you?"

"Hrk!"

Leone suddenly clammed up and said no more. I picked up my knife and fork and started eating.

After lunch, Leone and I left our seats to hold the rest of our conversation in private.

"Reincarnation! I should have known! Why didn't I think of that?!"

It was the one thing I hadn't considered. She had come from Japan long before me and had kept her memories when the rewind occurred. In her mind, it must have seemed as though she had simply been flung back through time for no reason. If this was my second time in this world, then I wondered if it was Leone's third.

I thought I was the only person who kept my memories. Is it because she's an outsider like me?

It was the only thing she and I had in common. What other explanation could there be?

"Well, there you have it," she said. "Now, what I want to know is how on earth you knew I was from Japan in the first place!"

"Trade secret, I'm afraid. Why should I tip my hand so easily to a fellow adventurer?"

"…You're not wrong. Still, I can't believe the goddess gave you a Tutorial Mode…"

"I just want to make sure, but you're not a kingdom spy, are you?"

"Of course I'm not! How many times do I have to tell you?"

"Just checking," I said with a shrug. "The nations of the world betrayed me in my first life, and even now Princess Orollea is on my tail. Can you really blame me for being cautious?"

"I guess not… So are you questing to find a way back to Earth?"

"Hmm, something like that."

Of course, that wasn't my goal at all, but I didn't want to raise her suspicions. Minnalis seemed happy to see her, so there was no need to burn bridges. Besides, it wasn't hard to imagine how a good-natured girl like her might react if she knew the truth.

"What about you?" I asked. "Do you want to go home?"

But Leone replied without hesitation. "No. I'm Leone now. This world *is* my home. The me from Japan died a long time ago."

It was an answer she could only have arrived at after a long journey of introspection. I had to respect that.

"...I see."

It was about time I started asking about the location of Minnalis's village. But just as I was about to cut the small talk and get right to the point, Dan, who had been casting the two of us impatient glances the whole time, finally got fed up and called over.

"Leone! We'd better get a move on, or the inns'll all be full!"

I glanced outside, where the streets were already growing dark. Dan the man was right. If we didn't get searching soon, we'd be sleeping in the gutters.

I called over to Minnalis and Shuria. "Let's stop here and find an inn. It'd be a shame to sleep outdoors after we came all this way."

Minnalis's village could wait. Leone wasn't going anywhere.

I also wanted to see if the merchant girl had heard any news regarding the kingdom. Orollea was where I had begun altering history. If the course of events was going to diverge from my memories, it would start there. From then on, it was only a matter of time before my knowledge became completely useless. I needed as much intel as I could gather to make up for that. There was no way the princess was sitting on her pretty little butt doing nothing.

"Yes, Master!"

"Okey dokey, Kaito!"

The two stood up from their seats, as did I.

"I'll leave you in peace, then," I told Leone. "But we'll continue this conversation tomorrow. Have you decided where you're staying yet?"

"The Cat's Grove," she replied. "But we're going to be busy selling off our goods tomorrow. Can we do it another time?"

"Oh yeah. I almost forgot. You guys are merchants, not adventurers."

"We'll meet back here four days from now, in the afternoon," she suggested. "By then, we'll have decided how much we're going to charge you for this info."

"I have to pay you?!"

"Of course! What kind of merchant gives anything away for free? All you specified in the contract was that I couldn't lie; you didn't say anything about how much it would cost."

...I mean, I guess she had a point.

"Fine. As long as I find out what I need to know."

I stood up and paid for our meal, as I had promised.

"By the way, Minnalis," I said. "You're not a slave anymore. You don't need to keep calling me 'Master.'"

"Being a slave has nothing to do with it. You're still Master."

"No, but..."

"You're still Master."

"..."

She wasn't willing to budge on the point, it seemed.

Before Leone left the restaurant, she called back to us, "Oh, we're going to be in town for a while, so if you need anything, leave a message with the landlady at the Cat's Grove."

"Will do. See you."

Well, that went rather well, if I do say so myself. It could have been a lot more painful than that.

Satisfied with the day's accomplishments, I followed Minnalis and Shuria out of the eatery.

Kaito Ukei.

The greatest traitor in the history of mankind, the former hero.

That was how I knew him. But meeting him in person, I found that the hero was far more reasonable than I'd been led to believe. I had assumed he was some sleazebag forcing himself on Minnalis and that Shuria girl, but that had just been an act.

My impression of him was that he seemed quite witty, if a little frivolous. He reminded me of the boys in my classes back on Earth, who always worked themselves into a frenzy about every little thing.

At the very least, I felt like I didn't need to act outright hostile toward him anymore.

"What about you? Do you want to go home?"

"No. I'm Leone now. This world *is* my home. The me from Japan died a long time ago."

It wasn't like I'd never thought about going home. But even if the option arose, I wouldn't be able to take it. What I'd told Kaito had been the unfiltered truth. I was not a displaced earthling—I was Leone.

"I see," Kaito replied, before placing a pile of coins on the table and standing up. He and Minnalis really seemed to get along well, as they were cracking jokes all the way out of the restaurant. It was hard to imagine how she must have felt after being sold into slavery and losing her mother. I'd half-expected her to have taken her own life by now.

But I was glad she hadn't.

"Oh, we're going to be in town for a while, so if you need anything, leave a message with the landlady at the Cat's Grove."

"Will do. See you."

Kaito gave a wave and turned to leave.

What a relief...

I felt that Minnalis had been saved. After all the hardships she had endured, she'd finally found someone for her. And though the kingdom was still on their tail, at the very least she could be happy.

So when I used my skill, it was only as an afterthought. A way of confirming what I thought I already knew.

...Activate Skill: Radiant Eyes.

I was already confident that I could trust Kaito with Minnalis. That she would be happy with him.

However, I saw in those three something that I had never seen before.

"...What? Wh-what is this...?"

Pitch dark flames, so black as to rob the light from the surroundings. So black I feared they would draw me in. Even just the glimpse my power offered was overwhelming, as though it would burn me to a crisp.

I could see the obsidian extend from Kaito's body like an aura, entangling his companions and draining them of light.

I had never seen anything like it. That shade of black was completely alien to me.

"How...how could this be?"

If that was pure hatred, then it made everything I had seen before seem pale and fleeting in comparison. All emotions grew faint over time. People couldn't harbor powerful feelings forever. But the thick black substance that composed the chains that bound the three of them seemed to keep the flames of their hatred burning.

"That's a fate far worse than slavery…"

Minnalis's mind was being tampered with. It was effectively brainwashing. Kaito had brainwashed those two girls, just like he'd brainwashed himself…

"Leone? What's wrong?"

My companions called over to me, worried, but I had no words to answer them with. I simply gazed down into my empty cup and muttered,

"…I have to save her…"

CHAPTER 3
Things that Obviously Need Stamping Out

T hank ye, come 'gain."

The shopkeeper mouthed his lazy farewell, and I stepped out into the backstreets of town. I had been going around gathering supplies for my upcoming dungeon run.

"Time to head back to the inn, I suppose."

Three days had passed since we arrived in Karvanheim. During that time, I had raised a decent amount of money by selling monster parts that I'd obtained along my journey, both to regular shops and on the black market.

The beds at Leone's recommended inn, the Angel's Perch, were every bit as wonderful as she'd described. Usually, Minnalis would borrow the kitchen to make us dinner, but here the food they provided was of such high quality that she didn't need to. Still, the fact that Minnalis had grown so skilled in the culinary arts that she regularly put professional establishments to shame was really starting to impress me. She could give any top-rate chef a run for their money by now.

"I'm back," I said as I entered our room.

"Ah, welcome back, Master."

"Welcome back, Kaito. Grrr…"

The two girls were sitting on their beds, practicing their mana control. Between them, Kuu was sleeping in a ball at the center of my bed.

It appeared that Kuu was considered my pet in this world, as I was able to store her in the Monster's Blade of Hatching. That came in handy because it meant we didn't have to walk down the streets with her, but Kuu said the inside of the soul blade was all "squickly" and "goobly," so she preferred being outside. I allowed it on the strict condition that she didn't try to leave the inn room.

Minnalis and Shuria were undergoing a sort of magical training, attempting to focus their mana into a small stick and use it to support a heavy weight on the end of a string. Too little mana, and the weight would cause the stick to snap, but too much, and it would explode into tiny splinters. It was a drill I had developed on my own time to make up for the fact that I couldn't practice casting spells, and it was a lot harder than it looked.

Minnalis had advanced in leaps and bounds, and it was starting to look like she was even more gifted at mana control than me. Shuria, on the other hand, had been struggling to muster even a modicum of precision, and the floor was littered with dozens of snapped twigs from her failed attempts at the exercise.

"Hmm, you've been coming along nicely, Minnalis. You too, Shuria. It doesn't need to be perfect. Well done."

The entrance examination was the following day, and Shuria was about on the level of the average candidate already. I saw no reason why they shouldn't both pass, and their subsequent lessons would iron out any further wrinkles.

"Heh-heh-heh. Thank you."

"Wait, don't stop concentrating, you'll…"

I heard the crack of the twig in Shuria's hand.

"Nooo! My record!" she cried, slumping in disappointment.

"Tomorrow's the big day," I said, "so that's enough practice for tonight."

"Yes, Master!" "Okay, Kaito!"

After the test, we would be meeting up with Leone again. It was going to be a busy day.

"Well, here it is."

"I'd heard stories, but I didn't think it would be *this* huge."

"It's got blue walls, too!"

The next day, we got up early to visit the academy, where there were already a smattering of people wandering the grounds. The campus was vast and included dormitories, all surrounded by the same blue walls that enclosed the city itself. The only other building with walls like this was the royal castle, which painted a pretty good picture of how important the academy was to this country.

"Never thought I'd be coming back here...," I muttered, following the signposted route until finally arriving at a large line of people.

"Oh hey, look who it is," I said.

"Ah, that explains why they were busy in the morning."

Ahead of us, mixed in with a crowd of people leaving the building, was Leone and her group. They noticed us and came over.

"Hey," said Leone. "I guess this means you're here to join the academy, same as us?"

"Something like that," I replied. "I'm just here to pay the tuition fees, though. These are the ones who'll be enrolling."

I clapped Minnalis and Shuria on the shoulders.

"That's right!" "We are!"

"Hmm?" said Dan with a quizzical look. "You're not attending, Kaito?"

"I have...something else I need to do. Besides, I don't use spells."

Can't would have been more accurate, but whatever. The line moved as we chatted, and we eventually reached the front.

"Thank you for waiting. Are you here to join the academy?"

We went through the standard questions and had our names added to the register.

"Ahhh, Kaito, Minnalis, and Shuria. And Minnalis and Shuria wish to apply for the advanced class, is that right?"

"Yep, that's correct."

Leone seemed confused. She blinked in surprise at our entry sheet. "Wait, Minnalis, too?"

"Yep, they're both applying for the advanced course."

"Really?" said Zanck, looking over at her uncertainly. "But she's...you know..."

Having just taken the exam for himself, he obviously knew what it entailed. And he was as well aware as anyone that beastfolk were naturally disadvantaged when it came to magic.

"She'll be fine," I said. Minnalis and Shuria would have no problems passing the exam. That was because I had told them they could rely on their intrinsic abilities as long as they didn't do anything too drastic.

The receptionist guided us inside, and we arrived in a large, open room. The floor and walls were blue, just like the exterior.

"Very well," said the exam proctor. "Please stand inside the circle on the ground and attempt to destroy the target. You will be disqualified if you throw anything or step outside the circle."

"Understood." "Roger that!" The girls nodded.

First up was Shuria. She tossed a full set of plate armor onto the ground, then began casting a spell.

"Here I go! *Marionette!*"

Usually, Shuria didn't need to speak any magic words, but we needed to give the proctor the correct impression. Invisible threads flew from her fingers and latched on to the suit of armor, bringing it to life. It drew its sword and slashed at the target, slicing it in two.

"Is that some kind of alchemical servant?" he murmured. "Hmm, but I sense no Earth magic involved... Ah, I see, it must be telekinetic magic of the Misc. category."

In actuality, Shuria's Puppet Possession was no mere telekinesis; it was a sort of hex that imbued its targets with false life, but I was in no hurry to correct the supervisor's incorrect assumption.

"I guess that means it's me next," said Minnalis, entering the circle. *"Hear my ode to death's decay and sink into the rotting swamp."*

Her clear voice filled the room, and her mana flowed freely into the spell.

"Tainted Grip."

Her words caused a purple sphere to manifest in the air before her. All of a sudden, a hand burst out from the ball. It shot toward the target, squeezing it until it smashed.

"Oh my! Poison magic!" exclaimed the proctor. "You don't see that every day. And for a beastfolk to exert such force over so far a distance, you must be highly skilled indeed!"

The poisons created by Minnalis's intrinsic ability, Intoxicating Phantasm, didn't attenuate with distance like the rest of her mana did, so her skills had nothing to do with it. Again, though, I wasn't going to say anything.

"Very good, you both pass. In destroying the target, you have shown a sufficient level of magical control to benefit from our instruction. If you stay enrolled at the school, you may be allowed into the advanced course after six months." The examiner smiled and handed the two girls their certificates. "So many good external students this year; it brings a tear to my eye. Be sure to take these to your induction."

"Thank you very much."

"Kaito, Kaito, look at this! Look at this!" yelled Shuria, waving her wooden placard at me, which of course contained a rudimentary magic circle. Why did everything have to be magic in this place?

"I see it. Well done, you two."

Everything was going according to plan. Minnalis and Shuria could now begin their lessons. The only other thing I had to do today was speak to Leone about Minnalis's village.

What could possibly go wrong?

Leone had told us to meet her at a particular café, so after that flawless display of magic, we headed on over. The seven of us ordered the lunchtime special and got to talking.

"I see. So that's how Kaito ended up buying Minnalis."

"Yeah."

I ended up giving a rather abridged version of the whole account, as I didn't want them to find out I was the hero or that the princess was after me. The only one who knew all that was Leone, but even she was unaware of my true goal.

"Well, I must say, Minnalis, I'm impressed. I never knew you could cast magic so well!" Spinne said, hugging her tightly in her arms.

"Please stop that! I'm not a child anymore!" protested Minnalis, despite making no effort to escape.

"I never thought you'd be able to get into the advanced class, though," said Zanck. "I'd heard that beastfolk tend to struggle with long-range magic. How did you do it?"

"Oh, I wanted to know that too!" said Dan. "It takes years of skill before they let an outsider take those classes!"

"I'm sorry, but I can't say," replied Minnalis. "An adventurer must always keep their cards close to their chest."

"She's right, you know," said Spinne. "No adventurer worth their salt gives away secrets for free… Still, you can give me a tiny hint later when the boys aren't around, can't you?"

"I'm afraid not."

"Awww…"

Even through her refusal, I could see the smile on her face.

"Minnalis looks happy," I whispered to Shuria.

"Yes. It's nice to see."

Leone and her party were some of the few pearls in the thick, muddy swamp that was Minnalis's life, just like Leticia had been to mine, and Shuria's mother and younger sister were to hers.

"Well, I propose a toast," I suggested. "To Minnalis and Shuria's acceptance into the advanced class. Spinne, you mentioned you were self-taught, right? If the girls run into any trouble, could I ask you to help them along the way?"

Leone would be there, too, but I figured if anyone would have a grasp on basic theory, it would be the spellcaster of the party.

"Of course!" she answered. "I couldn't let these two fall behind! I'm only there to pick up a diploma anyway, so how could I say no to a couple of adorable kittens like these!"

"Waugh?!" cried Shuria.

"Unh…?!" I exclaimed.

I suddenly found myself wrapped in the same warm embrace that had assailed Minnalis just moments earlier. Shuria let out a cry of surprise, looked down at herself and patted her chest, seemed to think for a moment, then pushed Spinne aside.

"Raaargh! Get away from him! You're the enemy! This woman's the enemy!"

"Whaaa…?!"

Shuria glowered and growled like a watchdog. The Mai in my head was saying, *Brother, you mustn't get involved in this matter.* I took her sage advice and decided to change the subject.

"You two are...Daniel and Zanck, right?"

"Just Dan's fine."

"Zanck's the name, stabbin's the game."

"Ha-ha. Well, you can call me Kaito. So what brings you to Karvanheim Academy? Are you looking to pick up some magic to supplement your swordplay?"

"Yeah, pretty much," Dan replied. Then, patting his bicep, he added, "I'm hoping to learn some buffing spells."

"I'm thinking of picking up a few enchantments myself," said Zanck, rubbing the swords at his belt. "I noticed you enrolled at the school, too? Even though you said you wouldn't be attending."

"Yeah," I replied. "That's because I want access to the library and dungeon."

"Ah, a dungeoneer, huh?" said Dan.

Only students and staff could access the dungeon on the academy grounds. The same went for the establishment's library. There were many students, like me, who enrolled in the standard class for the sole purpose of gaining access to these facilities.

"That's the long and short of it. Leone, could I ask you to take care of them, too? I expect people will be quite surprised to see a beastfolk walking the halls, though it's not like there's never been a beastfolk student of magic before... And Shuria could attract some strange looks, too."

"That's right," said Minnalis. "She looks like a child, but she's actually a teenager already!"

"Grrr, I may like being teased, but I *hate* being treated like a kid!" Shuria fumed, prodding me repeatedly in the ribs.

"Ow! Ow! Ow! Stop it, Shuria! That hurts! Wait, no, it doesn't hurt, but it feels weird!"

I jumped and twitched uncontrollably every time she landed a poke.

"Oh, I'll take care of them all right," said Leone. "If some sleaze-bag tries to hit on them, I'll make sure he regrets it."

Leone had been silent for a while before making that comment. She seemed cheery enough, but something about her had changed. It was like she was…warier, somehow.

Hmm? Did I slip up and arouse suspicion?

I'd thought that things had gone pretty well the last time we parted. What had changed since then?

It wasn't like the first time we'd met when she was constantly on edge, and it felt like one wrong move would awaken the bear, but something seemed off about her nonetheless.

Well, she can be suspicious all she likes. I'm not going to do anything to her.

I would have liked to reminisce with her about Japan, but she didn't seem in the mood. Besides, I knew we were never going to be friends in any true sense of the word.

That was because we had no intention of showing her our true selves.

"Minnalis, Shuria, you there?"

I dusted off Soulspeak and reached out to the others.

"Yep, yep! We can hear you just fine!"

"What is it, Master?"

"Change of plan. It seems Leone's still wary of me. I don't dare ask her where Minnalis's village is now."

My reputation had been in tatters by the time I died at the hands of my former party. That wasn't something I could overturn through a single meeting. Perhaps Leone had thought it over and grown suspicious of my claims. In which case, there wasn't much point in asking about the village and straining that trust further.

"Can I ask you two to see how she feels tomorrow and ask her then? I feel like that's our best bet at getting an answer out of her."

Of course, I could always use force if I needed to. Our contract meant that she couldn't lie. However, Minnalis and Shuria were going to be seeing her every day from now on. I couldn't worsen our relationship while she had done nothing to deserve it.

"*But Master…*"

"*There's no rush,*" I replied. "*I know all about Leone the Mad Bow from my first life. Befriend her and get her to teach you as many of her legendary skills as you can. I know how you feel, but we have to take this slow to make this as easy as possible for ourselves down the line. Don't go closing doors before we've even begun.*"

Try to reach out and grab every opportunity you saw, blind to the world around you, and you would end up tripping over your own two feet. It was a lesson I'd learned the hard way.

"*…You're right, Master. It's too early. I was impatient, I'm sorry.*"

"*Besides, even if we know where it is, we can't go there yet! We need to get stronger first!*"

"Hi, sorry for the wait, here's today's special."

At that moment, our order arrived, putting our impromptu Soulspeak meeting on hold. We ate our meal and left without incident…

…is what I would have liked to say, but idiots sprouted out of the woodwork wherever I went.

"Urgh. What a shitty little place. I come all the way to this backwater country only to pick the worst café in town. Just my luck…"

A filthy, bearded man, all muscle, entered the store so loudly and rudely it had to be on purpose. Judging by his greatsword, he appeared to be an adventurer. He was clad in silver armor, with glistening black trimmings that matched the scabbard on his back.

Urgh, it makes him look like a cockroach. Disgusting.

"Oh, great. It's Blacksteel Gheele."

"Dan! Don't make eye contact," warned Spinne. "He'll see us."

"...Someone you know?" I asked.

"He's a powerful adventurer who hails from the empire. We tangled with him once, and he's had it out for us ever since."

Although Spinne tried to keep quiet, it wasn't a large establishment. There was no way he could miss us.

"Hmm? Well, well, well, would ya look at that! I shoulda known I'd find shitheads like you in a shitty place like this!"

"Oh, cram it," Leone shot back. "Who left their dog untied? All this whining is giving me a headache."

"Grrr. You've got a mouth on you, lass, same as I remember." Gheele scowled. "Oh, who are these?" he said, switching his sights to me. "Ain't seen your face before, pal. New members?"

I had been hoping to sit and listen quietly without being singled out, but unfortunately, I was subjected to the man's leering gaze as it swept across me and my companions.

"Hur... Don't give a shit about the dude, but those two chicks ain't half bad... In fact, they're just my type."

"Hey, quit it...," Leone began.

"Hey, why don't you two forget this loser and come with me? I'll show you a much better time than—"

For crying out loud. This world was swarming with these types. As Gheele reached out his greedy hand, I snatched his forearm.

"Listen," I said. "You've had your fun. Now buzz off to whichever shithole you crawled out of before I pull your wings off."

"Huh? Who do you think you are? Get your hand— Agh?! Gh! Let go of me! Rgh!"

His arm creaked as I squeezed it, and after a few seconds I released him. I had given him a little taste of my strength, enough to know that he ought not to cross me. But a man like him had a reputation to uphold, and so he couldn't let a slight like that pass.

"You brat! I'll slice you in— Rgh?!"

Gheele went for the greatsword on his back, but before he could draw it, I conjured up the Soul Blade of Beginnings and drove the point into his neck. Just enough to nick the flesh and let my sword taste blood.

"Leave now, or you'll lose your head."

"You…"

"Do you still not get it? The only reason you're still alive is because I don't want to dirty this place with your blood. Now get out of my sight before I change my mind."

I moved the tip of the sword, carving out a line of flesh. There was only one way to make thickheaded guys like him understand the gravity of the situation they were in.

"Don't touch my partners ever again."

"I—I wasn't bein' serious! Don't you know how to take a joke?! G-get outta my way! I'm leavin'!"

Gheele forced his way to the exit and left the café, covering his escape with laughable excuses. Once he was gone the place erupted into cheers.

"Nice going, dude!" "You sure showed him!" "What a sight!"

"That kid's a real wiz with the sword," said Zanck. "Guess that's 'cause he's got two lovely girls to take care of, eh Spinne?"

"Why do you look at *me* when you say that? You'll get my loins burning…"

Spinne giggled in a way that could freeze water solid.

"Those were some sick moves!" said Dan. "We gotta have a battle some time!"

"Sure, if I feel like it," I replied, turning my attention back to my meal.

☆

Shuria and I, along with Master, turned up at the school the very next day. We would be attending lectures here from now on.

"Right," said Master. "I'll see you two later. I'm heading to the library as we agreed."

"See you later, Master!"

"See you, Kaito!"

"Yep. You two pay attention in class, now."

Master waved at us and left.

"I guess we should get moving, too," I said.

"Yes!" sang Shuria.

We followed the signboards posted around campus to our designated lecture hall. Amid the crowd of people walking in the same direction, one group stood out. They all wore the same uniform and were of similar ages, just a little older than me. These were the elite students of Karvanheim Academy, as opposed to the adventurers from all walks of life who made up the external students like us.

Well, who cares about them? I can feel them looking down on us, but I just have to ignore it.

A swarm of flies in one's face was a nuisance, but nobody would think to squash each and every one that happened to buzz nearby.

The students all turned to the right, into a squeaky-clean new schoolhouse, while the rest of us turned to the left into a dirty, run-down building. We came before a door marked EXTERNAL STUDENTS and walked inside. There was a speaker's podium at the front and lots of desks arranged in tiers facing it. The lecture was not due to start for a while, so the seats were only sparsely populated.

"I think we might have gotten here a little too early," I noted.

"Better than too late," said Shuria.

While the students chatted among themselves, we headed over to the relatively free rightmost section and took our seats there. A few moments later, Spinne and Leone walked in.

"Oh, good morning," said Spinne, spotting us. "It's good to see you two cuties again."

"Ah, morning," said Leone. "You're early."

The two of them waved and came our way, sitting on either side of us to box us in. Looking head-on, from left to right, it went Spinne, Shuria, Me, Leone.

"Good morning," I replied.

"Morning!" said Shuria.

"Mmm! Even the way you say good morning is cute!" said Spinne, hugging Shuria. "I just want to stroke your little head!"

It reminded me of the times she used to visit the village.

She's always loved children, I thought. *Some things never change.*

Back then, I'd received the treatment Shuria was getting now. Me, Lucia and Kril. Today, those memories were like toxic spines jammed into my flesh.

"Do you remember visiting my village, Leone?" I asked. "Spinne was always like this, wasn't she?"

"...Yeah."

"Do you still go there?"

"No...not anymore."

"I guess that means you heard what happened there. That's why you weren't surprised when you found out I was a beastfolk."

"Hrk."

She twisted her expression in misery. *Oh no, Leone, that's not the way I wanted to make you feel at all.*

"You don't have to be sad. Master saved me. The past doesn't bother me anymore."

"What...about Maris...?"

"My mother died on the journey to the capital. And I would have followed her soon after if he hadn't turned up."

"I knew it...! I knew it..."

I'm sorry, Leone, but there are some things I can't forgive. That's why...

"Leone, could you tell me where my village is? I don't even know where I came from."

"...So you can get revenge on the villagers who wronged you?"

"No, I told you, remember? The past doesn't bother me anymore."

"Then, why...?"

...I'm going to have to lie to you, just a little.

"I want to know if my mother left anything behind. I have nothing to remember her by."

"..."

"Please, Leone. I have to know. If there's anything left in that village of hers, I have to know."

A dirty little lie, in my mother's name.

She's lying.

I didn't even need to use my skill. I could feel it in her words. Years of negotiations had sharpened my senses, so I was able to tell when someone was saying something they didn't mean. I understood how she must feel, but revenge wasn't the solution. It wouldn't make her happy.

The Minnalis I knew had been a kind and loving soul, someone who would always make time for everybody. And I could feel her guilt now. She didn't want to lie to me. Somewhere inside her was the old Minnalis, just waiting to be brought back.

However, the contract I had signed obligated me to respond to her question truthfully. And so, before she could ask me anything further, I answered, "...The village is in the northeast region of the Orollea Kingdom, close to the border with the Grigal Empire. The quickest path from here is via the empire, cutting through the mountain pass."

I didn't have to lie to trick her. A merchant could weave webs of deception without spinning a single falsehood.

"The northeast of the kingdom... That's going back on ourselves..."

"There's a town near the mountains called Gagarrad. If you ask there, they'll be able to direct you to the village. It's a bit of a detour, but the safest way is via a town in the Lunarian See called Lobelia."

It's just as I thought. Nothing happens as long as what I'm saying is true. Even if I'm talking about a completely different village.

The precise wording of the contract was my savior here. So long as I didn't actively harm those three, I could do whatever I liked. If it had prevented me from constituting an obstruction, then that would have been a different matter.

"I see... Thank you, Leone. That means we're probably not going to be going there for a while..."

I had bought myself some time, but that wasn't the end of it.

"..."

Why would Minnalis choose vengeance? It's not like her. I can't let her go through with it.

At that moment, the doors swung open, and in walked our instructor, a man in a flowing robe. The lesson began, but I found myself unable to concentrate. All I could think about was how to rescue Minnalis from her sad fate.

I glanced at the two girls with my skill, and they were still bound by the same dark flames, as well as those detestable black chains that I could only assume were the result of some mind-control skill. I'd expected to perceive their true feelings on the inside, trying to break free, but I could see nothing of the sort. It was as though they had accepted those chains willingly.

That meant that nothing would change if the chains disappeared. Even if I could remove them, the girls would put them back on. I had to begin by toppling their faith in vengeance. I had to make them see that it wasn't the answer.

And to do that, I first need to persuade him, the person at the center of those chains.

I knew that Kaito wasn't single-minded in his pursuit of revenge. He cared about the girls' well-being, like when he'd stood up for them in the café. At that time, I saw not his dark flames, though they were still there, but a second light, pure and impossibly bright.

He's a kind and honest person at heart. I've seen it. If I can change his mind, then I can change Minnalis's and Shuria's as well. As things stand now, they're only feeding one another's flames, and that's just not healthy.

Those chains served two purposes. The first was the production of that black tar that kept the flames of vengeance alight, and the second was to bind the three together, allowing them to share their emotions. All that negativity, all that hate, swirling around with no place to go.

It's just not right!!

I knew it. I could feel it in my bones. That was no way to live. I had to bring them back—bring them *all* back.

Yes, then the three of them could accompany me on my journey. Just think of all the people we could save with his knowledge and mine combined. This world was violent, yes, but it also held beauty.

It's not right! I swear I'll put them on the right path!

They could still be saved. They could still be happy.

Because hiding somewhere within those dark flames was the pale-blue light of sadness; I could see it, choked and wailing, tortured by the darkness all around it. They could still laugh and cry. Their hearts were still living. Even if that black flame never left them, other lights flourished.

I had to make them relinquish the darkness. It was holding them back. They needed to realize how wrong it was and give up on vengeance. It was for their own good.

"There's a town near the mountains called Gagarrad. If you ask there, they'll be able to direct you to the village. It's a bit of a detour, but the safest way is via a town in the Lunarian See called Lobelia."

Ahhh, at last. At long last.

…Tee-hee. Tee-hee-hee. Oh, I haven't had to use my skill in a while. I almost let my emotions slip.

I tried valiantly to hide my smile, knowing full well my efforts were in vain. Even if I couldn't go after the village immediately, I now knew where it was.

"…So that means most spells are classified into these seven categories: Fire, Water, Wind, Earth, Light, Dark, and Null. Other attributes such as Ice and Poison are derived from these seven basic elements. Magic which falls outside this system falls under the Misc. attribute. Famous examples of Misc. magic include the plant magic utilized by General Arzalyst of the Grigal Empire, or the hexes practiced by tribes in the northern imperial wastelands."

Ah, I mustn't get distracted. I need to listen to the lecturer.

I needed to learn all I could so that my vengeance would taste all the sweeter when it finally arrived. I looked down at my copy of a textbook on magical fundamentals that had been passed out at the

beginning of class. It was an old, beat-up thing that had clearly seen
many owners in its lifetime. Inside was information on topics I had
previously only known instinctually.

I tried to suppress my rising elation and listen to the lecturer, but
just then, the last grains of sand drained from an hourglass in the corner of the room, and I heard the sound of a ringing bell.

"Looks like that's it for morning classes," the instructor said, in
the same droning voice he used for the lesson. "We'll reconvene at
two PM."

After he left the room, we took out our lunch boxes and placed
them on our desks.

"Now what are you two doing for lunch—ah, I suppose I can
see," said Spinne.

Today's lunch was sandwiches of two kinds: sweet and salty fried
warblefowl meat and springrass, and wildcow cheese with smoked jig-
glepork. Master and I had prepared them together, so they were sure
to be a tasty treat.

"Wow, so beautifully put together!" said Spinne. "They look delicious! I always knew you were a good cook, Minnalis, but this is on
another level!"

"Wait, these look good…even better than what I can make," said
Leone with a troubled frown.

"They don't just look good, they *are* good!" boasted Shuria with
unwarranted pride, considering she hadn't helped at all. "I'll let you
have a bite of mine if you really want…"

She tore off a few pieces of her sandwiches and handed them to
the two women.

""Mmm… These are good!!""

"Naturally," I said. "I shan't allow anything less than culinary
perfection to pass Master's lips."

I felt a sense of pride and joy welling up inside me as I said it. It was nice to have my efforts noticed and commented upon from time to time. If only Master extended me that same courtesy...

"You must really like Kaito a lot, huh?" said Leone.

"Indeed. He's very important to the two of us."

"Yes!" added Shuria. "Oh, but we are currently besieging his emotional defenses, so don't let him know any of this, okay?"

"...Right. Of course, I won't," answered Leone, giving the girl an odd look.

"...Hmm? Is something the matter?"

"No, it's nothing," she said. "Should we go for lunch, too, Spinne? We don't want to be late for afternoon classes."

"Good idea. But man, is this first day turning out to be a bore. I know all this stuff already!"

"There you go again. It's important to review the basics, you know? It'll be too late to go over it again when you need it. All right, you two, we'll see you this afternoon. Come on, Spinne, Dan and Zanck are probably waiting for us."

The two left the classroom with a smile and a wave. We took that as our cue to resume eating.

"*Om-nom-nom.* These are delicious!"

Shuria shoveled the sandwiches into her mouth, sauce dripping down her chin.

"Don't stuff your face, Shuria," I said, wiping her clean. "People are watching."

"Mmgh?"

...This reminds me of when we all used to eat lunch together.

Back in the village, it had been Lucia who had cooked our lunches, not me. She would make us all lunch boxes, and whenever we got tired from playing around in the forest, we would sit in the shade of the trees and enjoy our lunch.

"Mmm. Perhaps a little more sourness next time…"

This salty taste was not enough to distract me from my reverie.

The streets were dyed a warm crimson by the time we made our way back to the inn. I couldn't tell whether walking with Leone's party had made the journey feel longer or shorter.

"*Phew.* I never knew listening to other people talk could be so exhausting," I said.

"Really?" asked Shuria. "I don't feel tired at all."

"Good girl, Shuria! Well done paying attention in class!" said Spinne, grabbing the girl and roughly rubbing her head.

"Eep! I told you not to do that! Only Kaito can pull my hair, beat me, and step on me!"

Oh dear, I'd told Shuria to be a bit more family-friendly when she was out in public to avoid situations like this.

"What? Does Kaito really do that to you?!" exclaimed Spinne.

"That's just not right," added Leone.

"Yeah, I didn't think he was that kind of guy."

The four looked at one another, uncertain. Shuria hadn't meant to get Master in trouble, but her naivete was part of the problem.

"Well, no, he…," I began.

"Shuria? Does Kaito really do those things to you?" asked Spinne.

"He sure does! Only Kaito is a big softie most of the time, so I really have to beg him to do it, and he usually refuses even then. By the time he does agree, though, he usually looks so fed up that it makes it even more thrilling! His frigid glare just gives me the chills!"

"Uh…eh…huh…?"

Unsure of how to react, Leone looked over to me for an explanation while Shuria locked herself away in a world of her own.

"...Leone," I answered. "When we were younger, Spinne told me there were all sorts of different forms of love in this world."

"O-oh? Did I...?" said Spinne, averting her eyes.

"I can't believe you'd say that to a child...," chastised Leone. She sighed. "So Minnalis, you think it's okay to just leave Shuria as is?"

"I'm afraid so..."

"It's a hard path to walk for one so young," commented Spinne. "I wonder if she can bear it..."

"Ah-ha-ha! Looks like the little madam's all grown up already!"

Zanck and Spinne chuckled together. Shuria, meanwhile, was still trapped inside a prison of her own imagination.

"Snap out of it already...," I muttered. "How long are you going to stand around embarrassing us?"

I forged a shard of ice and dropped it down Shuria's back, causing her to leap and squeal in shock.

"Eep?!"

"What am I going to do with you...?"

"That wasn't very nice, Minnalis...," she moaned.

"W-well, anyway," Dan cut in, eager to change the subject. "You two are both gunning for the advanced class, right? I bet you have to deal with much tougher material than we do. Spinne and Leone are one thing, but I'm impressed you can keep up at your age."

"Perhaps you should take a leaf out of their book, Dan," commented Zanck. "I can barely focus with you snoring next to me the whole time. It makes me look bad, too!"

"Z-Zanck?! I told you not to tell anybody about that!"

"Dan...would you care to explain this?"

"W-well, Leone, I...er...h-hey, what's going on over there?"

Darting his eyes around for salvation, Dan pointed to a small crowd. There in an open part of the street, a few vendors and street performers had set up shop and were calling out to people walking by.

"That's got to be the worst way of deflecting attention I've ever seen," sighed Leone. "Fine, we'll talk later. What's this, then? Some sort of fair?"

"*Come one and all! Who will be our next challenger? Blow a dart through the hole and win fabulous prizes!*"

"*Prizes, prizes! Come and play, come and play!*"

There were two hawkers: a tall, gangly man, and a much shorter, rotund one.

The game in question appeared to involve using a cheap blow-gun to fire darts at a plank of wood that holes had been cut into, with the aim of toppling dolls that sat on the other side. It was packed with would-be prizewinners bemoaning their poor luck or simply shoddy aim.

"Argh, so close!" "Just a little to the left!" "You suck!" "Try aiming properly!"

The coveted prizes were also lined up in plain view. Mixed in with the simple toys were daily necessities and expensive-looking magical ingredients, and it seemed the top prize was some sort of expensive potion.

"Huh, that's quite the impressive lineup," said Leone. "But…"

"…They never let you win the good prizes, do they?" said Spinne.

"Hmm? What makes you think that?" I asked.

"Take a closer look at that plank of wood."

I looked again at the hole-riddled board, but it seemed ordinary enough to me.

"Hmm? Actually, there is something strange about it," said Dan.

Shuria clued me in on the trick. "There's some weird mana flowing through it," she said. Her Scarlet Eyes revealed all. With her observation in mind, I tried concentrating on that plank of wood again. It was painted red and yellow with flowing patterns, and the holes were all different sizes, corresponding to the value of the prizes.

Just then, a challenger's dart made it through a hole. As it did, its trajectory changed so subtly that I would never have noticed with only a cursory glance.

"Huh."

I saw a faint pattern in the air for a second...

"Dammit," the challenger cursed. "I got through the hole but missed the prize!"

"I see," said Zanck. "I don't know how they're doing it, but those holes are changing the path of the dart so that it misses the target."

"The magic itself is nothing special, but they've done a great job of hiding it," added Spinne. "I'm surprised you could see it at all, Shuria. Good job."

"Hee-hee! Thank you!"

Grrr. Was I the only one who couldn't see anything? I wasn't very happy about that.

"Well, stalls like that are a copper a dozen. Let's move on," suggested Spinne.

"Huh? Shouldn't we inform the watch?"

"There's probably dozens of stalls at that fair all doing the same thing," said Leone, shrugging. "The watch know, but they won't do anything about it. They've got bigger fish to fry."

As I watched, another challenger tried and failed to hit a target.

"Bad luck, missy, care to try again?"

"Try again. Try again."

"Awww..."

The little girl walked dejectedly away from the stall. I saw deep sadness in her eyes. One I knew all too well.

"...Even when they're tricking innocent little girls like that?" I asked.

"Well, I mean... I don't like it, but..."

Leone was hard-pressed to respond. She must have been exposed to scenes like this every day, so often that they no longer weighed heavily on her mind. Those two men were running a scam, sure, but it was an insignificant one in the grand scheme of things. A drop in the pool of petty injustices that was all too easy to sweep under the rug. A shame that most people would simply it laugh off, belittling the feelings of those involved.

"...If you don't like it," I told her, "That's more than enough reason to do something about it."

"I'm disappointed in you," added Shuria, turning on her heel and following after me.

"Y-you two? Where are you going?"

Everyone does it. It's just the way things are. You can't change it. These were all just pathetic excuses. We *could* do something about it, and I intended to.

"Excuse me, young lady. Which prize would you like?"

"Huh?"

"You have your heart set on one of those prizes, don't you? Which one?"

"Um...we need medicine... My mother is hurt and in pain, and we can't afford it at the market..."

The girl pointed at the top prize, the expensive potion.

See, this is what I hated about the world. I couldn't fault Leone and the rest for their behavior. They were just doing what everyone else does: grasping for an excuse to not ask themselves some difficult questions.

"No! I didn't know about any of this!"

"That woman tricked me, too! Those stinking creatures lied to me!"

It was the same thing my father had done, and it caused him to turn on Mother and me.

"I see," I told the girl. "In that case, would you mind waiting here for a moment?"

"We'll get that potion for you!" Shuria asserted.

I hated this world. What kind of place trampled an innocent girl's feelings like that? I gave her a reassuring smile and headed over to the carnival stall.

"Roll up, roll up, who's next? It's getting late, so our next challenger will be the last!"

"Roll up, roll up. Come try, come try."

"Mister, mister!" begged Shuria. "Please let us try next, oh please!"

"You don't mind if we both try together, do you?" I added. "How much is it to play?"

"Why, just five large coppers each! But for you two pretty ladies, how about joining us for tea after instead?"

"Here's one silver for the two of us, then."

I tossed him the coin, and Shuria and I picked up our blowguns. It appeared we were each allowed to take two shots.

"Leave this to me, Minnalis!" said Shuria, warming up her Puppet Possession ability.

"No need," I replied, stopping her. "I have something I've been meaning to try." I thought back to that time not long ago, when Kuu had gone inside me, and I attempted to summon just a fraction of that power.

"Let's do this, Shuria."

"Agreed!"

She gripped the dart, channeling mana into it, imbuing it with the faintest shadow of life. Then we both fired, while the man looked on with his papier-mâché smile.

Our two projectiles shot unerringly toward the center of the holes. Shuria's living dart passed through without changing course, toppling the doll on the other side. Meanwhile, a small fly nudged my dart back onto the correct course after it went through the hole.

"Tee-hee-hee!"

"Hah! Did you see that?"

A useful power indeed. This will come in very handy in the future.

I had gained the ability to create small insects out of mana and control them. It was nothing compared to the powers I'd wielded when Kuu was inside me, but perhaps it could be used in combination with other skills.

"Wha—?!" "Wuh?"

Before the two operators could respond, Shuria and I lined up our second shots. Hers hit the target as intended, while mine caused the doll to fly off the pedestal and into a second one, knocking it down as well. Thus, we succeeded in felling five targets with four darts.

"Well then, we'll select our prizes, if you don't mind."

"So many prizes!"

"W-wait, hold on… Y-you shouldn't have been able to—"

"Shouldn't have been able to…what?" I replied innocently.

"W-well, er…"

The man merely stammered for a while before holding his tongue.

"In that case, let's go."

We took our five prizes, and I walked back to the small girl, handing her the potion she wanted.

"Er…um…I…"

"It's getting late. Go and take care of your mother."

"B-but…"

"Go. While she still has a life left to save."

"Th-thank you, maid lady and weird-looking girl!"

The child gave a beaming smile that seemed larger than her face and took off down the street to wherever she lived. I watched her go, satisfied.

"Ooh! I am *not* weird-looking! And how come you get to be a 'lady' while I'm just a 'girl?'"

"Let it be," I replied. Then I turned and called over to where

Leone and the others were standing. "Bye-bye for now! We have places to be, so we'll see you tomorrow!"

"Bye-bye!" added Shuria.

"Ah, Minnalis…"

Without waiting for their farewell, Shuria and I left.

"Now then," I said to her once we were out of sight. "You follow the girl. I think they'll probably come after me, but there's no telling what some people will stoop to."

"Understood! Leave it to me!"

Shuria went off by herself, slipping into the crowd, while I headed for the market. I took the scenic route through old backstreets, each diversion leading me into more and more deserted areas, until I finally sensed a hostile presence behind me.

"There you are. Honestly, I thought you'd be a little quicker than that."

"…"

The sound of footsteps behind me stopped, and a pair of grim faces emerged from the shadows.

"I hardly think I need to ask, but what might be your business?"

"Well," said the tall and thin one, "I know you said no and all, but I wondered if you wouldn't reconsider having tea with us, you see?"

"Teatime! Teatime!"

I knew it. I'd thought they might have better things to worry about if I stuck to taking the one bottle and a bunch of cheap prizes, but I suppose there was no accounting for stupidity.

"I'm sorry," I said, smiling, "but I don't have time to waste on the likes of you."

The two men seemed to take offense at my words, for their ugly faces grew even more unsightly as they struggled to conceal their rage.

"Yeah, I'm afraid that ain't gonna cut it. We're gonna need you to hand back those prizes you stole, got it?"

"Got it, got it? Hand back, hand back."

"Oh? I merely followed the rules to win these."

"That so? Well, that's a damn shame, lass, it really is. 'Cause we're gonna have to get a little nasty if you don't hand them back yourself, see?"

"Nasty! Nasty!"

"…"

"Try not to struggle too much. We still have to track down that little girl and get our potion back."

"Get it back! Get it back!"

"If you do that, you won't be long for this town, you know?"

"Yeah, you're right. And we just started makin' some real money, too. Heh, guess that just means we'll have to take a few prizes of our own. Startin' with you, then that little girl and her sick mother. We'll cut out your tongues and sell you as slaves. Doubt they'll fetch much at market, but you, on the other hand…"

"Sell as slaves! Sell as slaves!!"

I could only chuckle as they said the word "slaves."

"And yer mother's gone and snuffed it, too. Can't believe I'm out here lettin' you impact my bottom line."

"You really are scum," I said. "Why did it have to be slaves, of all things? *Wall of Ice.*"

"Huh? Wh-wha—?!" "Urh? Urk!!"

I conjured up two dome-shaped barriers that engulfed the two men.

"I can't have you screaming for help, or somebody might get the wrong idea," I explained. "Good thing I picked a quiet street."

"Wh-what have you…?"

"My legs, my legs! Can't move, can't move!!"

I began by freezing the two men's feet to the ground. The crystalized ice then slowly worked its way up their bodies.

"Oh, I am sorry. I would have let you off with a warning if you'd just asked nicely, but it's too late now! You picked the wrong day to get on my bad side; now that I've had a taste, I just can't stop myself! Tee-hee-hee-hee-hee!"

"Aaaarghh?! S-stop! Please stop!!"

"Cold, cold! Waaah! Waaah!"

"Please enjoy. This is the kind of treatment a man would die for! Hee-hee! Hee-hee-hee-hee!"

It wasn't long before neither of the two men could move a muscle; the ice had climbed up to their neck. A moment later, it grew outward to form a bowl around their heads, as if to encase them completely.

"W-we're sorry, we're sorry! Please let us go, please!"

"Sorry, sorry... Forgive, forgive..."

"Ah-ha-ha-ha! You're asking the woman you attacked of your own volition for forgiveness? Do you have any idea how insulting that is? You're so pathetic, it's adorable! Hee-hee-hee!"

The ice stopped growing, leaving only a V-shaped gap through which I could see their faces. The two men breathed a sigh of relief. Perhaps they were harboring some misapprehension that it was over. I gave them both the sweetest smile I could muster.

"You don't think that's it, do you?" I asked. "Your behavior crossed the line. I'm going to melt you down until not even a scrap of flesh remains."

"Huh? Uh...ah... No...please..."

"Help... Help..."

The two men's faces became masks of sheer terror as the ice started forming once more. Now the bowl around their heads was complete.

"If only you hadn't said the word 'slaves,' I'd have given you a quick and painless death. Too bad that's no longer an option."

I used Intoxicating Phantasm to create a powerful dissolving acid and poured it into the bowl.

""Gaaaaaaaaagh!!""

Then I sealed the top of the bowl with ice, as if to trap their screams within.

"It took this acid roughly thirty seconds to dissolve a goblin. I wonder if you can hold out any longer?"

"Gyaagh! Aaagh! Aagh!"

"Urg... Urg..."

The acid took effect immediately, burning away their flesh. I could hear the two men's muffled screams issuing from within their prison of ice.

Skin, muscle, bone. All were dissolved until nothing remained but a dark red liquid, held in human shape by the ice.

"Ha-ha-ha! Oh my! That was even more disgusting than I imagined!"

The ice shattered into tiny particles that instantly vanished, and the duo's remains splashed onto the floor, where they soaked into the street without a trace.

"I suppose I'd better be off, then. I wouldn't want to be late."

I walked off, trying as hard as I could to keep my high spirits under wraps. As I exited onto the main street, I saw many stores and stands closing up for the day. It seemed this place had been a market, albeit a small one.

Oh, I didn't know they sold ingredients around here. I ought to investigate next time.

I started down the street, only to stop in front of a stall selling fruits.

"I'm sorry for making you come with me, Minnalis. I just wanted Kril to have something to eat on his birthday..."

" ..."

"Hmm? Something the matter, Miss?"

"Oh, no…"

There was a box filled with yellow fruits the size of my fist on offer at the stall. By some coincidence, they were the very same fruits Lucia and I had been searching for when she'd discovered my secret.

"Could I buy three of those fruits, please?" I asked.

"Hmm? Sure. That'll be nine coppers for the lot."

"Here you go."

I handed over the coins and took the fruits, placing them in the magic bag Master was lending me. Just as I was leaving, however, the shopkeeper tossed me a fourth.

"Here you go, lass. On the house for a pretty girl like you."

"Oh, why, thank you very much."

I gave a small nod and went on my way.

"…"

I peered at the fruit in my hand as I walked along, then took a bite. The tart, sugary juices filled my mouth, and a sweet scent filled my nostrils.

"I've been just terrible today. I can't seem to keep my emotions under control."

I gave a small sigh as I walked on back through the crowd. Ever since Leone told me the location of my village, I'd been seeing sparks dancing before my eyes.

There was Lucia, Kril, and me. The man who I'd once called my father, and all the other villagers. It was a world my ignorance had built, one which the merest upset had set ablaze. That dim light seemed dazzlingly bright, and although I knew it was so far away, I felt giddy at the thought of holding it in my hands.

My body, mind, and soul—they all ached so, so badly.

Oh, how can I bring them the most suffering? Which poison, which method of torture, which tools should I use? That girl was always a dreamer, an even bigger one than I was. I'd better prepare something extra special.

"…I should head back to the inn before it gets any later."

I walked the twilit roads, bathed in the glow of the magical streetlights. Perhaps it was their warmth which made it feel like I was walking on air.

"Oh dear. That took far longer than I expected."

I dashed through Karvanheim's now-familiar roads. The magical streetlights were just starting to come on, and by the time I arrived at the fruit seller, he was already packing away for the night.

"Oh, nice to see you again," he said when he spotted me. "I thought maybe you'd been seeing some other merchant!"

"You know I wouldn't," I replied. "I've just been busy lately, that's all. So? Do you have any left?"

"Sure do. How many do you want?"

"Ten, please. I was thinking of making a pie out of them."

"Sure thing. Just give me a second to unpack."

The vendor went over to a crate near the back of his stall and removed the lid, picking out the fruit I sought one by one.

"Yes, these are the ones!" I said. "I can't wait to finally eat them again! I've been so busy."

"It's not just you who likes them, is it? So? When's the wedding?"

"Oh, you and your jokes! Well, the truth is…we actually *are* getting married, next month!"

"Well, congratulations! Let me throw in a few extra for the lucky man."

"Wow, thank you!" I said, taking the fruits. "What a haul! I'll see you next time, then!"

"You're welcome, *Lucia*. Give my congratulations to *Kril*, too, you hear?"

"I will!" I replied. "He's going to love this pie!"

I waved farewell to the man and hurried home. I couldn't wait to get back and bake Kril a lovely meal.

CHAPTER 4
And Then She Learned the Truth

*T*hough *their modes of living share striking similarities, there is a difference between the race of vampires and their monster counterparts, Vampyrs. Both are humanoid in appearance, and both feed off the blood of living creatures, but the Vampyr is a form of undead creature and cannot abide daylight or exposure to holy water. Furthermore, if it cannot feed regularly, it is unable to sustain its physical body and turns to ash.*

The vampire race, on the other hand, exhibits no such weaknesses. While their powers are curtailed if starved of fresh blood, they are otherwise able to mingle among humans and live perfectly normal lives.

Treated as monsters for their bloodsucking tendencies, these men and women usually attempt to conceal their own existence. They have grown skilled at employing techniques that allow them to hide their status board and are thus difficult to identify. It is quite simple for them to hide among humans.

It is often stated in folklore that the species produces new vampires through the biting of victims, but this is inaccurate; the bite merely places the victim under the vampire's control for a time. This misconception seems to have grown out of witnesses experiencing a bite victim's erratic

*behavior and erroneously inferring vampiric conversion. Vampires repro-
duce in the same way as humans do, and hence cannot spontaneously
generate others of their kind.*

*It is rumored that certain dark arts can turn human beings into
vampires. However, no credible accounts of this process exist.*

"...Finally got my hands on a decent book, but there's not a lot
here."

I ran my eyes across the pages of the dust-covered tome I uncovered in the library of Karvanheim Academy. I had been coming here
every day for a week now.

Books were expensive in this world, and this library was perhaps
the largest collection of them on the planet.

I heard the other library patrons discussing their findings with
one another. Back in Japan, it had been considered rude to speak in
a library, but there was no such etiquette here. Many of the patrons
were adventurers, chatting with their party while digging up information for quests they were on.

I, on the other hand, was here to find out what had happened
to Minnalis the other day. To that end, I was searching for any books
on vampirism I could get my hands on. Most of them were filled
with rather bland accounts and were of very little use. They mostly
told me things I already knew or conflated the race of vampires
with the monster variety and denounced their actions on religious
grounds.

I wanted to know if there was some sort of toxin or serum that
could induce vampirism, but I could find no mention of it in books
on either vampires *or* poisons. Nor could I find anything that shed
light on Kuu.

"Well, guess it was never going to be that easy," I muttered, ruf-
fling my hair and letting out a brief sigh.

If I couldn't find anything on vampires in this library, then I would have to consider asking one directly. Perhaps that egotistical bastard could help sort things out.

"But I really don't want to talk to him. I just can't deal with him."

I sighed yet again, grimacing at the thought.

Vampirism could be a powerful tool, but I'd need to know precisely what it was capable of first. I could always experiment and find out, but it never hurt to have more information.

"Anyway, I think I've turned up all I can here. Tomorrow I'll head into the dungeon and...hmm?"

Just as I was about to close the book, I noticed there was still one page left.

"Ah, not this crap again."

The True Vampire is the most ancient being ever to walk the globe.

—T. Kuroi

These words were apparently profound enough to merit an entire page to themselves.

"Man, the people in this world act like they're from a video game. Then again, they basically live in one."

Why was it that every book here seemed to have some sort of gimmick? A treasure map hidden in the binding, or a page held up to the light to reveal a secret message? Or if you were feeling really ambitious, a tome that appeared completely normal until someone channeled mana into it, whereupon it started glowing, the words changed, and a disembodied voice went "*Those who seek power, slake thy thirst...*" or whatever. Yeah, I really don't want to remember any more about my cringy teen phase than I need to, thank you very much.

I sighed and closed the book. By now it was quite late. I wandered around the bookshelves, replacing all the tomes I had picked up in the course of my research. Just then, I heard a voice.

"Ah, there you are!"

"Hmm?"

I turned to see Leone standing there.

"What's up?" I asked. "You need something?"

I hadn't spoken to her since the day of the examination, though I had, of course, been keeping tabs on her via Minnalis. She seemed a lot calmer now than she had back then and was no longer showing me the same reproach. As I wondered what could have caused such a transformation, she opened her mouth as if to respond, let her jaw hang there for a moment, then closed it again.

"…I have something to ask you," she said at last. "Will you come to the tavern with me? We can discuss it over drinks."

I pondered her suggestion for a moment before replying. "Sure," I said, "but I'll pass on the drinks if you don't mind. I need to get back to the inn fast, Minnalis is cooking tonight."

"…I see."

Leone looked somewhat upset by my reply, but she turned and started walking.

She doesn't seem angry at me. Still, I have a feeling there's more in store for me than just a pleasant chat.

I couldn't help feeling anxious as I followed her out of the library.

The tavern Leone took me to was already busy, even though it was early in the evening, and the hall was filled with sounds of people talking.

"Hey, waitress! Can we get another beer over here?"

"…So when are we going to stop drinking and get to why you called me out here?"

"Oh, quit bein' such a bore. You 'ave any idea how long I was waiting outside the dungeon for you to show up? Why didn't ya tell me you were going to be in the library?"

"I don't recall promising to keep you apprised of my location. If you wanted to get in touch, you should have asked Minnalis to take a message."

"I can't tell her this! You know how awkward it would make her feel?! What kinda... *hic!*...girl d'ya think eyam?"

"So we're talking about something awkward, are we? Anyway, I think you've had enough. You're babbling like a baby."

"From the mouth of babes comes truth. That's why beer is mankind's greatest invention, 'cause it turns you into one! C'mon, I'll buy you a mug as well!"

"I told you, I'm not drinking! What's gotten into you?"

I had entered the tavern ready to hear anything, but I hadn't expected Leone to immediately start ordering flagons of ale. After just one, she was rosy-cheeked and rambling, and the chances of having any sort of decent conversation seemed slimmer by the second. It was past the point I could be angry at her. By now I just wanted to go home.

"I've had enough. I'm leaving."

I stood up, leaving the fruit juice I had been sipping on the table.

"Hold it!" Leone protested, grabbing my arm. "You're not goin' anywhere!"

"Come on, give me a break..."

"You're like a withered-up plant, you are!!"

"..."

"You're like a withered-up plant. All dried up. I suppose I shall have to take good care of you."

I knew Leone hadn't meant anything by it, but her words stirred a memory in my heart.

"...I'm withered-up? ...What does that even mean?"

I let out a sigh and slumped back into my seat. Those feelings and Leone's dogged persistence left me too tired to argue. I was woefully unprepared for what came next.

"I'm talking about your true goal, the one you've been hiding from me. I'm talking about the vengeance lurking in your hearts."

It was like a needle in my back. A needle filled with deadly poison.

"Grh."

Leone's cheeks were still tinged red with inebriation, but her eyes bore right into my soul.

"I can see it, you know. I can see the hate that fills your hearts and the chains that bind it there."

"...Oh?"

My voice came out in barely a whisper. For some reason, I had no desire to ask her how she knew.

"Minnalis is a good girl, I know she is. Even Shuria's just an innocent child, deep down. And I'm certain you care a lot about them. That's why I want you to give up on this revenge stuff, Kaito. It's not right."

"Not right, you say?"

"Yes. Even if they asked for it, what you're doing is brainwashing."

"...Brainwashing. I see. So that's how it seems to you."

She wasn't wrong, technically. But that was the oath we'd each sworn in private. It wasn't for her to debate the righteousness of it.

I felt invaded.

"It's not the only way," she went on. "You still have one another, and you've been given a second chance. Forget what happened to you the first time around. It doesn't matter! What matters is that we know what's coming. We can make things better!"

"..."

"We can't waste time on petty vengeance. In just six months, the barrier the Church maintains over the continent will collapse, and the world will be plunged into conflict. Think of the people we could save if we put our minds to it! That's the best way forward, not only for the world, but for you guys as—"

Splash!

I threw my drink in Leone's face.

"This conversation's over."

I had meant to hear her out to the end, but I just couldn't stand the way she talked.

"Wh-what was that for?!"

"I didn't come here for a sermon. If it was that easy to make the pain go away, we wouldn't be here."

Something I had tried with all my will to suppress reared its ugly head. Now it was spilling forth unhindered.

"Who cares if revenge isn't the way forward? Who cares if it won't make me happy? Oh, you make me sick, fantasizing about my life when you don't even know what I'm going through. It's easy to talk sunshine and lollipops when you only have to stand and watch from the outside, but you wouldn't talk like that if you knew what I've been through. Do you have any idea what it's like? To hate someone so much that merely killing them isn't enough?!"

I wasn't just fed up with her anymore. I spat and glared at her with all the hate I could muster.

"Where do you get off, preaching justice to the downtrodden?"

"That's not fair!" she shouted back. "I'm only thinking about you!"

Leone was utterly undaunted by my fierce gaze. She hadn't come here flaunting some half-baked philosophy; she had thought long and hard about her position. I could see the old me in her eyes, the me this world had killed…and so mixed in with my anger was a sliver of self-pity.

"It doesn't matter how logical your argument is," I replied. "You'll never be able to change my mind."

"Grh!"

"The things you say can never be. We've accepted that, while you've gone on running in the wrong direction."

"What's that supposed to mean?" she asked.

"It's not that we think what we do is good, or that we revel in doing evil. It's that we chose to be agents of retribution, even if that meant letting go of everything that was important to us," I explained.

"But why would you choose to live that way?! You admit that those two girls are important to you! So why are you still obsessed with the past instead of the future?!"

Leone looked so frustrated I feared she was going to crack her teeth.

"You've still got this totally wrong," I told her. "We're not *looking* to the past, we're stuck there. When we found ourselves in hell's deepest pit, we swore that wouldn't be the end. We haven't taken a single step since. The thought of a bright, happy future is nothing more than a sick joke to us."

A play so tragic that all you could do was laugh.

A suffering so deep that our tears had long since run dry.

An anger so strong that it threatened to tear us limb from limb.

To forget that and merely wait for our scars to heal was the life of a spineless sheep.

"I know we can't go on living like this—and that's exactly why we have to see it through. That's why we seek revenge—to move on with our life, not to end it."

Though the world had tried to prematurely draw the curtains, our tale was far from over. We would show the others what hell followed that final act.

The woman's conviction, however, remained firm. She stood up from her chair, pounding her fist on the table.

"It's not like that!" she cried. "You can still move on! We have a chance to make things right! People died in the run-up to the war! Some of them lost their lives protecting me, and I'll be damned if I'm just going to sit back and let that happen again!"

Her face was still bright red, but I could no longer tell if it was from inebriety or anger. The fire in her eyes, though, was as strong as ever.

"The two of us can change history together! We can make sure that nobody has to go through the grief Minnalis faced! Don't you understand that?!"

"I do. We're the only ones who can rewrite the script. Make it so it's not the weak and innocent who suffer, but the evil bastards who orchestrated everything."

"You don't get it at all!!"

The light in her eyes was burning with righteous indignation. Perhaps she really did believe that she could save everyone she'd lost the first time. It was an arrogant notion, but one I could empathize with. The only problem was that I could no longer force myself to feel that way. Her heartfelt appeal aroused nothing in me but a wallowing self-pity, and she was brushing dangerously close to a nerve I wanted very much left alone.

"I understand you want to get your revenge," she said, "but we're wasting precious time! Can't you see that? We can stop the things we had no choice but to accept! We can save the lives we couldn't save!"

"Shut up."

"Gh!!"

"Just…shut the hell up."

I was annoyed. I had tried to stay quiet, because I knew those old wounds would otherwise reopen. But I'd failed. Why couldn't things just go my way for once?

"You don't understand me in the slightest. If you did, you wouldn't talk like that. I'm sick of listening to you go around in circles."

"Wh-what are you—?"

"I'm saying that you're never going to get through to me. You came woefully unprepared to this discussion, and you only have yourself to blame. Don't speak to me again. Don't even *think* about me. You'll leave us alone if you know what's good for you."

I stood up, dropped the money for my drink on the table, and started walking off.

"Where are you going? I'm not done talking to you!"

"Yes, you are, Leone. You're through insulting us."

"Grrr… Listen to me! What's all this 'us' business?! You're a danger to those girls! You're denying them a happy future!"

"That's for them to decide, not you."

I left the tavern without another word. Bathed in the light of the setting sun, the streets outside looked as though they'd been stained with blood.

"What a joke. Saving the lives we couldn't the first time?"

I hated myself. I kept on making the same mistakes, never learning, never growing, my ideals always just out of reach. I told myself that I needed only vengeance, but even I was aware I was *jealous* of what others had. I knew it was wrong, I had sworn an oath. And yet try as I might, I couldn't let those feelings go.

"Turn back the clock as many times as you like. You can never bring back what we've lost."

Yet even my awareness of that fact and my determination to live up to it weren't enough to keep me from harboring regrets about how things had gone the first time around. And for that, I loathed myself.

"...It's not right. It's just not right. Once he takes revenge, there's no going back."

After Kaito left, I fell to the dirty tavern floor. I had failed to persuade him.

But I'd learned something in the process: I knew he wasn't dead inside.

How many people have I seen?

In the years that followed the demon war, I had traveled to towns all across the land, bringing goods to impoverished regions.

I'd seen wives who'd lost their husbands. Children who'd lost their parents. Brothers who'd lost their sisters. Soldiers who'd lost their friends. I'd glimpsed the darkness in their hearts, and I saw how they patched it up just so they could go on.

And I also witnessed what happened to the people who chose revenge, screaming out for it as their bodies wasted away. Saw the cruel manner in which they met their ends on a bloodstained blade. Saw their faces, warped by anger and spewing blood, cursing the world and everyone in it to the bitter end.

I saw the ones who'd succeeded, too. I saw them at the end, clutching the knife of vengeance, utterly consumed by an anger they gave their entire life to fuel.

Each and every time, they'd been crying. As if the cycle of hurt went on. After it was all over, there was only a hollow laugh. No joy, no sadness—just a voiceless, wailing cackle that seemed to go on forever.

"…But if Kaito's saying he wants revenge so that he can live, that means there's still a chance."

This avenger wasn't like the others. He hadn't given up on life just yet.

"I won't back down."

If this was a business discussion, this obstacle would be enough to get me to cut my losses and back out, but it wasn't. This was about somebody's life. And where there was a will, there was a way.

I thought of the towns I'd encountered, devastated by the demon lord's armies. I thought of the people I'd met, starving and afraid. I thought of Minnalis, wasting away in a dirty cage god only knows where.

I thought of myself, hiding in terror on war-stricken plains, hearing another scream off in the distance and wondering if it was one of my friends who'd died this time.

"I don't want to live through that horror again."

I wanted to be able to smile. I wanted to be able to be happy.

I wanted to hear true laughter, not a hollow mockery of it, devoid of either coldness or warmth.

"I don't want them to cry because I didn't try hard enough."

No matter how difficult it was, I couldn't give up. I clenched my fists tightly.

"Water, check. Rations, check. Potions, check. Adventuring gear, check."

Looking over my equipment, I gave a satisfied smile.

Minnalis and Shuria had already left for school. The two girls were taking in information like sponges, and it reflected in their magical understanding. Previously, they'd had only an intuitive grasp of spellcraft, and casting anything was like performing long division without knowing the multiplication tables.

A good example of this was how Minnalis was quite adept at Ice magic but struggled with what should have been the simpler forms of Water and Wind magic. An intuitive understanding could only bring her so far. Anything above the most basic spells had been an unsustainable effort. No amount of natural-born talent could substitute for that effort; it was only through book learning, the distillation of the work of thousands upon thousands of history's greatest wizards, that Minnalis and Shuria could grow any stronger.

The two girls had been hesitant at first, but once they realized how it could make them better at slinging spells, they became rather eager.

"No more hanging about, then," I muttered to myself, standing up. "Time to go."

My destination was yet again the academy. But as of the day before, I was done with the library. This time, I had my eyes on the dungeon.

To be honest, I didn't feel like I'd gotten my effort's worth out of the library, but I couldn't waste any more time searching for information I might never find. Besides, after that conversation with Leone yesterday, I was feeling ready to hide underground for a few days.

I picked up the lunch box Minnalis had made for me and placed it in the Squirrel's Blade of Holding, then left the inn, giving a short nod to the taciturn landlord as I stepped out.

Walking the busy streets outside, my thoughts turned inward.

What a stroke of luck to run into Leone. She's taught me more than I ever expected.

The world was in a state of impending war. Every single nation was strengthening their armies in preparation for the demon invasion, and though my absence was only one factor of many, the effects were beginning to show. The beast lands of Gilmus was the only country whose behavior was completely unchanged.

Without me to act as their secret weapon, the Orollea Kingdom lacked the means to quell rising anti-monarchist dissent. They had apparently given up on summoning a hero, opting instead to hold a ceremony whereby they would pick a champion from among their people. In other words, they were choosing a sucker to act as my replacement.

And so, with the supposed blessing of the Great Spirits behind them, the kingdom was in the midst of holding a tournament where the winner would be awarded the title of Hero. When I heard that, I was incensed. Why did they summon me when they could have done that all along? I wanted to go tear down the walls of that damn city at the earliest opportunity.

As for the Church, it was much the same as before, with supporters of the archbishop growing in power. But with me out of the picture, the kingdom hadn't been able to strong-arm the Church into providing assistance, which left the Church free to divert all available manpower into conquering a dungeon within the See called *Coffin of the Undying*. Heading the charge was apparently the priestess, whose holy magics were extremely effective against the undead.

I'd have thought they'd be all over whoever the kingdom picked as my replacement, but it seemed the Church drew a subtle but important distinction between summoned heroes and those simply chosen from within this world.

As for the empire, they were tackling a dungeon of their own, acquiring powerful weapons and magic items while training their soldiers for war. It was a dungeon I myself had visited the first time around. Apparently, their campaign was going well, despite the large numbers of casualties among the conscripted slaves who composed the front lines.

The beast lands could focus on little but taking care of skirmishes with infernal creatures within their territory. Geographically speaking, they were the most exposed to the demonic threat, and so they had to deal with significantly more attacks compared to the other nations. The barrier stretching across the entire continent prevented them from suffering any major damage, but it was only a matter of time before everything came tumbling down.

I need to face the fact that my exclusive knowledge isn't going to help me much longer.

Well, whatever. It didn't change what I had to do. My top priority was getting back into shape, and that would all start here.

"…Here it is."

I had come around to the back of the academy, where there were two dungeon entrances. The ground here was sunken in a circle, like a bowl, and surrounded by a fence of thick logs. There were only a few people around at the moment, and none of them seemed like they were heading in any time soon. That was fine by me, since I'd purposefully picked a time when I wouldn't run into anybody.

As I passed by a wooden checkpoint, a guard seemingly employed by the academy called out to me.

"Halt. Do you wish to enter the dungeon?"

"That's right," I replied. I took a deep breath and steeled myself for the fight ahead. This labyrinth was of a much higher level than the one I'd tackled alongside Minnalis near the royal capital, and even the one near Dartras where I had obtained the dungeon core that kickstarted the Mana Storm.

"Do you have anything that identifies you as an agent of the academy?"

"Will this do?"

I flashed the man my enrollment certificate.

"Very well, you may pass. Ahead of you lies Karvanheim, the

Temple of Darkness. As a solo adventurer, I'd advise you stick to the first five levels. From then on, the dungeon becomes far more dangerous."

"Yes, I know."

I walked through the checkpoint and down the gentle slope of the basin, arriving in front of the dungeon entrance. It was carved out of a rock face nearly five meters tall, with snakelike carvings all around the opening. The gate alone had the distinctive flavor of mana particular to dungeons.

The light-green walls within were covered with grooves, and here a guard stood watch over two doors. Behind one of these doors was a dungeon unlike any I'd ever faced before. It was an ancient place, the very literal and metaphorical foundation of the city that bore its name. It had been growing far beneath the ground for eons by the time the first settlers arrived, and now it totaled fifty floors deep.

It was also not my destination.

"Hmm? Excuse me, sir. That's the entrance to the Tutorial Dungeon, a training dungeon for beginner students. The Temple of Darkness is through the other door."

"Is that a problem?"

"Huh? Well, no, it's not an issue… But there's only one kind of monster in there, the Mad Puppet. There won't be much of interest to an adventurer of your caliber."

"I know. Trust me. This is the door I want."

The guard was only trying to be helpful, but I waved off his remark and entered the Tutorial Dungeon. As soon as I stepped foot inside, the whole atmosphere seemed to change.

"Krikk… Krikk… Krikk…"

A monster appeared that looked somewhat like a clay figurine. This was a Mad Puppet. It was a misshapen creation formed of some terracotta-like material, with a voice that sounded like the movement of rusted machinery. It seemed to be actively falling apart as it attacked. I lopped off its feet and headed deeper into the dungeon. More attacked, but I dispatched each one in the same way.

"Right, that's enough warming up. Time to head to the *entrance*."

After I'd had my fill of the Mad Puppets, I descended to the lowest floor of the dungeon, to what appeared to be the deepest chamber. In the center of this large room stood an engraved pedestal, atop which sat a crystal sphere that shone a reddish-orange. This was the dungeon core, or at least, that was what the academy believed.

"Grooough! Graaargh!"

"It's taken me nearly an hour to get down here... I'm short on time."

The creature before me was known as a Lesser Mad Golem, but it was basically just a larger Mad Puppet. Lazily and without sophistication, it swung an enormous fist at me.

"There's no doubt about it, I really am getting sloppy."

I took half a step back, straightening my body sidelong to evade the blow. Then I leaped on top of the arm and began running along it. Dispelling the Soul Blade of Beginnings, I conjured up the Ruined Sword of Gigantism, a katana with a chipped edge. I channeled mana into it, and the blade grew to be as long as the golem's arm itself. I guided its massive weight down to slash the golem diagonally in half.

"Gruuuugh..."

Its core bisected, the creature crumbled into a pile of clay.

I used far more mana than I needed to just now.

Slowly, but surely, I was letting down my guard. I'd killed Eumis, I'd killed Grond. I was growing satisfied. Happier. I was enjoying myself, doing the things I wanted to do. Crying, laughing. Letting the light take over the darkness in my heart.

I was finding the pearls mixed in with the sludge at the bottom of the pit. They were exactly what I was fighting for, and yet they caused me to crack. To slip. I picked them up, one after the other, even though I knew they were tearing me apart.

"Right, then."

Sidestepping the clay pile, I dispelled my soul blade and approached the pedestal. I took out a knife and sliced into my palm, letting the blood trickle onto the dungeon core. As the core absorbed it, the roots growing around the base of the pedestal pulsed ominously. Soon a magic circle appeared before me, shifting through red and purple light.

I stepped into the circle without hesitation and saw the world twist around me. I waited for everything to return to normal.

I had not felt the effects of teleportation in a very long time.

I arrived in a strange location that resembled the guts of some gargantuan creature. The walls and ceiling were soft and fleshy, and the air smelled distinctly of blood. Above all else, the mana I sensed in this place was leagues stronger than that of the previous dungeon.

"Never thought I'd come back here," I muttered. "But it's the perfect place for what I have to do... Oh?"

"""Hissss?!"""

Three monsters known as Granomir Snakes tried to sneak up behind me. I turned and decapitated them all with a single swing. They were powerful B-rank creatures, with an intrinsic ability that allowed them to go undetected by sight, smell, and hearing. Once slain, they released a purple gas and began to crumble.

"Ha-ha, coming at me with the hard stuff right off the bat. Just what I need to wipe the grime off my heart."

I felt a chill run down my spine for the first time in far too long. Death was close, I could feel it. One wrong step away, one wrong breath away, one wrong move away. I could almost hear it laughing at me.

"""Gibble!"""

Before I could even catch my breath, a pair of oozes appeared. They were monsters known as Immortal Slimes, and they contained multiple miniscule cores within their gelatinous body. The only way to defeat them was to destroy each and every core at the same time.

"Come on then. You're nothing but another warm-up."

I conjured the Ivory Blade of Snow, a rapier whose blade and grip alike were pure white, decorated in such a way as to look almost ceremonial. It had the ability to slow down all creatures within a fixed radius.

"Gibbooo!" "Gibbieee!"

As the Immortal Slimes rushed toward me, I channeled mana into my blade.

"Stained in white. Biting light. Let my domain arrest thy flight. *Ivory Garden.*"

I turned the point downward and plunged it into the ground. A pale white dome instantly spread out around me, engulfing the two monsters. Inside the dome, a light snowfall danced on the air, and everything was pale and blurred. The oozes' tentacles reached toward me bit by bit, but soon their heat, the movement of every one of their atoms, was drained from them.

I slashed with my sword as if dividing the very air itself. After a moment, the two ice sculptures before me crumbled into dust.

"Yes. This is it. This feeling."

This was my mission. To conquer this dungeon that nobody knew. That didn't even have a name yet.

When my second life began, I'd been reborn with purpose. Before that, I had been living without a cause, clinging only to the promise I made with Leticia. Vengeance gave me hope, but it was a poisoned chalice. The more I sipped that sweet nectar, the more complacent I became. Soon, I would be unable to complete that which I'd set out to do.

So I had to go back. I had to feel that despair once more. I had to sink to the very pits of it, surround myself with nothing but bitter foes.

"…It's time to take a walk through hell."

The imperial citadel towered over the city of Garigal, capital of the Grigal Empire. If the royal castle of the Orollea Kingdom was a stone-wrought beacon of history and tradition, then this building was a testament to the wonders of technology, a fortress of iron and fire.

"Hrm. It was my belief that you were currently preoccupied, heading the conquest of the Coffin of the Undying. Perhaps I am growing feebleminded in my old age."

I stood before an aging man who nonetheless oozed a powerful aura from every pore. He was Gorodir Grigal, ruler of the Grigal Empire, a nation which bought its legacy with blood and steel.

He appeared almost immortal, divine, exuding a radiance matched only by the solemnity of his surroundings as he sat upon the imperial throne.

"Lunaris has bestowed upon me many wisdoms," I replied, "but Her motives are not mine or any mortal's to question. I am merely an agent of Her will."

"It matters little. I welcome you to my domain, Lady Metelia."

"Much blessed I am to receive your gracious hospitality, Your Majesty."

Such a miserable man. He's just as unpleasant as I remember.

Our meeting was off to a predictable start. Backhanded comments hidden in our words, poison lacing our smiles. I couldn't say I condoned testing the limits of one's potential allies in such a way, but when in Grigal, I supposed.

"Perhaps you'd care to enlighten me as to the purpose of your visit, my lady."

"...The seeds of discord are ripening. Dark forces seek to cast a shadow on Our Lady's light. The time draws near. If we do not strike this evil at its heart, the oath-sworn grace of Lady Lunaris that protects this nation shall be lost. The world must stand united against this threat, or else we shall surely fall apart."

"Hmm. Indeed, demon sightings within the barrier have increased in frequency as of late. Furthermore, it appears to be happening across all regions that lie at the edge of the continent. I can't say I put much stock in this 'oath-sworn grace' of yours, but the fact remains that the barrier's power is fading fast."

Chin resting in one hand, Emperor Gorodir nodded deeply.

"And so you wish for all nations to band together, as they did in the past?"

"Quite right, Your Majesty. No one country can stand alone against the demonic threat, no matter how mighty. Thus, I have come to propose a treaty. As we speak, my messengers are also extending the same offer to the kingdom and the beast lands.

"I see. Very well, then. My court officials will work out the details."

"I thank you for your understanding, Your Majesty."

"You are leaving tomorrow, correct? In that case, I hope you find the remainder of your stay relaxing."

"Thank you, Your Majesty."

I curtsied and left the room.

""""Welcome back, Lady Metelia.""""

I returned to the chamber provided by the emperor, where my attendants awaited me. There was an intoxicated, almost euphoric look in their eyes, a result of their careful upbringing that had instilled in their hearts a complete devotion to serving me.

"Has the letter been delivered?" I asked.

"Yes, my lady."

"That is a relief. Very well."

There was no indication that the princess had left the kingdom, and at this time the target of my correspondence ought to still be seeking work. There was no doubt he would reply.

I softly brushed my attendant's cheek, letting an almost imperceptible amount of mana flow into her.

"Ahhh...ahhh...my lady..."

"Lady Lunaris seeks to put the world on the right path. You must join me in writing the ending to this tale that was always meant to be."

"Y-y-yes, my lady!!"

The attendant's look turned to one of rapture. Her faith was much becoming of an apostle of Lunaris. Ready to give her life for mine and Kaito's future without complaint. They were surely deserving of a place in our perfect world.

After all, Kaito often said that happiness was to be shared with other people.

"I think I shall take a bath. Please ensure I am not disturbed."

""""Yes, my lady!""""

I picked up a sack and headed to my assigned bathing quarters. The empire's offerings were considerably austere when compared to the wide-open bathrooms of the kingdom's royal castle. As one bound by a vow of poverty, I very much preferred this style. Even the suffocating walls reminded me of the arms of my beloved Kaito.

Empty Container.

I spoke the command words, and the sack I'd brought dispensed its contents: dozens upon dozens of Kaito dolls. My very own Kaitos, each lovingly stitched by hand. Happy Kaitos, angry Kaitos, sad Kaitos, blushing Kaitos.

"Ahhh, every bath becomes a dip in paradise so long as I have these..."

I sank into the warm water, surrounded by happiness, and I felt a throbbing deep inside.

Kaito was looking at me. Me, and only me.

"Hee-hee-hee... You're making me blush, Kaito... Ahhh, if only you could really be here... ♪"

I pulled my life-size Kaito doll close, burying my face in the back of his neck.

"I love you, Metelia."

"Aaah... Aaah, Kaito..."

I closed my eyes, imagining him in my arms. The more I touched, the hotter my body grew, and soon I was running my tongue all across the doll's shoulders.

"Mmm... Ngh... Mmm..."

I squeezed the doll tightly, then turned it around, as though he were lying over me.

"I love you, Metelia."

"I love you, too, Kaito. I want you. More than anyone. More than anything... Mmph... Mmm..."

I placed my lips softly on his. Time and time again.

"Mmm... Ah... Mmm... Soon you won't just be a doll, Kaito. I can't wait to see how the real you feels... Hee-hee-hee... Let's start over again, just us..."

Soon, there would be no more obstacles in our way, and the two of us could walk the correct path together.

Couldn't we, Kaito?

The empire was a dark place. Under their meritocratic system, might meant right.

But that same rule existed everywhere in this godforsaken world. Swindling, ambushes, traps, hostages, betrayal. These were the bread and butter of every nation on the continent. The winner took all; it didn't matter what underhanded tricks they resorted to in pursuit of victory. History was written by the killers.

I'd become an assassin because I saw it as the purest profession in the world. I wanted killing to be my life, my enjoyment, my purpose. It wasn't enough to be an adventurer, a knight, or a mercenary. Those people were not pure killers.

I didn't want to kill to live; I wanted to live to kill. That's how I became known as the Lord of Murder. I had no interest in epithets, but I felt the title validated my way of life nonetheless.

"Oh, Gordo. Out for a walk?"

"Why, yes, the weather *is* lovely today."

"That's not what I said, Gordo. You still goin' senile?"

"Why, of course! Ten coppers apiece, was it?"

"Listen to me, you old fogey... Besides, that barely covers my costs!"

"You see, I have a date with Yunmei tonight!"

"Yunmei? Ain't that the name of one of the neighborhood dogs?"

"Ho-ho-ho."

I tossed the coin to the fruit seller, and bit into the cheap, ripe fruit I had purchased.

"Ahhh, this sweet flavor warms my heart... Oh?"

When I returned to my haunt, I found traces that someone had been there while I was out.

"Oh, dearie me. Looks like I missed a visitor."

If this was a burglary, then it looks like my next target just came up.

"Hmm? Ah, just a letter, it seems."

What I found waiting for me at the table was an ordinary folded-up sheet of paper.

"...Addressed to me directly. From the priestess? Very fishy, very fishy indeed... I had always wanted to kill the priestess..."

I chuckled, giving a toothy grin.

Ever since I first laid eyes on her smooth, pale skin, I wished to know what it was like to shove a blade into it.

I unsealed the letter and read it.

"...Karvanheim, the City of Magic? That is west of here, and rather chilly for these old bones."

Now, how would a hero's flesh feel in death, I wondered?

"*Sigh...* Leone didn't show up to school today, either."

Shuria and I were walking back from the academy with the rest of Leone's party.

Usually, classes only ended once the streets were dyed in the orange glow of evening, but the sun was still high today. Supposedly, the oh-so-special internal students were scheduled to have a mock battle, so afternoon lectures had been canceled.

With no concern for *our* schedules, of course. Had it been just one week earlier, I could have spent the afternoon with Master, but he was currently underground. What a useless school.

"I know," said Spinne. "She seems to be having some trouble getting in contact with her business partners at the moment. Yesterday she came back crying 'Where is heee?!' and had drunk so much she woke up with a hangover. I told her if she's going to make me sit through all these boring lessons, then the least she could do is make an effort to turn up herself, and she said she just couldn't! How is that fair?"

Spinne grumbled to herself, fuming.

"I'm more worried about this one," said Zanck, turning to Dan. "This is what he's like after trying to keep up with lessons for just half a day."

"Bwuh…"

"Even just the basic course is difficult," Shuria complained. "I have to focus really hard just to understand, and when I get home I need to go over it again with Minnalis."

"Oh, you do self-study?" asked Spinne. "That's very admirable. What kind?"

"We just go over the material in preparation for the lecture and review it again afterward," I explained. "We use our textbooks, along with the notes I take in class, to… Huh?"

I fished around in my schoolbag for that day's notes to serve as an example, only to realize they were nowhere to be found.

"Oh dear," I said. "I think I left them on my desk… Go on without me; I'll catch up. Shuria, we'll start our study session when I get back!"

"Ah, Minnalis?!"

I turned back and retraced my steps to the academy. The daily lessons must have been getting to me. I'd never forgotten anything in my life.

…I just haven't been able to calm down since coming to this city…

Perhaps it was because of Leone and her group. Meeting her had caused old memories to come flooding back. Because of that, my "Manipulative Mask" skill had been very useful lately. I didn't want Leone knowing what I was fantasizing about during lectures.

"Oh, thank goodness. Here they are."

I returned to where I had been sitting to find my notes still spread out on the desk. I filed them away in my satchel and made to leave the classroom, when suddenly I heard a girl and boy racing down the hallway, apparently in some rush.

"Well, maybe if you weren't so slow all the time!"

"Wh-what's the hurry? It's not like Lucia's going to lose!"

"Don't you know who she's up against? She and Kril are going to have to pull out all the stops if they want to win!"

"…Huh?"

Those names were like a spike in my brain. What did this mean?

"Hurry up! The match is almost over!"

"I-I'm coming!!"

No, It can't be them, I thought. *I mean, the village is all the way in the northeast of the kingdom…*

Like a butterfly to a flower, like a moth to a flame, I felt drawn to those students. Washed away, as if by a raging river. I found myself walking after them, filled with emotions I couldn't even begin to untangle.

"…Why? Why are they here?"

It was some kind of mistake. It had to be. It couldn't really be them.

I soon arrived at a battle arena the academy set aside for the internal students. It was much larger, and far more beautiful than the colosseum we external students used for practical magic courses. The stairs leading to the upper gallery were dimly lit, and the far exit was filled with such a blinding light that I couldn't see what lay ahead.

My ears rang, and my chest tightened. Darkness clutched at the corners of my vision. Each step I ascended felt steeper than the last. And when I finally moved into the light, it was like falling underwater. All the color and sound of the world drained away.

"W-wow! Both sides are evenly matched!! This is shaping up to be a fight for the ages! The four most prodigious students to ever walk these halls, Team Square!"

My ears were plugged with cotton. My eyes felt dim and shaky. It was them.

There you are there you are there you are there you are there you are there you are there you are there you are there you are there you are there you are there you are there you are there you are there you are there you are there you are there you are there you are there you are.

"Lucia… Kril…"

She had grown into a fine, proud woman. Her face was more mature, her hair longer. But no matter how different she looked, she couldn't hide herself from me.

"Haah…haah… Time to finish this! Haaaaaagh! Hellfire Sword: Blazing Inferno!!"

"Go for it, Kril! Force Up! Fire Spirits' Blessing! Medicality!"

They were standing right before me. Countless nights had I dreamed of this day, and now it was finally here.

"I won't go down so easily! Snowdrift Spear: Raging Blizzard!!"

"You think you can defeat us? Physical Conversion! Boosted Enchantment! Spiritcalling: Voices of War!!"

The opposing teams of two rushed toward each other, letting out a loud ringing of steel and a great dust cloud that engulfed the arena. When the dust settled, it revealed two boys, exhausted by their clash, and two girls, worn out by their comprehensive suite of support spells.

"Haah… Hahhh… Krh… Raaaaaaaaaghhh!!"

"Kril!"

"Grh… Hrh… Grrr… Rrrraaaaaaaahhh!! Krh! Gh!"

"*Eugace!!*"

The two boys struggled to their feet once more, but then one of them fell to his knees.

"*The match is over! The last team standing is comprised of Lucia and Kril!!*"

Oh, what on earth was going on?

"*Krh. You win. You're a tough guy, Kril.*"

"*Ah-ha-ha. I couldn't have done it without Lucia. She's my true strength.*"

"*Ha-ha-ha. Look at you, showing off. You know the whole room is listening, right?*"

"*Ah…*"

What was happening?

"*Eh-heh-heh. Thank you, Kril, but it's because of you that I can do my best.*"

"*Haah. I guess this makes another loss for us. How many is that now, Lucia?*"

"*Don't be like that, Cataleya. You could say the true victor here is mine and Kril's love!*"

"*Ever the lovebirds. I hope I'm invited to your wedding!*"

"*Of course you are! Thank you so much, you two! I'm so blessed to have such good friends!*"

What in heaven's name was I looking at?

"*What a heartwarming scene from the academy's top performers, Team Square. I hear that they plan to represent our magnificent nation by joining the Karvanheim Defense Force upon completing their studies. Kril and Lucia will also be celebrating their wedding next month. I hope you'll all join me in offering my warmest regards to the happy couple.*"

"""*Huuurrraaaaaahhh!!*"""

"Oh… Ohhhh… Ahhh… Ahhhh…"

The storm of applause. The stage bathed in sunlight. It was all as fake as my pristine snowscape. A beautiful land glimpsed through the looking glass. A pale, empty world.

"...Hee-hee. What trash..."

How could it be you standing there? How could you?

"What a load of rubbish..."

How could you? How could you do this? How could you expect me to allow it?

How could you how could you how could you how could you how could you how could you how could you...?

This could not be. It was impossible. And so, there was only one thing to do.

"...You need to be destroyed, don't you...?"

Like filth. Like waste. Like vermin. Tread it into the earth until it's all gone.

"..."

I took a deep breath to clear my head and focused my gaze on their laughing faces, as if through a lens.

Don't laugh. Don't laugh. DON'T. LAUGH.

"You make me sick."

I turned my back on that distant world and walked away. The gears in my head, clogged with gravel, tore themselves apart. Bereft of their teeth, the cogs rattled and whirred, clattering and sparking like flint against steel.

"..."

It was all too disgusting to even look upon. I left the arena and began walking back toward the school building. I needed to check something. Something I feared to even speak aloud. It was not my old lecture hall I retreated to, but the building reserved for internal students. Many of them were watching the match, so the halls were eerily quiet. Still, as if on cue, a female staff member exited one of the rooms. She didn't look the fighting type.

"Oh? I haven't seen you around before. An external student, I assume? What are you doing here?"

Already she was looking at me like a nuisance, wondering how to get rid of me. Here in Karvanheim, where magic itself was a virtue, it was easy to see the disdain people held for those like me who were naturally disadvantaged when it came to magic.

It was something I'd grown accustomed to over the past weeks. It didn't bother me anymore.

"Eek?! Wh-what are you—?"

"Just drink it," I told her. "And don't you dare scream."

I pressed my knife to her throat, forcing her to imbibe the truth serum I had prepared.

"Mmm... *Glug*... Uhm... Gh..."

Soon, her eyes clouded over, and all the strength left her.

"Answer me," I told her. "What are the names and birthplaces of the four students in today's mock battle?"

"Eugace Wyndia, from the capital. Cataleya Francois, from the capital. Kril, from Quiquitto Village. Lucia, from Quiquitto Village."

Quiquitto Village. That was the name of my hometown.

"Where can I find Quiquitto Village?" I asked,

My throat dried up. Lucia and Kril were internal students, of that there could be no doubt. But the only ones who could become internal students...

...were Karvanheim nationals.

"Quiquitto Village is five days' carriage journey southwest from here."

"...That will be all," I said. "You are free to go. And tell no one of our conversation here, understood?"

"...Yes."

The female staff member walked shakily down the hall. I slipped into the classroom, and closed the door behind me.

"Aah… Aahhh… Aaaah…!"

It was close. So close I could taste it. It hadn't been all the way on the other side of the Orollea Kingdom at all.

"She betrayed me, then. Just like all the others."

Just like Lucia. She lied to me. She cheated me.

"Which means to say, Leone…"

…You're my enemy as well?

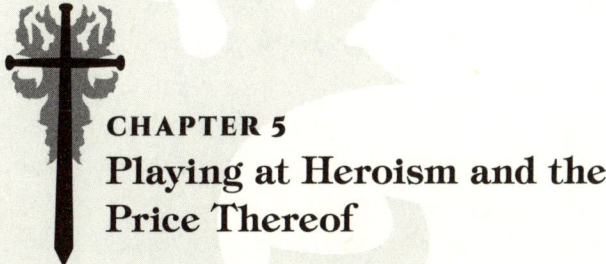

CHAPTER 5
Playing at Heroism and the Price Thereof

Two weeks had passed since I'd entered the secret dungeon below Karvanheim. The only way out was to defeat the boss, and after weeks of fighting, I had finally reached the Guardian Room.

"Hark, the ground roars! *Palace of the Earth Dragon Lords!*"

I brandished my soul blade, the Sword of Earthbound Wyrms, and swung it into the ground. When the sword, modeled after an eastern-style dragon, hit the blood-red rock underfoot, out came a dozen winged serpents formed of the stone.

""*Groooaaaaarrrghhh!!*"""

The dragons obeyed my will and attacked the variant monsters that surrounded them, the fifty-foot-tall Lizardman Kings. These were the ultimate form of the basic Lizardman enemy, possessing a breath attack that rivaled a dragon's, the intellect to command a troop of other Lizardmen, and astonishing skill with spear and blade considering their enormous size.

However, I was up against something far stronger: a Unique Monster. This Lizardman King was no mere variant species or evolutionary branch. He was an individual whose capabilities far outstripped his fellows. In contrast to their black scales, his were dyed red and could repel magic, and as if one head wasn't enough, this guy had three, each commanding a different type of breath attack.

Furthermore, the spear in his hands was enchanted by his own magic, imbuing it with elemental power.

I had been fighting this troublesome foe for nearly three hours now, and although I had deprived him of his left and right heads, the battle showed no signs of winding down.

Breath attack in two seconds. Start chanting the moment I dodge, then four seconds after it ends, take half a step to the right and attack. Follow that up with a blow to the left.

"Graaaaghh!!"

"Hrh."

The remaining head unleashed a breath attack that shot straight forward, like a beam of plasma. Easy enough to dodge. I cartwheeled sideways, placing myself exactly where I wanted to be, while switching soul blades to the Teardrop Blade of Lightning.

"The Cloud Emperor weepeth. Harken unto his grief. Know his pain! *Imperial Cry!*"

This blue-colored sword was made of seven crescent-moon blades stacked atop one another. As I swung it, a thick bolt of blue-green lightning shot out from the tip and engulfed the Lizardman King.

"Graaaaaggghhh?!"

The monster let out a scream as black smoke rose off his body, and I watched him fall to the ground. However, I didn't let down my guard just yet. I began running, this time switching to the Eccentric's Scissor Blade.

"*Execution: Guillotine.*"

The handle of this sword was coated in eye-catching pink and green feathers, such that the rusted blade that severed the Lizardman King's final head seemed quite out of place. It fell to the ground with a wet *thunk*, announcing the end of my long struggle, before the rest of the body pitched forward and toppled over. I checked the beast was fully dead before relaxing my guard.

"Phew... What a fight..."

My body and mind were both screaming out for rest. I swigged a couple potions and slumped to the ground. I had been taking them regularly throughout the last week in order to get things over and done with as quickly as possible, and I now had only half of my original stock.

I guess I should get in touch with Minnalis soon...

Minnalis had sent me a message shortly after I'd entered the dungeon, about a week ago. Our mental connection, Soulspeak, didn't carry that far into labyrinths, but we had come up with a different way of staying in contact: the Slimophone. The idea was that we would have Slimo split himself up and use the smaller slimes as intermediaries for Soulspeak.

I left one with Minnalis and told her only to use him in case of emergencies, but soon after I entered the dungeon, I received my first transmission.

She had located the targets of her revenge.

"All right, Slimo. Here we go."

"Kupie!"

Slimo waved his little feelers in the air and shrunk down so he could fit in my hand. As I channeled my mana into him, his gelatinous body quivered.

"Ahhh. Testing, testing. Minnalis, Shuria, can either of you hear me?"

The two girls responded immediately.

"I can hear you, Master."

"Coming through loud and clear!"

"I've finished conquering the dungeon. This is more than enough experience points to unlock Lust and Sloth. The teleportation circle is

right where I remembered, too, so I'll be out as soon as I'm finished up. How about you two? Is everything ready?"

"*Yes,*" came Minnalis's voice. "*And my target is none the wiser. She hasn't changed a bit, you know. It's enough to make me laugh. I've gathered as much as I can from within the academy, and I have a good idea who we're going to use for the opening act. I've been taking my time getting everything ready.*"

"*I've run into a little bit of trouble,*" said Shuria. "*Kitty has marked the boundary, and I've scraped together the MP potions we'll be using, but I wasn't able to find a cursed item...*"

"*I see,*" I replied. "*Well, they're not exactly easy to come by.*"

"*Should I take time off school to go and find one?*" she asked.

"*No, stay there,*" I told her. "*Someone needs to keep an eye on Leone. We don't technically need a cursed item, just objects with a lot of negative mana. Have you managed that?*"

"*Yes, lots!*" she chirped back.

"*In that case, no problem. If we use that as a basis, we should be able to make something work. We're on a fairly tight schedule, but it sounds like things are going well.*"

"*Thank you so much, Master. You too, Shuria.*"

"*Don't thank us. Your vengeance is my vengeance, remember?*"

"*Kaito's right, Minnalis! It's our job to make sure everything goes exactly according to your plan!*"

"*You just tell us what to do, Minnalis, and we'll handle the rest.*"

I heard her take a deep breath, and then...

"*...You're right, Master. We signed a contract, didn't we? In that case, please do everything in your power to uphold your oath and exact my vengeance.*"

"*You got it. I'd be a pretty lousy partner in crime if I couldn't do that.*"

I smiled. *"I'll be back as quickly as I can. I wouldn't want to be late for the opening act, and if we don't hurry, Leone might start to catch on."*

"...Yes. I'll be waiting for you, Master."

With that, I cut the connection. I was plenty rested by now.

"The sooner I get started on this, the better."

I stood up and walked over to the door at the back of the Guardian Room. Through it, I beheld the true Dungeon Core, as well as a treasure chest containing one of the main reasons I came here. The walls in this chamber no longer resembled the bowels of some giant creature, but were carved of pure white marble, just like the first dungeon.

I opened the chest, and inside were my trusty old garments, the Clothes of Dark Spirits. As I reached out to take them, a flash of black lightning shocked me, as though the clothes themselves were rejecting my touch.

"Whoa! Rowdy, aren't we? Well, I'm afraid we'll have to skip the pleasantries this time; I'm in a hurry."

I reached out once more, enduring the lightning and snatching the garments.

"What's up, Leone? You're spacing out again."

"Huh?"

Minnalis's voice roused me from my daydreaming at the end of the school day. It had now been two weeks since I'd tried and failed to convert Kaito. I thought at least I'd learned to find him in the library, but the next day he wasn't there.

I asked around and eventually discovered that he had entered the school dungeon and not returned since. My resentment turned to ennui, and lately I had been drowning my cares in drink. It appeared he planned to be down there for a while, so I made my return to classes. Since I'd come back, however, Minnalis had started acting quite strangely.

She would be absent for the entirety of our lunch break, and when classes ended, she would go off somewhere by herself. I hadn't told her about my spat with Kaito, yet she seemed more distant than usual; in conversation, she was curt and noncommittal, like she was avoiding me. As the days went on, she seemed to grow more and more restless, until I finally made up my mind to ask her about it.

"...Minnalis, I noticed you've been going somewhere after school lately. What's going on?"

"Oh, that?" she replied. "I'm afraid you've spotted my secret training. Master will be coming back from the dungeon soon, so I've been heading to the library to research a recipe that will really impress him."

"Ooh, I can't wait to taste what Minnalis is cooking up!" said Shuria.

"Yes, well, this country has all sorts of unique and peculiar cuisines," she went on. "I'm sure it'll be quite a treat."

The two girls giggled without a trace of discomfort.

Almost as though they had planned their responses all along.

At that moment, Spinne appeared over my shoulder, along with the two boys.

"That guy doesn't know how lucky he is," she said.

"I gotta admit, I'm a little jealous," added Zanck.

"I can't believe how much our Minnalis has changed," said Dan. "Guess that's just a part of growing up."

"Oh, look at you, Dan. You'll never understand what goes on inside a woman's heart. Isn't that right, Leone?"

"Oh, er, yeah..."

I mumbled a response, but my mind was far away.

…I don't think she's been going to the library at all. But what could she be up to that she feels the need to lie about it…?

It didn't make sense. My only theory was that she'd found out about my argument with Kaito and was avoiding me. But then, wouldn't she be more obvious about it?

"I think I'll pay the library another visit tonight," she said. "Could I ask you four to look after Shuria for me?"

"Grrr, I'm not a child, Minnalis! I don't need looking after!"

"Oh, Shuria! You're so adorable when you're angry! Come here!"

"Rargh! Get those oversized milk bags out of my face, I say!!"

"Tee-hee. Thank you very much, Spinne."

The rabbit girl gave a pleasant laugh and waved good-bye.

"Wait, Minnalis!"

"Hmm? What is it?"

However, after calling after her I found myself with nothing to say.

"Oh, er…it's nothing. Have fun."

"I will."

With that, she turned and left.

What are you up to, Minnalis? What are you doing?

All I had were my own uneasy thoughts for comfort.

After making my excuses to Leone's party, I went and met up with a man. He worked every day to pay off the debt his friend had racked up.

"Everything in your life is his fault, isn't it?"

"…Yes, you're right. It's all his fault… I didn't do anything wrong…"

"I can help you get revenge. You won't need to feel guilty. It's all his fault for doing this to you."

"...He planned this... He wanted to saddle me with this debt all along..."

He was ready. I peered into his dark, muddy eyes, and smiled.

"Yes," I said. "It's all *Kril's* fault. And you are not the only one he's hurt. We shall carry out his punishment in two days. I'll tell you where to go."

"...Ahhh, thank you..."

The unhealthy-looking man staggered off, his eyes burning with hatred for a man he barely knew. Alone in the alley, I let out a small chuckle.

That's everyone I had in mind for the opening act. Leone is clearly on to me by now, but it's too late for her to stop me. Master should be return-ing tonight, and by tomorrow everything will be in place. There's nothing anyone can do about it now.

My toothless gears would soon engage once more. I took out a blue crystal from my pouch. It was an image crystal that would play a crucial part in my revenge. I channeled mana into it, whereupon a see-through window like a status board appeared, and a scene began to play.

"Don't play dumb. Out with it! I know you've been making eyes at Kril!"

"I...I don't know what you're talking about! I've never looked at your boyfriend that way!"

"Then stay away from him. If you ever make a lunch box for him like you did before...well, I hope I don't need to explain. Suffice to say, my friend Cataleya knows people. The types who can make your life very difficult, understand?"

"Y-you wouldn't! What have I done...?"

"I won't say it again. Stay away from Kril, or there's going to be trouble."

"O-okay, okay..."

There the recording ended. I let out a breath and glanced upward. All I could see was a white dome that blocked out the rays of the sun. Beneath that now-familiar sky, I chuckled to myself.

"It won't be long now. Very soon you'll see what I have in store for the lot of you!"

Kril, Lucia, and all the other villagers.

I would paint each and every one of them white. As white as the snow-covered world I remembered. A white that concealed the churning mire beneath.

"Oh, I wonder what you'll say when you see me...?"

A frozen world, unreachable, untouchable.

A deafening silence.

And only the falling snow.

"...And beneath it all, your suffering. Let me be the one to cover it up... Tee-hee. Tee-hee-hee-hee!"

I couldn't help speaking it aloud. My sigh-laden voice mingled with the cold night air and disappeared.

And so, we came upon the eve of our vengeance.

"...*Phew.* Looks like I made it back in time. Hey guys, I'm done."

I returned to our shared inn room, wearing a long cloak, so dark it seemed to absorb the light. I had done what I could to make the Clothes of Dark Spirits accept me, and now it was time to move on to the next step. In my hands I held a kukri knife. Its thick, sturdy blade, primarily for chopping, was so deep a crimson as to be almost utterly black.

Shuria lifted her head at my voice and rubbed the sleep from her eyes.

"Hwah? Is this what you were working on? Whoa. I can see dark mana around it."

Shuria's Crimson Eyes shone, like two pinpricks of light burning in the candlelit gloom.

"The Bloodcurse Blade," I said. "It's not as powerful as the Greatsword of Grief, but it should be enough to feed Sloth."

One of the Swords of Sin I wished to use had a very specific activation condition that required the sacrifice of a cursed weapon. Vanishingly few items possessed the depth of corruption required, but articles approaching that level weren't impossible to find if one knew where to look. Masks, furniture, and old cutlery handed down through generations. The city was full of them, and those were what Shuria had been gathering up. By using the Box Blade of Fusion, I could combine them with the fragments of the Greatsword of Grief, the cursed sword I'd won in the dungeon near the Orollea Kingdom capital, to produce this weapon, the Bloodcurse Blade.

"Good work, Master," said Minnalis, who had apparently gone off to make me some hot milk. She placed the wooden cup on the table, and I stood up to pat her head.

"Thank you, Minnalis. Everything's ready now. We just have to wait for tomorrow."

"It will be okay," said Shuria, squeezing her hand. "I am sure everything will be fine."

"Yes, it will," said Minnalis. "At long last, they're all going to get what they deserve…"

Minnalis's smile looked cold and fleeting, as though it could melt away at any moment. The two of us snuggled up on either side of her.

"I'm heading back to the village now, Kril."

"All right, don't cry *too* much while I'm gone! You've always been lonely, ever since you were a kid."

"Come on! I'm not that little girl anymore, you know that!"

I watched as Lucia climbed onto the carriage bound for the closest town to Quiquitto Village. Her cuteness never failed to take my breath away, no matter how many times I saw her pouting face.

We'd met all sorts of new people after being invited to become students of the academy. Many men attempted to court Lucia, and it was out of jealousy arising from those interactions that I came to recognize my own feelings toward her. Once we graduated, we were to be wed at last.

"I'll set off soon. Just two more days, I promise. Say hello to everyone in the village for me."

"I will. Let's make this a wedding to remember."

Lucia gave me a smile.

The journey to the nearest town was three days, then it was a further two days by horse to the village itself. The villagers were preparing for the wedding in ten days, but there were some things the bride had to be present for. That was why she was leaving now, while I remained in Karvanheim to take care of a few things.

I watched the carriage disappear down the road until it was completely out of sight.

"Ah, marriage. I can't believe it's happening."

I felt pride welling up inside me. Lucia and I had finally managed to escape that tiny little village. It was all thanks to a troop of magical soldiers from the nearby town who'd recognized our magical prowess while visiting and invited us to enroll at Karvanheim Academy.

"You mustn't leave town until you reach adulthood. Monsters walk the streets out there."

It wasn't like I hated our sleepy little hamlet, but I'd wanted to see the big, wide world. I wanted to leave and spread my wings. I wanted to see the world the grown-ups spoke of. And that day came sooner than I'd ever imagined.

Ever since I was a kid, I'd loved the stories my parents told me. Tales of heroes wielding magic swords, rooting out injustices, however small, triumphing over incredible odds, and eliminating evil from the world. I pored over those storybooks until the bindings were in tatters, and I yearned to be a hero like the ones I read about every night.

Because of that, I always used to stick my neck out; this got me in trouble on more than one occasion, but I'd also forged strong bonds of friendship because of it. Now I was even more determined than ever to make my dream a reality.

Stretched out before me was a road that led straight there. A path to greatness, even for someone like me who didn't know the names of the nearby villages and towns. It had been a long road, but I was nearing its end.

Just then, I passed a beastfolk mother with her child. Judging by their foxlike ears, they seemed to be Vulpids.

"Mommy, I'm hungry!"

"Patience, little one. It'll soon be time for supper."

The sight of that little girl and her mother reminded me of another old friend of ours. One that we'd chased out of the village about a year before we left.

I remembered that day with a heavy heart. It was hard to believe that someone I'd grown up with would end up betraying me like that.

That fateful day, I'd learned there was a beastfolk among us. One of the monsters the grown-ups had warned me about.

When I first arrived in this city, I was surprised to learn that all beastfolk were not monsters, and that this notion was simply a misconception rife in our village. But the fact remained that she had lied to me and that she had bullied Lucia in secret.

Her behavior was inexcusable, but Minnalis had been my friend for so long that I couldn't help but feel for her. Wherever they were now, I hoped she and her mother were living respectable lives. Everyone deserved a second chance to correct their mistakes, after all.

"She probably didn't know how to control her beastfolk strength. She was still just a kid."

That was all more than five years ago now, and Minnalis wasn't an inherently bad person. We'd both grown up, so surely she had as well.

"I expect I'll be traveling a lot once I'm in the army. Perhaps I should try keeping an eye out for her."

I didn't expect Lucia to forgive so easily, having been the one mistreated at her hands. But those old wounds of hers would surely heal with time. Then all three of us, Lucia, Minnalis, and I, could be together again, just like old times.

Think of how magical that would be.

"All right, guess I'd better start clearing out our dorm."

Unlike regular recruits, people who joined the army through the academy were not forced to live in barracks. Lucia and I planned on moving in together after graduating, so there was a lot of work to be done in preparation for the move.

I walked the familiar route back to the academy dorms and

arrived outside my room. But just as I put my hand on the doorknob, I sensed something within.

...Hmm? Is someone inside?

Eugace, my roommate, had gone home last night and wouldn't be back until tomorrow. I also distinctly recalled locking up before I left. Besides, it was difficult to imagine why any of the other dorm students would want to break into my room.

Could it be a prowler? Eugace may be the son of a wealthy family, but he's hardly going to leave his valuables here.

As I struggled to comprehend the intruder's motives, I placed my hand on the sword at my hip and slowly pushed open the door. Standing there was a figure in robes, their back turned.

"Who are you?" I asked. "And what are you doing in my room?"

"..."

I received only silence in response.

"Speak. Are you a burglar? Sorry to disappoint, but there's nothing of value he—"

Suddenly, the figure spoke, and when they did, I was flabbergasted. It was a woman's voice, and one I remembered well.

"*The Dawnsung Hero.* I remember this story. I can't believe you've kept it with you all this time."

Only now did I notice the books that she had strewn across my desk.

"...It's been so long, Kril, but you haven't changed a bit."

The figure dropped her hood, and out flopped a pair of rabbitlike ears. Standing before me was my old childhood friend, on the cusp of womanhood, looking more beautiful now than I ever remembered.

"Minnalis...? Is that you...?"

"How long has it been, Kril? Five years? Six? How time flies."

She grinned. I could do nothing but stand there, stunned.

"Y-yes! Wow! It...it's great to see you again, Minnalis!"

"Come. Let's talk over lunch. I imagine we have much to discuss, no?"

Minnalis took me to a café hidden on the backstreets of the town. Though it was currently peak hour, she and I were the only customers.

"But, wow, Minnalis. I hardly recognize you. You've really grown up since back then."

"Hmm. Well, I had to. Let's just say I've had my fair share of life experiences."

She cast me a gentle smile.

Oh, I'm so glad you've come into your own, Minnalis.

Our parting being what it had been, I was afraid she might come back spiteful and petty. But I could see she was a respectable woman now, in both mind and body. She wasn't the clumsy and awkward girl who used to bully Lucia anymore.

"So what are you doing these days, Minnalis? From your clothes, I'm guessing you're a live-in servant of some sort?"

The needlework on her uniform was really top-notch. I hoped she had found gainful employment with some rich and noble merchant of good standing.

"You could say that. In fact, it's related to why I wanted to speak to you tonight."

"Hmm? You have something to ask of me?"

"Kril. And Lucia, too. The fact is...I've been tasked by the government with keeping an eye on you for the past year."

"Wh-what? You've been watching us? For a whole year? That's unbelievable!"

"Hee-hee. Do you remember this person?"

"Wha—?!"

Before my eyes, Minnalis's face shifted and became that of someone else entirely, a merchant who regularly visited the academy.

"It's an illusion," Minnalis explained. "Beastfolk mana falls off strongly with distance, but it's perfect for little tricks like this."

Minnalis dispelled the illusion, and her face returned to normal.

"As for the results of my investigation, I'm afraid to say there's an issue with Lucia. One that may have ramifications for your future together."

"What?! Wh-what do you mean by that?!"

"...Take a look at this image crystal I recorded."

Minnalis produced a blue crystal, and my eyes were drawn to the scene playing out within it.

"Don't play dumb. Out with it! I know you've been making eyes at Kril!"

"Stay away from him."

"My friend Cataleya knows people. The types who can make your life very difficult."

I saw Lucia bullying a girl I knew from school.

"Wh-what is this?"

"This isn't the only one. I have more here, if you'd care to see."

As I watched recording after recording, I began to grow faint.

"I can't believe it... I never knew Lucia was so..."

She was kind, cheery, childish, and beautiful. This wasn't the Lucia I knew. The girl in the recording was spiteful and ugly... It was a side of her I had never seen.

"Looks like our food's here."

Seeing the waiter with our dishes, Minnalis put the image crystals away.

"I don't plan to make these recordings public yet. If Lucia

apologizes before graduation, the military is willing to see this as a mere indiscretion by a minor."

"…"

"Your food is going cold."

"…Oh, er…"

I picked up my spoon and sipped my soup, but it tasted of nothing at all.

"…I get it," I said. "You want me to encourage her to change her ways."

"…"

"Leave it to me, Minnalis. I'll see to it that she renounces her wicked behavior. Everyone deserves a second chance; a chance to make things right!"

"That's from *The Dawnsung Hero*, no?"

"Yes. I believe with all my heart that people can change."

If Lucia had strayed from the path, all I had to do was correct her. Defeating evil, and bringing back anyone it misled—that was my duty.

"People can change, you say? Hee-hee…"

"Huh?"

I suddenly felt an eerie shiver run down my spine. Every instinct in my body threw me out of my chair and made me recoil in fright.

"Hee-hee… Hee-hee. Ah-ha-ha-ha-ha! Ah-ha-ha-ha-ha-ha-ha!!"

Her dark laughter started small, then grew until it filled the room. It felt like it would pull me in if I tried to reach out and touch her.

"M-Minnalis…?"

"People can change? Oh, you do make me laugh, Kril! Why, you haven't changed in the slightest!"

"Wh-what do you mean…?"

Minnalis suddenly seemed like a completely different person. I broke out in a cold sweat, and my hand instinctively flew to my sword. She continued laughing for an unsettlingly long time, before she suddenly stopped and spoke in a soft, yet bizarrely arresting tone.

"You really are exactly the same, Kril. You don't care about justice. You don't care about change. And you don't truly believe that everyone has the power to grow."

"Wh-what are you talking about? Of course I— Hrk!"

Suddenly, there was a deeply unpleasant sensation in the pit of my stomach. I wanted to stop Minnalis from saying anything more, at all costs.

"If you did, then why was your first thought *I'll make her change*? Why not *Lucia would never do such a thing*, or *Did that really happen*? All I showed you was a recording, which are quite simple to fake."

"What? You mean you tricked me?!"

"That's the best part—I didn't. These all really happened. But you don't care about the truth, do you, Kril?"

The corner of her lips curled upward, like she was mocking me, like she was above it all. Like seeing me flustered was amusing.

"Grrr! Shut up! Stop messing with me!"

"You just want to see yourself as the great hero who casts out evil. You don't care if those you oppress are actually wicked or not. That's why you were so eager to turn on Lucia without doing any research yourself."

She was like a demon, laughing as she toyed with people's hearts.

"I said shut up! That's not who I am!"

"How many more people did you 'save' while I was gone? Did you ever think about *why* they needed saving? *If* they needed saving? It's all just sport for you, isn't it? What a hypocrite."

166

She peered down her nose at me, as though she were observing a cockroach wriggling about on the earth. Her words were dripping with scorn.

"...And how many stones have you thrown at the undeserving? At people like me?"

"I said SHUT UUUUUP!!"

"No. After all, this is our last conversation together."

"What do you— Urk?! Wh-what's happening?"

A sudden numbness ran through my legs, and I fell to my knees.

"I'm afraid the soup you just drank was poisoned. It's starting to take effect."

"P-poison?! M-Minnalis... You invited me here just to poison me...?"

"You really are slow to catch on, Kril. How dull-witted do you have to be to talk to me for this long without realizing the depths of my hatred for you?"

As I watched Minnalis heave a disappointed sigh, I realized it really was our last farewell. She hadn't changed at all. She was pure evil.

"...This isn't the end!! You think this poison's enough to kill me?! Cleanse my taint! *Clear Body!!* Now take this!!"

Evil had to be stopped. And I, the hero, had to be the one to stop her. I cast a spell to cure the poison and drew my sword. However, there was a piercing ring as my blade stopped mid-swing.

"Wh-what?!"

"Aren't you embarrassed, shouting things like that in the middle of town? Aren't you worried what people will think?"

I couldn't believe how easily she stopped my blow. My instincts were right; this girl was a threat!

"Sink beneath the shifting sands. Leaden beetles tie your hands. *Summon Gyrmecia!*"

"Beetles?!"

Suddenly, a hole appeared in the ground, out of which came tens, hundreds of shimmering beetles, their carapaces a deep green mixed with crimson. They were a species I'd never encountered before.

"Grrr! *Hellfire Sword, Blazing Inferno!*"

Even though I was in a public place, I couldn't afford to hold back. Fortunately, there didn't appear to be anyone around, and the staff would easily be able to escape out the back door before things got out of hand.

I just have to burn away all the insects and escape into the street. It's too cramped for me to fight indoors.

However, I didn't get time to put my plan into action.

"What's this?!"

The beetles seemed unaffected by my fiery blow. Through the cracks in the swarm, I saw Minnalis grinning at me. Then, as if in response, the insects all scurried toward me at once, from all angles.

"No, stop! Stay away from me!"

I swung desperately, but there were so many of them that I couldn't keep the beetles at bay with just my sword. They started crawling up my clothes.

"Grh! Why are these beetles so heavy?! Grrrrrrgh!! Dammit! Dammit!!"

Each one felt like a bucket of water. They clung to me, dragging me down, pinning me to the ground. Minnalis walked slowly over and crouched down in front of me.

"Dammit! Dammit! Don't you know what you've done?! People will be here any minute!"

"Why, yes, you're absolutely right, they will."

"Hrh?!"

Once again, it felt like I was being skewered on a giant icicle. She was smiling, but there was no pity in her eyes for me. No mercy. It was the coldest, most ruthless look I had ever seen.

"Wh-what are you...? Grh! Agh!"

Minnalis produced a dagger and steeped its edge in a violet serum. Then she drew the blade across my cheek. Immediately, my whole body felt numb, and any strength I might have yet possessed left me.

"Now everything's ready," she said. "Your death...will be slow."

She shot to her feet and spoke, gesturing wildly.

"The table is set, the places laid. Come, one and all, enjoy your meal!"

What could only be described as a horde of specters responded to Minnalis's call. The hatred burning in their eyes was not of this world. They were men and women with sunken, hollow sockets and pale, stretched skin.

Their eyes seemed the only thing living about them. They glared daggers into my soul, muttering curses under their breath.

"It's all his fault. All him."

"Give it back. Give my life back to me..."

"...Kill you. I'll kill you..."

"Wh-who are they?"

Darkness seemed to be leaking out from them, polluting the very air around us. My heart felt as though it had been steeped in ice water, freezing my bones from the inside out.

"Why, they're all people who hate you. People who want to see you dead."

I didn't get it. What was happening? It just didn't make sense. Why were they looking at me like that?

"They hate me? What for? What have I done? I've never seen them before in my life!!"

At that moment, the air in the room grew heavy.

"What do you mean…you don't know us?"

"How could you possibly forget what you did?!"

"Aaargh! Die, die, you piece of trash, DIIIIII*IIE!!*"

I heard a sound like flint sparking, and my eardrums nearly burst from the screams.

"If you don't have weapons of your own, feel free to use these."

Minnalis giggled and handed out rusty swords and knives to the people who had gathered around me. One after the other, they raised them above their heads.

"Oh, Goddess have mercy! Earth's power, suffuse me! *Metallic Body!!*"

"Give me back my store…!"

"You killed her! You killed my baby!"

"Die already! Why do you yet live?"

"Hrgh! Gh! Gaah?!"

A wave of violence descended on me like a bursting dam. The ghosts showed no hesitation or mercy at all. Their rusty blades sliced and pierced my flesh. Though my spell turned my skin as hard as steel, a dull pain washed across my entire body.

"You abandoned my friend and left him to die!!"

"You killed my brother!!"

"Curse you… If only you hadn't been there… If only… Curse you!!"

I could not comprehend what was happening. Try as I might, I couldn't remember doing anything deserving of this much anger and hate. The words spilling from their mouths made no sense to me.

"Tee-hee-hee. How does it feel, Kril? To see the world through my eyes?"

Her voice! Urgh! She's in my head…!

"Ahhh, this is nice. The beetles not only allow us to communicate,

they also let me feel your confusion, your fear. What will your despair taste like in the very end, I wonder? Tee-hee-hee."

Just then, one of the blades shattered, and the fragment flew into my eye.

"Aaargh!"

A burning sensation, not even pain, engulfed me.

Why was this happening to me? Why?!

What had I done to deserve this? Why did all these people hate me so?!

"Tee-hee… ♪"

A soft titter escaped Minnalis's lips. Not inside my head this time, but a genuine laugh. It was as cold as the evening snow, ready to freeze all who heard it.

"You haven't done anything. They've all been lied to."

Her voice was in my head once more, brimming, spilling over with joyous rapture.

"They've been lied to…? Gaaaagh!!"

My words only unleashed another torrent of violence upon me.

"Lies! You let my child die!!"

"My business was going perfectly until you showed up!"

"If you'd just given him a spare antidote, you could have saved my friend. Now he's dead, and it's all your fault!!"

My incantation didn't make me invincible. Even the miniscule damage from these grief-driven blows would add up and take its toll eventually.

"Yes, they've been lied to. There's no great evil responsible for their misfortune. Most of them are just victims of bad luck. All I did was give them a scapegoat, someone to blame for their problems. Let me show you what I mean."

There were no words to describe the wicked grin that flashed across her lips as she began to speak.

"Now, all of you. This man is the root of your woes. He's responsible for all the evil in the world. Why don't you show him how that makes you feel? You don't have to feel guilty; everything is his fault. And you have to make sure he doesn't hurt anyone else, don't you? Worry not, for justice is on your side."

"Yes…it's all his fault!"

"Everything's his fault…"

"It's all your fault, you hear me?! All your fault!!"

"Listen to me…you've been lied to…" I protested.

"Silence!"

"It's all your fault!"

"If only you didn't exist!!"

My words failed to reach them. The wave of anger crashed against the rocks once more. Minnalis's voice carried like a ripple on a clear pool, riling up the crowd's fury.

"Now do you see? They're not interested in hearing the truth. The only thing they need, the only thing they want, is a justification. A pretext to kill."

Shut up, shut up, shut up!!

The senseless violence caused a wave of anger to surge within me as well.

"How could it all be so meaningless?! Erupt from my body, *Final Flame!!*"

"Wraagh!"

"Eek!"

"What?!"

Orange flames enwreathed my body, and the crowd stepped back in shock. This was my ultimate technique. It boosted my stats and neutralized all status conditions. Of course, it would exact a hefty toll, so I'd sworn only to use it against the most formidable foes. However…

"Grh! Wh-what's wrong? Why isn't the poison going away?"

"Ah-ha-ha-ha-ha! My poisons aren't like those you get at market! I'm prepared for every pathetic trick you can dream up!"

"Curse you... This isn't...the end..."

"I'm afraid it is. Start absorbing, Gyrmecia."

"Wh-what?! Aaagh! It buuurns! Aaagh!"

As I struggled to my feet beneath the weight of the beetles, my strength suddenly left me. The insects started nibbling at the flames, devouring them. The more they ate, the hotter they grew, until it felt like I was buried under a mound of burning coals.

And once it was clear I was weakened, the storm of violence descended upon me once more.

"Hah! You'll pay for scaring me like that! Die, die!!"

"Murderer! Murderer!"

"I'll see you suffer more than you ever thought imaginable..."

The hate was relentless, interminable. I heard myself crack.

"This is the end for you."

"Die, die, diiiie!"

"Grh... Guh..."

Minnalis's voice pierced me like an icicle of frozen poison. My heart, which I thought was made of steel, was beginning to crumble like dirt.

"Feel what it's like to have no one. To be *no one. All for a crime you didn't commit."*

"I can never be happy as long as you're here!!"

"S-stop...please..."

She drove that icicle into the cracks, prying them apart.

*　　*　　*

"Pleasant memories, a happy life, a promising future, all carried away on a wave of senseless violence. Your pathetic tale ends here, hero."

"Why do you live while he's gone?! Give him back! Give my friend back to meee!"

"Please…gh…I can't…gah…"

There was nothing I could do to stop it. I was falling to pieces, like a sand sculpture in one's hands.

"Feel what it's like to have the last page of your story ripped out."

That witch drove her long nails into my heart, and I heard something snap.

"GET THE HELL OFF ME!! Get off! Get off! Get off!!"

I couldn't die here, in some back-alley café, because of people I'd never met! I was meant for greater things! Much, much greater!

"Tee-hee-hee! Oh, that's magnificent, Kril. You fear death so much, don't you? I can feel it."

"Minnalis!! Stop this at once!! How dare you come back to me unrepentant! How dare you get in my way!!"

"Tee-hee. That's the spirit. Perhaps it's time for me to stop taking a back seat and join the show. It's getting hard for me to hold back now! Ah-ha-ha-ha-ha!!"

Saying this, Minnalis took out a sword so blunt it was little more than a steel club and entered the fray.

"Gah! Curse you… You'll pay for this!"

"That's right, feel it. Feel it!!"

"Guh!! Gah…ghh… W-wait!!"

"Why should I? Did you wait for me back then? Why should I stop when it feels so good? Tee-hee-hee! Ah-ha-ha-ha-ha!!"

Her blow broke through my reinforced skin, sending a ripple of pain through me. I couldn't believe this. How could she have grown so powerful? How could she make a fool out of me?

"Please...no. I don't want to die..."

How had it come to this? In just a few days, I was supposed to be heading back to Quiquitto village to be with Lucia.

"You don't, do you? Well, that is a shame. I would have liked not to be sold into slavery either, yet here we are. Do you know what my mother said just before she died? *I'm sorry*, she told me. *I'm sorry I won't be there for you anymore.* But that's just life, is it not? We can't always get what we want."

"S-slavery? What are you talking about?"

"...Oh, I guess they never told you. But then, it never mattered to you, did it? I was just an actress who finished playing her part. You really do get on my nerves sometimes!!"

"Gah! Grhh...ghhh!!"

The world around me churned. Crimson threads teemed at the corners of my vision. Please. I couldn't die. Not here, not yet. Not before getting married. Not before being accepted into the military. Why? Why?

"I expect the pain is beginning to dull. All right, everyone, please stop for a moment."

Minnalis raised her hand, and the angry men and women calmed a little. Then she emptied the contents of a small vial over my head.

"Huh...? Mph! Wh-what's this, a potion...?"

I felt the pain across my body vanish. My wounds miraculously healed, and my hazy consciousness slipped back into reality.

"You...saved me...?"

"Bah-ha-ha-ha-ha!! Saved you?! You're still holding out for salvation? How stupid can you get?"

"I don't... Gaaaaaaagh!!"

Shredding any last bit of hope I might have had, Minnalis drove her rusty blade into my shoulder. The pain was fresh despite my dying nerves.

"I told you, didn't I? Your death will be slow. You're going to suffer and suffer and die in despair. Tee-hee-hee. Ah-ha-ha-ha-ha!!"

What had I done to deserve this? Was it really my fault?

"We'll disembowel you. We'll drill holes in your hands and legs. We'll roast you alive. Over and over again. As long as time permits."

This wasn't the way things were supposed to go. Minnalis was supposed to be living a happy and respectable life somewhere far away. I knew something had been wrong with her from the moment we met, but I was still willing to forgive and forget if she apologized for her past behavior.

So why? Why had it ended up like this?

"We've only just begun, Kril. There's a lot more healing potions where that one came from."

Had I done something wrong?

"Writhe in pain. Let the blood clog your throat. Weep at the gross iniquity of it all. And wait for the sound of your world falling apart, as I did for mine."

She lifted her knife into the air. And as she did, a malicious smile spread across her lips. It was as if she was possessed by the reaper himself.

Just then, I heard a voice.

"...Minnalis? What...are you doing?"

But by then I was too steeped in despair to listen.

"Ah, Leone. You're earlier than I expected. Did you skip classes to come find me? Still...you picked a good moment. I've just finished the first course."

That day, I chose to investigate the unsettling feeling I couldn't shake to put a stop to my doubts once and for all. So as soon as classes broke for lunch, I went to find Dan and Zanck, then brought all four of us around the back of the school building.

"H-hey, Leone, where are you taking us in such a hurry?" asked Dan as I pulled him along.

"I wish you'd at least tell us where we're going…," added Zanck.

"Don't look at me," said Spinne. "I don't know any more than you two."

"Minnalis and Shuria were both absent from school today," I explained, turning to face them. Minnalis had been acting suspicious lately, but I had been content to give her space. However, she didn't even show up at all today.

"I-is that it?" asked Spinne. "That's not really enough to…"

"I don't like it," I insisted. "Something's up, I just know it. I always do."

I bit my lip in frustration. Just then, who but Shuria walked by.

"Hmm? Where are you four off to in such a huff?" she asked.

It was as if I was personally being invited beyond the point of no return.

"Shuria…"

She was smiling sweetly, just as she always did. But something was wrong. I just knew it. This was a far cry from the Shuria I was used to. There was no warmth for us. It was like she was staring at a group of complete strangers. Her tanned skin now seemed dark enough to suck in the light.

"…Hmm. I have a feeling you are not in the mood to chat," she said. "Very well, as a reward for your clever guess, I will show you the way. Follow me, if you please."

Shuria turned before we could respond and began walking, without looking back.

"Er... What do we do?" asked Spinne.

"Leone's right," said Dan. "I've got a bad feeling about this."

"Let's just follow her and see where this goes," said Zanck, and the four of us walked after her before she could disappear from view entirely.

Shuria walked silently ahead of us, leading us down darker and darker streets until we arrived at a desolate café, in a district so poor and run-down it was practically a slum.

"What's up with this café? asked Zanck. "There's a silencing ward across the entire premises..."

"I'm surprised you could tell at just a glance," said Shuria. "Well done."

"Well, it's not exactly hidden," explained Zanck. "Even I can—"

"I wasn't talking to you. I was speaking to Leone."

"..."

I hadn't said a word, but it seemed Shuria had noticed my unease regardless. Against my better judgment, I had activated my Radiant Eyes skill, and I could see a flood of colors spilling out of the building. Red, blue, green, yellow, purple, pink, orange, gray. All mixed together, and all robbed of their brilliance. It was a cauldron of different emotions, all warped nearly beyond recognition.

However, those warped colors seemed somewhat familiar.

"..."

As if in a trance, I approached the door of the café and slowly pushed it open...

...Entering into the domain of the demoness, wreathed in rotten, rusty laughter.

The words left my lips in a daze before I could stop them.

"...Minnalis? What...are you doing?"

179

"Ah, Leone. You're earlier than I expected. Did you skip classes to come find me? Still…you picked a good moment. I've just finished the first course."

Someone was lying facedown on the floor, surrounded by dozens of hollow specters. And the leader of those ghouls was none other than Minnalis. She turned her pretty face toward me, and I saw blood splattered across her cheeks.

"Wh-what is going on in here? Who are all these people?!" yelled Dan.

"Minnalis? What have you done?" asked Spinne.

"Leone was right about you," said Zanck. "Now, who's this poor guy?"

"Answer me!!" I screamed at her, my head pounding. "What are you doing?!"

"What am I doing? Isn't it obvious? I'm doing exactly what you've been trying to tell me not to! Tee-hee-hee. Tee-hee-hee-hee-hee!!"

As she spoke, Minnalis spun the knife in her hand and drove it into the body lying before her.

"GAAAAAAAGH!!"

"Who is that? Oh, Goddess have mercy! Is that Kril?! What is he doing here?!"

"You really are a scatterbrain, Leone. You didn't stop to think that he might be living in this city when you lied to me about Quiquitto Village?"

"Grgh! Ghuh… Agh…"

Minnalis drove the knife into Kril again and again, laughing merrily to his screams. Her enjoyment roused the crowd of strangers into a frenzy, and they joined in with her.

"Hey, cut it out, you lot!" cried Dan. "The kid's gonna die!"

"This is not looking good," agreed Zanck.

"Snap out of it, Leone!" said Spinne. "We have to stop them, even if it's by force!"

"Grh... Minnalis, I didn't want to do this...!!"

I have to put a stop to this violence before anything else!

We reached for our weapons, when suddenly we all heard a voice.

"Feel the weight of the earth and sink. *Titan's Tomb.*"

That voice, dripping with darkness, caused us all to be rooted to the spot, immobile.

"I'm afraid nonparticipants have to wait their turn. You're not supposed to be in this scene yet."

It was Kaito, clad in pitch-black robes that concealed his over-flowing mana, holding a double-edged longsword. The blade was forged with a wave along both edges, colored white at the base before darkening to a deep brown at the tip.

It suddenly felt like we were carrying the weight of the world on our shoulders, and we collapsed to the floor.

"Grh. A naughty child like you needs punishing! *Water Bolt!* Drench and shock my foes!"

"Indomitable Wall: Hammerstorm."

"No! How did he deflect it so easily?!"

Spinne's spell, a bolt of water wreathed in lightning, ricocheted into the ground as if struck by a giant invisible hammer.

"Grh... Now's not the time to hold back. Beast Mode, activate!!"

A pair of white horns appeared on Dan's forehead, and his skin turned crimson, while red steam rose off his body. He was using his intrinsic ability.

"I'll back you up!" cried Zanck. *"Force Up! Physical Up!"*

Zanck's magic mixed with the steam, causing it to glow. Even the inexperienced Dan of the present day could easily go toe-to-toe with an Iron Golem in this state. He slowly got to his feet, but Kaito had other ideas.

"Feel the weight of your sins and repent. *Titan's Hammerfall.*"

"Grhh! Gaah!"

Dan collapsed to the floor once more under the weight of this new technique.

"Apologies," said Kaito, "but let's just say I've been doing some intensive training. I'm not the Kaito you knew from two weeks ago, and I'm afraid the four of you are no match for me now. It's time for you to exit stage left. You're going to be helping me out backstage, and let me tell you, these final three days are going to be a real doozy. Don't worry, you'll make it out with your lives...probably."

From out of nowhere, he produced a semitransparent sword of indigo and green, brimming with magical power. A magic circle spread across the floor beneath us, and the sword began to glow.

"All right, Minnalis, Shuria and I will go ahead. Let me know when you've finished up here."

"Yes, Master."

"Grr, I'm sad I didn't get to torture this man very much."

It was only now I realized Shuria had been among the people tormenting Kril, mincing the flesh of his legs with a barbed knife. When had she and Minnalis gotten so sadistic?

"Be grateful you got a chance at all," said Kaito. "I was busy dealing with these nuisances. Minnalis, be sure not to overdo it, you hear? We'll need him alive for the next step."

"I know, Master. Tee-hee. Tee-hee-hee..."

I felt the darkness closing in around me, second by second. I reached my hand out toward her, as if attempting to salvage what I could. I screamed, my eyes blurry with tears.

"Minnalis, please. Stop this. Vengeance isn't the answer!"

"No," she answered curtly. "I won't stop. Not anymore."

I didn't get a chance to speak further. A bright light swept everything away, including Minnalis. The last I saw of her was her face, that of a weeping child.

The Transcendent Blade of Translocation gave off a light that enveloped the party of Master, Shuria, and Leone, carrying them away.

"I've been falling. Down and down, ever since then. And now I've finally reached the bottom."

Ever since that cold winter day, when my mother had drawn her last breath, when my world had shattered into fragments. The moment I took vengeance's dark hand and swore it wouldn't be the end.

"Now, where were we? I hope you're not thinking of giving up yet, Kril."

I took my second potion and poured it into his mouth.

"Wha—? Glg…glg…"

Then I stomped on his face.

"Gaaaaagh?!"

I turned to my *tools*, all standing around me. "You should enjoy this while you can," I said. Then, softly, to myself, I muttered, "…Because you're all going to forget everything that happened once the serum wears off."

"Agh…gh… Rggh… Someone…anyone…help…"

"Let me give you some friendly advice, Kril, as someone who's been in your shoes. No one's coming to save you."

"Grh!! I'm…sorry! Minnalis, whatever I did, I'm sorry! Argh!!"

"Your apology's more than five years late, Kril. But don't worry.

I'll stay by your side, right up until you break. Tee-hee. Tee-hee-hee. Ah-ha-ha-ha-ha-ha!!"

I sat at the center of a world of pitch-black darkness. And I laughed. I laughed and laughed and laughed. I cackled with my whole heart. An inky laughter to match the depths of the depravity around me.

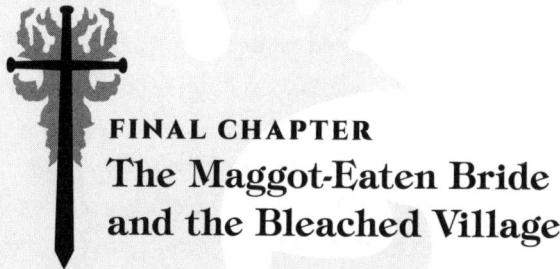

FINAL CHAPTER
The Maggot-Eaten Bride
and the Bleached Village

There were six days remaining until Lucia and Kril's wedding. I had said my farewells to Master and Shuria, then set off alone on a pilgrimage back to my birthplace, pulling a wagon behind me.

"Ho, *trader*. Back again?"

A traveling merchant on their way to sell wares to the village. Such was the guise I had assumed to hide my true identity. A huntsman with a leg-bound rabbit slung over his shoulder had called out to me. His was a face I had always been happy to see as a child. Now, the sight of him only brought me a sick sense of nausea.

"Yes, I figured you could use some basic necessities," I said, concealing my displeasure behind a fabricated smile. "With the wedding coming up, you'll surely be in need of wine aplenty!"

"Ha-ha-ha! That's a merchant for you, ever on the lookout for an opportunity. I seem to recall you doing much the same thing during our last wedding!"

"…You're quite right, I did."

"Well, speak of the devil, here's the happy couple now! Hey there!"

Suddenly, the huntsman spotted the newlyweds of which he spoke over my shoulder and called out to them. The man was accompanied by a far younger woman, and the two clung so closely to each other it was obvious of their relationship.

The face of the man was one I would never forget.

"Well, who do we have here?" he asked, walking over. "Perfectly timed, if you ask me."

My, Father. *Gotten a few gray hairs now, I presume? I'm afraid I cannot tell, for when I look at you, all I see is the face of utter contempt that was scorched into my mind forever. I can hardly bear to stand in your presence a moment longer.*

"Been a good while, hasn't it, merchant?"

Why are you smiling? How could you smile after what you did? Have you forgotten how you cast my mother and me aside? Do you think this new woman of yours can absolve you of your sins? Answer me, Father.

"How's the newlywed life?" I croaked, fighting the urge to leap at him immediately. Threads of logic bound my screaming heart, and my illusion magic spun my voice into something approaching respectable.

Oh, just go to hell already.

I couldn't even find the words. My mind went blank as I saw him get all cuddly and giggly with his new wife. Pure white, like frosted snow, as if a part of my brain had been sliced out. My blood dripped down my nails, alerting me that I was clenching my fists hard. The cuts were deep, but I felt no pain. Only emptiness. I licked my palms, allowing the blood to linger in my mouth. That rusty taste swept across the canvas of my mind, painting everything red in an instant. If I didn't have Master and Shuria to consider, I would have torn him to shreds right then and there.

"Well, I have you to thank for providing for such an amazing wedding," he said.

"And our new home is looking prettier than ever, because of the furniture you supplied," said the wife.

"Not to mention this bow I bought off you. Never had one like it. It took down a warblefowl nearly three meters long the other day! You should have seen it! One shot, straight through the head!"

"Oh, honey. How many times are you going to tell that story?"

The woman giggled. I was not particularly surprised to see this neighborhood girl filling my mother's shoes. I still remembered how gleefully she'd thrown her stones.

I wanted nothing more than to rip the two of them limb from limb on the spot. To watch them die. To watch the light leave their eyes. However, I had to be careful not to say too much, or I would ruin everything we had worked for.

"I'm just glad to see you two spending a happy life together."

Stay calm, stay calm. Just for this moment. Try to guide the conversation toward eliminating this nuisance huntsman as quickly as possible.

I waited for my chance, and soon one arose.

"I was thinking of swapping out the leather strap on this bow. Have you any to sell?"

"...Of course. I've finished my negotiations with the elder, so I have a few left over that I would be delighted to show you."

"In that case, why don't we invite him to our place, dear?"

"Excellent idea, honey. It's getting late—how about stopping over at our house and continuing your journey on the morrow?"

All laughter, all smiles. What are you so pleased about? By all means, enlighten me.

"I would be most grateful for your hospitality. Pray, lead the way."

Ahhh, so close now. So close I can almost taste it. Bear with it and be grateful that these fools have so unwittingly invited destruction into their own home.

"Gladly. It's just down this road here..."

I walked a familiar path, my father and his new wife leading the way, and soon we arrived at my childhood home. I passed through the door expecting to be overcome with nostalgia, but reality shattered that illusion.

I didn't recognize a single item of furniture. It had all been replaced, and the smell I remembered was completely gone. My mother had always preferred plain wooden tables and chairs, but the new stuff was decorated and smelled of iron.

This was the place my mother and I had lived. But it was no longer our home.

"How's the room? Splendid, don't you think? 'Course, I know next to nothing about decorating, so I let the missus take care of that. You should have seen the old place. Let me tell you, it looks a lot more livable now than it did back then!"

"Yes, the old look was so musty. It's not a big house, but I hope you'll make yourself comfortable."

"Of course, thank you."

The pit of my stomach felt like boiling acid. Yet it was not their happiness that brought me grief. For if they were happy, they were full of hope. If they were happy, they perhaps believed that tomorrow would be brighter still.

...So it would be all the more delightful to show them the hell that truly awaited them.

Dear Father, it's your turn next. Look how much life rewarded you for abandoning us in our hour of need.

Don't you think it's time that dream came to an end? Don't you think it's time you faced the consequences of your actions?

"*...Corrupting Needle.*"

Each of them felt a tiny pinprick on their skin as my needles of frozen poison found their marks.

* * *

"Pardon the intrusion, so to speak."

"Hrh...huh...? I feel...so tired..."
"Wh-what's...happening...?"
The two collapsed to the floor. It was the sound of my shackles falling loose.

"Have you enjoyed these last five years? I sure hope so, because I'm afraid that's all you're going to get."

As I spoke, I dispelled the illusion, revealing my true identity.
"Wh-what...?"
"No...this can't be..."
"Hello, Father. Now it's my turn to be happy."
"M-Minnalis...? Th-that's impossible...," he said, looking up at me witlessly.

I smiled. "Enjoy your final rest, Papa. When you wake up, you'll be entering a world of endless pain."

Welcome to the hell I've been living in ever since you turned your back on me.

Hey, Kril. Do you remember that time we got in trouble sneaking into a hunting lodge on another one of your adventures?

Hey, Lucia. Do you remember that time we "practiced being wives" together by making food for the whole village?

Do you remember how I laughed and smiled back then? I can't. I've already forgotten.

Even after torturing Kril to within an inch of his life, I can't recall anything.

"Don't you think it's about time you stopped pretending to be asleep, Father? We need to talk."

"...M-Minnalis...? Gaaaaaagh!!"

The sound of my name from his lips so incensed me that I plunged my knife into his hand. We were deep in the forest, where I had dragged them after leaving the house.

"What about you, Father? Do you remember how I used to laugh?"

"Goddess, no...the pain...curse it all!"

My father rolled around on the forest floor like a grub. His palms were slashed, his right arm burned, his left ankle pulverized, his right leg twisted in the opposite direction, and countless poisoned needles had been stuck into his waist. From the neck up, I had left him untouched, as I wished to hear his screams for as long as possible. His face was a perfect mess of drool, tears, and anguish.

"Then, again," I admitted, "that was so very long ago. Perhaps you've already forgotten, just like you forgot about us. Is it that refreshing to be living with a new, young wife? Perhaps the sound of her screams will jog your memory?"

"What?!"

I walked over to where the woman lay faceup and stepped on her. I had fastened her in place by her arms and legs, then stripped her naked. Now her skin was covered in welts, holes, and unsightly blotches where I had burned off the upper layers of flesh. When the skin turned blackened and crisp, I cut it out with a knife, and pressed dirt from the forest floor into the wound. The welts and holes were from where I had lashed her countless times with a needled whip.

I'd kept feeding her potions so she wouldn't die, and the further her torture progressed, the more delightful my father's screams became.

"Please! Don't hurt my wife anymore!"

Ah, why is it only now I'm hearing those words?

"Look at you, acting all brave," I taunted. "As if I have any interest in what you have to say now."

Even merrier than before, I resumed his wife's torment.

"Ghhhhh! Stoff! Lady, have merfy!! You're cruffing meeee!!"

As I stomped on her abdomen with my hard-soled boots, there was a crunch, and she started foaming at the mouth. I must have destroyed some of her organs.

"Whoopsie-daisy! I guess I overdid it. My mistake! ♪"

I didn't want her to die so early, so I poured another potion into her gaping mouth.

"P-please...not her. She means the world to me," the thing that used to be my father begged. Begged me not to kill her.

It was the last thing I wanted to hear out of his foul mouth. Where was all this when *we* had been suffering? Had we not been important enough to him?!

"...Does she, now? Then let's make her suffer even more! ♪"

"Guph?!"

I walked over to the man who was once my father and unleashed my emotions on him, kicking his face upward so he could watch. Then I went back to the woman and lit a flaming torch, bringing it close to her face.

"Eek?! Pleafe...no...not my fafe— AAAAAAAGHH! NOO-OOOOO!!"

"Stop... Please...stop... No more..."

"Tee-hee-hee! ♪ Nope!"

The woman's protests, the man's delicious groans. Neither of them quelled the anger in my heart.

"Come on," I jeered, "how stupid do you have to be to spout rubbish like that?"

191

The woman's features looked truly ridiculous now. I dusted my hand with cooking salt and rubbed it all over her face.

"Mmfff!"

"Spare her? Why? Because you care more about her than your own life? So what?! Hey, listen to me! *So what?!*"

"Mmmff?! Mmff! Mmmmff!!"

I twisted my hand, grinding the salt into her. She screamed in agony as the crystals scratched at her sensitive flesh.

"Listen, your dear, dear wife is crying out in pain. Do you want me to stop?"

As I asked the question, I saw his face light up with the faintest hope, almost as if he thought there was some chance of salvation.

"P-please, st—"

"Nope! Sorry!"

I picked up the torch and thrust it at what was once my father.

"Gyaaaaaaaagh!!"

"Ah-ha-ha-ha-ha! ♪ Surely, you're not that stupid! Did you really think I was going to let you go?"

"Gah... Ghh... Grh..."

He could only manage to mutter incoherently in the face of my scornful laughter. Perhaps it was time to turn up the heat.

"Do you know how long my mother suffered? How many times she apologized? What good do you think it did her? I'll tell you: as much good as it'll do you."

The flame of hatred burning within me was much, much brighter now. Like a roaring bonfire.

"...We have a long, long way to go. I'm waiting for you to reach the depths of despair, the very pits of what this world has to offer. Then, and only then, will I kill you."

"Ugh...uurghh..."

"Now, I know we're just getting into it, but how about we take a short break? After all, leaving this poor woman alive a second longer would be an insult to my wretched mother."

"Mmmff?! Mmmfff?!"

From my bag, I produced a large pair of gleaming scissors. I opened the blades wide and stuck the points into the ground so that they were positioned across the woman's face. Then I cut free the woman's cloth gag with my knife, letting it drift softly to the ground.

"P-pleafe... You don't haff to do thif...," she begged.

"Oh? Are those to be your last words?"

"No...wait! Helf! Helf me! I'm forry! I'm forry!"

"Stop it! STOP IIIIIT!!"

With both hands, I squeezed and the scissor blades gouged in the earth and closed them around her head.

"Stof it...it hurtf...thif isn't...funny— Ukk."

The blades swung together and ended the woman's life.

"Aaaaughhh!! Aaaaughhh! Aaaaaaaaaughhh!!"

"Tee-hee-hee. Now it's your turn, Father. The pit you're bound for is darker yet, by far. A swamp of blood and despair without end."

"Th-this isn't right... Th-this can't be happening... I-it's a dream...it m-must be... It c-can't be real... I've n-never done anything to deserve this..."

The man I once respected, my ex-father, gave a hollow laugh.

"I need you to go to sleep now," I said. "A restless slumber, without solace... From nesting place in haunted soul, your wretched wingbeats end it all. *Summon Whiteclear.*"

My chant produced a milky-white maggot about five centimeters in length that squirmed in the palm of my hand. It was special, far more magical than my other insects. I kicked the man onto his back and dropped the worm into his open mouth.

"Don't worry, Father, you won't be alone. You'll be bleached white, just like the rest of them! Tee-hee! Tee-hee-hee-hee! ♪"

*   *   *

A while later, I was letting myself cool down when the others returned.

"Minnalis! We're all done on our end!" said Shuria.

"I'm finished with my part, too," said Master. "And it looks like you're almost done here."

"Yes," I replied. "Nearly there. There's only the finishing touches to go."

Master was looking a little pale after activating the Sword of Sin. I had attempted to persuade him that such suffering was not necessary, but he had told me that he would endure any fleeting pain for the sake of my eternal vengeance, and I couldn't very well say no to that.

"Okay," said Master. "Then it looks like we're on track to begin tomorrow, as planned. I can't wait."

"I've seen to it those worms stay on their best behavior," said Shuria. "So I'll be waiting in the wings from now on. I'll make sure no one comes to interfere!"

"Thank you so much, both of you."

As I spoke, a frigid wind blew, and soft flakes of snow drifted down from the sky.

"Ah, snow," I remarked. "Of course; I suppose winter is drawing near."

From the consistency of the flakes and the way the snow was falling, I expected the next day to be clear skies, with a thick blanket of white upon the ground.

"It's like I'm picking up right where I left off..."

So fall, snow, fall. Recreate the conditions of that fateful day.

"Tee-hee-hee. Tee-hee-hee-hee."

Look, Lucia. This is how I laugh now. Will it feel strange to laugh with you like this? Will I remember how it used to be?

"Oh, I just can't wait for tomorrow. My past will finally meet its end in a hellish winter wonderland."

And your life will be bleached clean, like everything that lies beneath the pure-white snow.

It was the morning of the tenth day after I'd witnessed Minnalis's act of violence and Kaito had taken me away. The cold air stung my cheeks, rousing me from shallow slumber.

"Ah, Leone, you're up. How are you feeling?"

"…Lousy, obviously. Why are you pretending you care?"

"Who said I don't care?"

Kaito was keeping me in an abandoned hunter's lodge on the outskirts of Quiquitto village. It was a dilapidated shack, just enough to keep the wind and rain at bay. In these colder months, it saw relatively little use, so he and the rest of my party were the only other people around for miles.

Thick rope bound my hands and feet, and I sat in a pile of straw, occasionally assailed by a gust of cold air that blew in through a crack in the walls.

"I'd say you made it pretty clear you don't care by bringing me here!"

"That's your own fault; you ignored my warnings. I told you to stay away, but you didn't. The only reason you're here is because you chose to be. You could have easily decided not to meddle, and you'd be passing your days peacefully in Karvanheim right now."

"…If you weren't so obsessed with revenge, it wouldn't have to be this way."

Kaito gave a gleeful chuckle, as though it were none of his concern. "Well, I can hardly do anything about that, can I?" Then he took a sip of the tea he had boiled over the fireplace.

"What do you mean, you can't do anything about it? You're strong enough to choose your own path, aren't you? So why this?"

He sighed. "Why? Let me tell you a little about myself. I tend to sleep in a lot, and my little sister always used to come into my room and pull the sheets off my bed to wake me up. My dad was the same; my mother had to drag him out of bed by the ear. She was always clumsy and could never make toast just right. When I walked to school with my friends, we used to goof off and show up late. There was one teacher who always gave us a beating for it. "Mr. Corporal Punishment," we used to call him. Those people were important to me, you know. I cared about them."

"...Then you need to do them proud. What would they think if they saw you now?"

"Oh yeah, they'd hate it. They'd be embarrassed to see what I've become."

That was what Kaito truly thought. I didn't need to use my skill; the wistful look in his eyes was all I needed to see. He had said the purpose of his journey was to find a way home, and I still thought there was a grain of truth to that.

That was why I could never persuade him.

"Give up on this. I'm sure you'll find a way back someday..."

"But it doesn't matter what they think of me. They're all dead. The price of my summoning was the two hundred people physically nearest me at the time, as well as half a dozen members of my closest family."

My hollow words fell on deaf ears.

"...What...the hell?"

"At the time I was called to this world, I had been in school. We were joking around before classes started, when a magic circle appeared underneath me from out of nowhere, and I was enclosed in a sphere of light. The people around me at that time…were my friends and teachers."

Each of his words sounded like he was driving a knife into his own heart. I knew I had to say something, but whenever I opened my mouth, nothing came out. It was like the ground beneath my feet was beginning to crack, and I feared taking a single step farther, lest it give way completely.

"You said I've been given a second chance," he said, his voice as black with hate. "So tell me. How do I get them back? My friends, my family, my life. Tell me. If you think you know me so well, then tell me how to get them back. Make it all go away…"

"…I…I…"

"…I'm sorry. This has nothing to do with you, Leone. I'm just jealous of you, you know. You're hopeful. Optimistic. Everything I used to be and more. It drives me mad."

At that moment, I saw a longing in Kaito's eyes. A longing for something far away he couldn't have.

"I know it's not right. I know it's disgraceful. I tell myself that every day. And yet…and yet…"

Despite it all, I found myself pitying the man. But I couldn't speak, couldn't find the words, and soon I heard the sound of a far-off door swinging shut.

"…Break time's over. For you and me both. It's time to go back into the box."

A shiver traveled down my spine. In an instant, he was no longer a lost child. He was my captor, a dark flame in his hollow eyes. He opened his lips, and a voice that was not his own escaped them.

"Let us play. Let us play. In my box you'll find the way.
Any garden, any hill. Anything you need to kill.
Fester, sicken, splutter, cough. I won't let you flutter off.
Is it dream, or is it real? Tell me how it makes you feel.

Pretty colors on the wall. Soon enough you'll hear the call.
In my box you'll be my friend, and in my box you'll see the end.
Sword of Sin: Lusty Little Girl."

The moment he finished speaking, there was an oppressive silence, like the air had been sucked out of the room.

"Ah-ha-ha-ha-ha! I'm free, I'm free! ♪"

A girl who looked roughly seven years of age appeared out of thin air. Her long, straight hair had red roots and violet tips, and it cycled through all the colors of the rainbow in between. She had an angelic smile, wore a thin white dress, and there was a band around her wrist connected to Kaito's right hand by a multicolored string.

"Hey Kaito! Can I play? Please, please, pretty pleeease?"

Her innocent voice scared me. It was the voice of the devil. Behind me, I heard my three companions waking up. They had all been tied up like I was.

"Urgh... Dammit, this hurts."

"Ugh... Not this again."

"If this is a nightmare, I'd sure like to wake up around now..."

Kaito turned to the girl. "Yep. They're all yours, Lust. *Multicolored Toybox.*"

""""Hrh!!""""

Suddenly, a seamless glass box closed around us. It was filled with a sticky, transparent fluid that was neither warm nor cold, which miraculously allowed us to breathe. The first time this happened, it had felt like paradise, like swimming in a boundless ocean. But now it made my skin crawl, because I knew what was coming next.

The fluid began sucking the mana out of our bodies. The pleasantness would only last until it was done. It was like our last meal before a painful execution.

"Gaaaaaaghh!! Grhhhh! Make it stop! Please, I'm begging you!!"

Dan was the first to run out. His MP reserves and magical resistance had always been the lowest among our group.

Then it was Zanck and Spinne.

"Gh… Grrrrh! Gaaaaah! Grhhrhh…"

"Ahhh…ahhh! Please…no more…"

"Stop this!" I shouted. "Do whatever you want to me, but leave my friends alone!"

"I'm afraid I can't do that. Your pain alone isn't enough to suit my needs. Keeping Sloth active requires quite a lot of MP, so I need to stock up. There's no use complaining."

Kaito refused, and as I began to drift out of consciousness, I felt my own mana reserves, restored through rest, reach their lower limits once more.

"Don't worry. This is the last time. After this I'll have all the mana I need. Then you can sit and watch until it's all over."

As he finished speaking, my MP hit zero. The pleasantness across my whole body suddenly flipped, and I felt like the surface of my skin was being stripped away, making me one with the world. As my essence flowed out of me, I thought I felt something else making its way in.

It hurts make it stop I can't take it can't bear anymore please help me I'm scared I'm all alone I need saving I want to cry it's so dark it's so cold I don't want to be alone I want to go away I want to disappear I want to die I want to die I want to die I want to die I want to die I want to die I want to die.

"Hrrrgh! No, stop! Stay out of me!!"

Fighting its way inside me was a darkness so pure, a single drop would stain my whole mind like a cancer. It was crossing my skin, soaking into my flesh, shooting through my veins, making its way to my heart and spreading through my entire body. It was a pain I was deeply familiar with by now, but I could neither block it out nor adapt to it. Once exposed to the sensation, it was difficult to even stay sane, let alone think of a way out.

"*Everyone loves the inside of my box,*" said the little girl. "*Take everything I have, and I'll turn it all into mana.*"

"…I think you're coming on a little strong, Lust. Lay off a little, or they won't last three days. I've got plenty of your mana stocked up in the Clothes of Dark Spirits already, and I need these four to be able to watch. Keep it up until they're on the verge of passing out, but no further."

"*Aww, but I was just getting started! I won't stop now, I won't, I won't!*"

"Don't be selfish. Just do what I say."

"*Hmph. Okaaay…*"

The girl with rainbow hair pouted and spun her finger, and the oppressive feeling backed off.

"Krh…*Cough!! Cough!!*"

I was still in excruciating pain, but at least I could think again. I gasped for air, not even knowing what it was the box had taken from me.

"…Have your fun, Lust. *Picture Box.*"

As Kaito spoke those words, the hut disappeared, as though a large box had been drawn around us.

"What's…this…?"

When I came to my senses, I was looking down on a small village surrounded by snow-flecked trees.

"*Oh, is this mine? Can I play with it, Kaito? Wheee! ♪*"

"Wait, stop!"

Ignoring Kaito's words, the girl gestured in the air with her hand as casually as she might scribble on the wall, and all the trees in one location were knocked flat.

"*Ah-ha-ha-ha! Look at that, I squished them— Hrk!*"

The girl's laughter suddenly stopped as the multicolored thread grew in length, wrapping around the girl's throat and squeezing.

"Listen to me, Lust. This isn't a toy, understand? It's not for you to play with."

"Rrrgh! Rrrgh! Rrrgh!"

The girl struggled, flapping her arms and legs, swinging her head from side to side. Meanwhile, Kaito turned to us, a vicious smile on his lips.

"It's time for Minnalis to begin her revenge. This way, you guys can watch, too."

"…You mean, this is…?"

The gears of my hazy mind began to turn, and I realized what I was looking at. As I turned my gaze toward it, the scene came closer, as though revealing itself to me. From the confines of the clear box, I was looking down on Quiquitto Village.

Using the power of my soul blade, I had created a miniature version of Minnalis's village so that Leone and the others could watch along. I'd panicked when Lust suddenly destroyed some of the trees, but on second glance, the location was far from the town, and also far from the area where Shuria had corralled the innocent village children. Shuria also informed me via Soulspeak that she was already on her way back and hadn't been harmed.

Reassured, I glance down at the village once more, just in time to notice a church collapse, its tall towers falling into piles of rubble. Minnalis had already begun, and it was time for me to play my part. I'd done all this to give her the best stage possible on which to play out her revenge.

A voice belonging to someone else issued forth from my lips.

"Let me linger, let me languor. Do not raise your fist in anger. You're the one who bothered me; it's only fair you leave me be.

Make it simple, make it quick. Run around and never stick. All this rushing to and fro. Can't you see it has to go?

See what effort you can save, when you dwell within my cave. Here you'll rest all through the day, until my workshop goes away.

Sword of Sin: Grotto of Death's Neglect"

A huge man appeared, the size of a troll, but with dwarven features. He was dressed like a blacksmith, with a tarnished gold and silver hammer hanging from his waist.

"...What is a smith without materials? I'm going back. Put me back."

Although the lot of us appeared to be floating in the air above the village, he slumped down onto his side as if there was a floor beneath.

"You can't go back until you've done your job, Sloth. Here, just one thing, then you can go back to sleep."

Before Sloth could shirk his duties completely, I took out the Bloodcurse Blade I had prepared earlier and tossed it to him.

"...This isn't as good as what you gave me last time."

"That was Lichie's Staff of Despair. You don't see quality materials like that every day. Be grateful for what you get."

I sighed, remembering what a hassle it had been to obtain. Then I looked down once more at the diorama my soul blade had produced.

"Get to work already. *Blackwheel Workshop.*"

"Urgh. What a drag."

Sloth took the cursed item and held it over the miniature village. Then he lifted the hammer from his belt and swung it down on the Bloodcurse Blade with a clang. Suddenly, the item disintegrated into countless shimmering motes, and a wall of black gears, slowly turning, appeared around the village.

Now the entire region was in the domain of the Blackwheel Workshop. I turned to Leone and told her this:

"Now all of you are going to see just what it is you've been working so hard to prevent."

"…"

She didn't answer. I turned back and sat down, watching what happened next. All I had to do now was make sure the workshop stayed up; otherwise, I could sit back and enjoy the show. That was the reason we had been funneling mana from Leone and the others into the Clothes of Dark Spirits.

"Over to you, Minnalis."

"…And so, the warrior slew all the evil monsters with his magic sword, and he and the village girl got married and lived happily ever after. The end."

"Aww, it's over? C'mon, Lucia, read us another one!"

"I'm afraid that's all we have time for today," I said, closing the picture book in my hands. "You have to go to bed soon or you won't be able to get up in the morning. You have to be up bright and early to celebrate my wedding."

"Hey, how come the warrior didn't marry the princess at the end? He woulda become the king then! Isn't a king super powerful?"

"That's because he loved the village girl. Love is more powerful than anything else, and it gives you the strength to conquer every obstacle in your path. Just like mine and Kril's love does."

I tucked the children into bed and blew out the candles before sitting next to them and stroking the tops of their blankets as they fell asleep.

Tomorrow was the big day. Kril was supposed to be back in the village already, but he had sent a message saying something had come up, and he would instead be arriving on the day, alongside Eugace and Cataleya.

Kril was always getting waylaid by this or that, so this came as little surprise, but I thought he'd at least be on time for his own wedding, so that we could spend our last night together not as husband and wife, but as lovers…

"Hee-hee! ♪ I'm going to be a wife! I can hardly believe it!"

I was getting married to Kril. It was something I'd dreamed of all my life. All my hard work was about to pay off. I'd made him notice me, fall in love with me, and cherish me more than anything else. I learned how to cook for him and how to make myself look pretty for him. I'd toiled and toiled and toiled. I studied magic, made my connections, and used any means necessary to eliminate all threats to our union. And Kril still trusted me through it all.

I cast my mind back to our *other* friend, the one who'd been chased out of the village. She was surely lying dead in a ditch somewhere by now. The grown-ups had tried to pretend she was living somewhere far away with her mother, but I knew that they had really sold her into slavery.

And good riddance, I say. Now nobody could stand between Kril and I.

I'll wake up early tomorrow to pick fruit and bake a lovely pie. He loves his fruit pie.

I thought back to the pastry I'd made that day, when the nuisance was gone from our midst. No effort was too great for the sake of Kril's smile.

Hee-hee. I just can't wait for tomorrow!

The red fruit of happiness would be in my hands tomorrow.

*   *   *

Dawn broke on a clear sky the next morning, and I stepped out into snow as deep as my ankles. I was up a little earlier than I needed to be, so I was taking a walk around the village to kill some time, reminiscing about everything in my life with Kril that led up to this point.

I walked by the plaza we'd used to play in, passed the abandoned house where we used to play hide-and-seek, and arrived in front of the church where we made our silly vows. Later today, it would be the place where we exchanged them for real. The village priest was usually up early; I wondered if he was about.

I gently pushed open the door and entered the chapel. It was empty, and a solemn silence presided over the inside of the building. I approached the altar and clasped my hands together in prayer.

"Thank you, my Lady, for watching over Kril and me. I swear to live a happy life with him."

Suddenly, I heard the door creak open behind me, and in walked a gentle old man with a graying mustache.

"Oh, Lucia? What brings you to the house of our Lady?"

"Good morning, Father. I woke up early today, so I thought I'd come and offer my prayers."

"I see, I see. Worry not, Lucia, for our Lady is always looking over you. Her mercy shall fill your lives with happiness."

The priest's warm smile was filled with love and kindness. I imagined the entire village standing around us, offering their support.

"Thank you, Father. I promise to lead a happy life."

…However, the blueprint of my happiness was not long for this world.

*　　*　　*

"So you should, Lucia. You've come so far. I'm still sorry I never noticed that beastfolk living among us. I'll always regret not noticing your mistreatment earlier. Now that monster is gone from your life, you can move on and— *Hurk?!*"

...A few drops of blood trickled down onto the blueprint, staining the whole page red.

"Oh, Father. You always were an early riser. But I'm afraid I can't have you interfering in this."

"...Huh? Wh-what...?"

With a sound like slicing fruit, the priest's attacker retracted their bloodstained blade from his back.

"Ngh...ugh... The blood... I'm dying... Help...me..."

"Oh, don't be such a crybaby. I didn't hit anything important. You'll live...for a while."

"Ughh?!"

The woman holding the knife smiled as though she were looking fondly upon an old friend. She kicked the priest aside, and he collapsed to the ground.

"Agh...please...I don't want to die..."

"Don't worry. Isn't your goddess watching over you? What happened to Her mercy?"

The priest floundered on the floor, clutching the hole in his torso. I could do nothing but watch on, stunned. Then she turned to me.

"What do you think, Lucia? Personally, I wouldn't be happy with a goddess who merely watches and does nothing to help. Do you think you can sympathize with that?"

"M-Minnalis...?"

It was her, the childhood nuisance I'd tried so hard to get rid of.

The same flaxen hair and eyes, the same rabbit ears atop her head. Only now, she wore a bewitching smile and a maid outfit that showed off her slender arms and womanly charm.

"H-how? I thought they sold you into slavery!"

"Oh? That's interesting. Kril didn't know about that, but you do. Listening in on the grown-ups again, were we? Don't you remember what they used to do when they found you?"

She giggled, sending a chill down my spine.

"Wh-what business do you have here?" I demanded. "I don't recall sending you a wedding invitation."

"Oh, but I simply must give the new bride my regards," Minnalis replied. "What kind of friend would I be if I didn't make an appearance?"

She smiled, but the malice on her face was plain to see, almost as though she saw no reason to hide it.

"Is that so? Well, I hate to break it to you, but murderers aren't allowed to attend... Save myself, of course. Festering tongue of earth and fire, answer to my heart's desire! *Lovers' Snake!!*"

The air suddenly flickered with heat, and a large serpent of molten lava appeared.

She's a beastfolk, so she'll dodge it and try to get close. When she does, I'll roast her alive with Wall of Flame.

However, my prediction was quickly overturned.

"I haven't murdered anybody," she said. "Yet. *Icicle Spear.*"

"What?!"

Minnalis's ice magic collided with my own, and the completely frozen snake clattered to the ground.

"A combination Fire and Earth spell," she noted. "Not bad at all."

"How did you do that?! Beastfolk shouldn't be able to summon spears without even chanting!"

"Because beastfolk mana gets weaker the farther it is from the source? Don't be silly, Lucia. It doesn't drop off *that* quickly. You've heard of beastfolk warriors who enchant their weapons, haven't you? Don't they teach you that at the academy?"

"Grrr. O, fire sprites who dance at dawn, by sacrifice your breath is drawn! *Breath of the Fire Spirits!!*"

This spell possessed the same destructive force as dragonflame and could burn away everything it touched. The fire rushed toward Minnalis, but she didn't even bat an eye. She ran inside the building, leaping out of the way.

"Oh, Lucia. Giving up the initiative so quickly with a long chant? And your spirit magic is impressive in might only. Do those mock battles actually teach you anything or are they merely for sport? They could replace you with a fixed cannon and lose nothing in the way of flexibility."

"Grrr! Shut up and die already!!"

The tide of battle was turning against me. This was not good. Mine was merely a support role; I couldn't compete with a beastfolk in terms of physical ability. If Kril were here, he'd be able to protect me, but since he wasn't, I would need to kill Minnalis before she got close.

I have no choice. The next spell has to take her down!!

I still didn't know why Minnalis had come here, but it didn't matter. There was no place for her in our world. She wasn't even supposed to be alive!!

"Tee-hee-hee. You haven't changed, either. Remember how you always used to fall behind in our races? Here, I'll help you, just follow the sound of my voice! Tee-hee-hee!"

"Grrr! I didn't want to have to use this, but your face is really starting to tick me off!!"

I reached into my item pouch and pulled out a stone brimming with Fire magic called a Fire Orchid Stone, which was used as catalyst to call upon the full power of the fire spirits. They didn't come cheap and were good for only a single use. Plus, unleashing it here would likely destroy the building we were in. But right now, I couldn't afford to hold back.

"Fire and brimstone, be my shield! Let thine anger be revealed! *Wrath of the Fire Spirits!!*"

For a moment, all the mana in the surrounding area was sucked into the stone, and it glowed with an incandescent light. The next moment, white-hot flames spread out from me, devouring everything they touched. By the time the dust settled, I was standing in a pile of rubble and debris.

"I...I won? Ha...ha-ha... Stupid woman, coming here only to die."

I felt a wave of relief wash over me and breathed a heavy sigh. No ghost of the past could kill me now, not when I was on the verge of realizing my dream.

"Oh, but now the church is ruined. What am I going to do about the wedding?"

"I think you have other things to worry about."

"Ah..."

The voice, *her* voice, carried softly into my ear from behind. I spun around to face her, when she plunged a knife into my shoulder.

"Aaaagh! No!"

It hurts... I have to do something!!

I took a few steps back from her before falling to my knee and chanting a healing spell.

"Grh! Ghuh! O s-spirits free, hear my plea! *Heal!*"

"I'm always appalled by how callous you can be, Lucia. Weren't you worried about the poor priest? Or is your wedding more important than his life? Hee-hee-hee! ♪ It's a good thing I rescued him, or else he might have gotten off easy!"

The soothing green light slowly caused my pain to recede, but it did nothing about the chill that gripped my heart. Minnalis glared at me like I was merely a worm wriggling in the dirt, and that filled me with dread.

Just then, the other villagers began to appear, drawn to the noise.

"Wh-what happened here?!"

"The church! It's been destroyed!"

"Has anyone seen the children?"

"What's going on here? Hey, look! Isn't that Minnalis over by Lucia?!"

However, Minnalis didn't seem afraid. If anything, she looked happier than ever.

"Tee-hee-hee. The stage is set. It's time to begin."

"B-begin what…? Grh!"

Just then, a black wall suddenly appeared around the entire village. Embedded in its surface were ebon gears, slowly clunking and turning. The mere sight of the obstruction was enough to instill in me a deep feeling of dread.

"Tee-hee-hee! Tee-hee-hee-hee! At last! At long last! Lucia, it's your turn next. I'm going to destroy everything you hold dear! Tee-hee-hee! Tee-hee-hee-hee! Ah-ha-ha-ha-ha!!"

For the first time in my life, I was not angry or disgusted at Minnalis. I was afraid of her. Deeply, deathly afraid.

A crowd was forming. The villagers stared at me with eyes filled with curiosity, save Lucia. Hers were filled with terror.

"How has it been, my old family? I do hope you've been well. Tee-hee. For my part, I have been keeping exceptionally well, if I do say so myself! Tee-hee-hee! Ahhh, what a beautiful morning. It's like—"

"Hey, what's this stinkin' beastfolk doin' back in our villa—? AAAAAAGH!!"

Minnalis's spear of ice flew into the man's foot, pinning him to the ground and causing the soil beneath to run red with his blood.

"I believe I wasn't done speaking," she said. "Do they not teach basic manners in this village anymore? Why is what you have to say more important than anyone else's, hmm?"

"You! You'll pay for— Gaaaaagh!!"

"Where do you think you—? Aieeeee!!"

Two yapping dogs, deeply lacking in imagination, started running toward me, each earning themselves an impaled shoulder.

"Please, exercise a little self-preservation. Or can you just not comprehend that the little girl you persecuted is now in a position to fight back? You really are a bunch of fools."

Some of the other villagers rushed over to protect those that I'd harmed. In their eyes I saw a mixture of bewilderment and anger.

"Ahhh, those are the eyes I've longed to see," I said, letting a chuckle escape my lips. The red and black distillation of my heart's desires worked its way up and out of the inner recesses of my soul.

"I have one thing to tell you all before we begin," I explained. "I do not intend on holding back in the slightest. There is not one reason why I should show mercy to a single one of you. My partners in crime have worked tirelessly to ensure that I can cut loose completely tonight. Allow me to provide a demonstration."

"Guh! Ghhh...gfff?!"

Before the man creeping up behind me could swing his ax, I spun around and stabbed him in the heart with my sword.

"I should have known it was you, Calif. Simpleminded as ever. Shouldn't you be a little more careful now that you have your family to worry about?"

"Calif?! Noooooooo!!"

I kicked the poor soul off my sword, and his wife Yuria came running over in despair. Anyone could see that his wounds were fatal—and if luck was on his side, he would already be dead. But strangely, Calif kept on yelling.

"Aaaaagh! It hurts so bad! I'm gonna die!"

"C-Calif...?"

The wound was so deep you could almost see right through him, and blood was pouring out of him like a flood. Yet he was still writhing in pain, kicking and screaming.

"Oh, don't worry, he'll live...for now. That's the nature of this magical prison. It prevents your souls from leaving your bodies, which means you'll have plenty of time to suffer! Tee-hee-hee! Tee-hee-hee-hee! ♪"

"Huh? Oh...uh?"

Yuria seemed unable to comprehend that her husband was not in fact deceased. That, or perhaps her brain was simply refusing to accept the cruel reality that he would be stuck in a waking nightmare forever. And so, I turned back to Lucia to give her a hint.

"Come on, Lucia. Calif is going to die unless you use your healing magic."

"Y-you're insane!"

"Oh, now that's not nice. Hee-hee. Who do you think made me this way?"

She glared at me with abject hatred. No appreciation for my kind and thoughtful words.

"Okay, then in honor of our friendship, I'll give you a little motivation. How about this? *The village children have all been taken prisoner somewhere.* That sounds like what a hero would get involved in, doesn't it? I know you always liked that sort of thing."

"What?! What have you done to the children?!"

"What do you think I've done?" I said, with a suggestive smile.

"Why, is that still not enough for you? Then how about this one? *There are too many wounded for us to deal with alone.*"

"No...stop!"

I sneered and drew a handful of throwing knives, tossing them into the crowd.

"Gaaah!!"

"Aaaargh!!"

"Aghhh! My leg!"

"H-how could you be so cruel?! You know I just expended all my mana! Have you no sympathy?"

"Ah-ha-ha-ha!! I'm afraid you destroyed that a long time ago! Each and every one of you! You broke it into tiny pieces with your stones!"

Ahhh, this was it. I could feel my heart crying out for more. It was time to taste the fruits of my diligent harvest.

"Why don't you try paying attention?" I asked. "It's starting."

"Huh...?"

Something was happening to the wounded.

"Look, it's nearly here," I said. "The seeds are beginning to sprout."

"Ghh! Ggh! What's that...? Get it out...!"

"S-stop...what's happening to me...what the hell is happening to meee?"

"Wh-what are they...?"

"...They're my darling maggots! ♪"

I grinned a vicious grin as the villagers descended into a hell far deeper than any they knew.

"Eurgh!! Gaaaagh!!"

Like pus, dozens of milky-white maggots spilled out of the towns-people's deep knife wounds.

"C-Calif? Wh-what's happening to you?!"

"Y-Yuria?! Oh, craaa— Aaagh?!"

213

"Tee-hee. Oh, it hurts, doesn't it? That makes me so happy! Tee-hee-hee!"

Their eyes were filled with a sublime mixture of malice and fear that I couldn't get enough of. It was like they'd finally realized their place: as swine who were beneath me. But my little piggies had a long way to go. They had reached but the first perch on the cliffs of a steep chasm. I couldn't wait to see the looks on their faces when they saw how deep the bottom really was.

"Lucia, please! Do something for Calif! If you don't, he'll... huh...?"

Yuria's impassioned plea turned to dismay, and all the villagers, Lucia included, watched in shock.

"You're married, aren't you?" I said. "And couples ought to share everything. Isn't that right?"

I watched gleefully on, my lips arcing into a crescent smile, as Calif drove his maggot-ridden teeth into his own wife's neck. He rubbed his face into the wound as if trying to push the larvae inside her.

"Eieee! Stop...Calif! That hurts! OwowowoOOOWWW?!"

"Aah... I'm sorry...Yuria... I can't help iiiit!!"

"Aaaaaaagh!!"

"Aha! ♪"

That scream was the first note of the ensuing symphony. Once it began, a host of other voices joined the resounding chorus. The next to join in was the stingy, mean-tempered old lady who ran the apothecary.

"...Gh... Agh...? What's...happening? Aaaieeee!!"

Her wrinkled skin bulged like an overfilled water balloon, revealing the shape of the maggots multiplying inside her. They burst out of her flesh, slurping up her blood with sounds as disgusting as their appearance.

The wriggling creatures spilled from her eyes, her ears, her nose, her mouth, clogging her throat as she tried to scream. After her, it was the hunter's wife, then the elder's son. Then the old trapper, and so on, and on, and on… One after the other, the villagers began experiencing the same symptoms, until about one in five of them were infested with the maggots.

One man, unable to endure the sight any longer, tried to run, when another victim lying on the ground grabbed him by the leg and sunk their teeth into his calf, allowing the maggots to enter his body.

"Eieee! What are you doing?! Get…get off me! Aaaagh!"

"Tee-hee-hee! It's a village-wide game of tag! I think you'd better start running; you've seen what happens to those who get caught, haven't you?"

"Nooooo!!"

"Run awaaaay!!"

"Wh-what the hell is going oooon?!"

The townspeople all fled in different directions, screaming their heads off, while the few who didn't immediately run became food for the beasts. Once the maggots entered them, they began roaming around, seeking to infect others in the same way.

"Tee-hee-hee. Now then, I'd better see where Lucia went."

Leaving the villagers to their own devices, I went off in search of the girl who had conveniently disappeared in the confusion. Just as I'd suspected, I found her attempting to engage in some deeply shameful behavior.

"Dammit! What's this wall made of?!"

She clawed with futility at the black wall that surrounded the village. The sight was so amusing, I couldn't help but laugh.

"There's no use trying to escape," I explained. "According to Master, even the evil dragon couldn't escape this wall. A grub like you doesn't stand a chance."

"Grrr… Minnalis…"

She turned and glared at me, and I chuckled again. Just then, I noticed another villager a short distance away, beating his fists against the barrier. It seemed he had the same idea as Lucia and came face-to-face with the walls of the pen Master created.

"This can't be happening!! Let me ooout!! No! S-stay back! Noooo!! Gh!! Gaah!! Grhh… Gggh!!"

With no way out, the man was quickly surrounded, and the slavering beasts descended on him. Moments later, he was another one of them. Lucia winced at the sight before turning back to me and giggled. "Ah, Lucia, there's no need to worry. The townspeople won't come after you; I've got something far more special planned for my good friends. Doesn't that make you happy?"

"…Do you really think you're going to get away with this? This is essentially an act of treason against Karvanheim itself! Plus, my friends from the army will be arriving at any moment. They'll put you to death for this, mark my words."

"…Hmm. Well, I can't say I expected that."

"Give it up, Minnalis. I'll put in a good word for you. Maybe then you won't face execution."

As soon as Lucia saw the look on my face, she gave a sneer of superiority. She was looking down on me again. *Yes, that's it. Let's start from there. Right where we left off all those years ago. That's the only way I can get closure on the world I lost that day.*

"What I mean, Lucia, is that I never expected you'd be this slow to catch on. Do you not get what's happening here? You do remember I said I have something special planned for my good friends, don't you?"

"…Huh?"

Her face froze. Using the power of the Transcendent Blade of Translocation, granted to me by Master's activation of the Sword of Lust, I called over the pet I had so lovingly trained for this moment.

"Hee-hee-hee. One must take good care of their friends, mustn't they, Lucia?"

"Wh-what…is this? What are you doing…?"

A magic circle roughly a meter across appeared beside me. The spell was imperfect and only brought him to me slowly.

"At first I considered doing the two of you together, but then I thought, *I mustn't get greedy.*"

"Wh-what…do you mean? What did you do…?"

Bit by bit, tiny motes of magical light began forming together within the circle.

"I mean, it just isn't fair to either of you if I split my focus, is it?"

There he stood, head hung, his skin a ghastly color. He was covered in dried and blackened blood, and his arm bones zigzagged wildly, while his legs had swollen to an unnatural size.

"I think it's time to show you what's become of Kril," I said. "After all, I need to make sure both of you get tortured equally."

"K-KRIIIIIL!!"

That's right, show me how it feels to look upon the suffering of the one you love so much.

"Ah-ha-ha-ha-ha!! Did you think he was coming to save you? Well, too bad! I've already had my way with him, and this is what he's become!! Ah-ha-ha-ha-ha-ha!!"

"Wh-what did you do to him?! You're…you're insane!!"

"Tee-hee-hee. Well, first I beat him to a pulp…"

That's it, show me.

"Ahhh, no, no, this can't be happening…"

"Then I carefully broke the bones in his arm and healed them back into place. After that I buried his legs beneath scalding rods."

Show me more, more.

"Then I poured boiling water mixed with slime powder over his entire body to make it nice and sticky."

"S-stop… How could you…?"

Yes, run your fingers through your hair. Let your voice quaver.

"Then I left him with a frozen block of my special potion. If he stretched his tongue, he could just about reach it, and it would relieve the pain for a while. What he didn't know, however, was that the potion caused his insides to rot and bruise like moldy fruit!"

"Aaahhh… Ahhh… Aaaahhh…"

Show me a face warped with grief. Let me hear your hopeless wails.

"And do you know what I did after that? I filled him with maggots, just like I did to the villagers. But I knew you wouldn't be able to recognize him if I let them eat him. So what I did was, I covered him in a special serum to preserve his skin. It made him go a little off-color, but you can still tell who it is, right?"

"MINNALIIIIIIIIIIIIS!!"

"Ah-ha-ha-ha!! That's it! That's the face I've been waiting for, Lucia!!"

She was furious, like a child whose favorite toy had been broken. She launched a fireball at me, but as a result of her temper tantrum it was sorely lacking in both power and accuracy, and I neutralized it without any effort.

"Why do you always, always, always get in my way?! I was finally, finally happy!! Why did you have to show your ugly face again?! I was so close! So close!!"

"Yes, I know. That's why I'm here. I'm here to destroy that dream you worked so hard for! Ah-ha-ha-ha-ha!!"

Ahhh, what a glare. What defiance. But it wouldn't last long. She was out of MP now.

"…Krh… I…can't…"

Lucia crumpled to the floor like a limp puppet. Sitting there in the mud, on her hands and knees, she looked just like my miserable mother.

"…Just end it already," she said. "That's what you want, isn't it? To kill me."

"Yes," I replied. "I do. You wouldn't believe how much I've wanted to end your life."

But it was still too soon. She was perched on an upper cliff, while I stood far below. It was time to give her *exactly what she wanted*.

So I could trample all over it.

"…Tee-hee-hee. Go on now. Lucia's waiting for you. Be by her side."

"Bubuhh…buuhh…"

He opened his mouth to respond, spilling maggots, and staggered over toward his fiancée. He pushed on, even after he tripped, crawling on hand and knee to reach her.

"The maggots start out by nibbling away at the host's flesh, ignoring the brain. Anything they devour they replace with a sort of false flesh that gets incorporated into the body, which becomes food for the other maggots. Once they fill up, the host is driven to find somewhere for the excess specimens to go. The reason they bite is because the mouth is where they breed quickest."

"It's…too much… Too much…"

"I'm sorry, Kril… I'm sorry I couldn't protect you… I'm so sorry…"

Lucia reached out toward him without hesitation.

"Tee-hee. Oh, that's right. It's your wedding day, isn't it?" I teased. "Why don't you give him a lovely kiss?"

"…You'll pay for this, I swear," she shot back in a voice thick as mud. "You really are a monster. A fiend in human skin."

"Ah, well then I suppose you had it coming. What sort of person crosses a monster and doesn't expect to meet a grisly end?"

I saw resignation in her eyes, along with a burning hatred she would never be free of. *Oh, Lucia. I can see straight through you. Maybe I could have fallen for your wiles in the past, but not now.*

"I love you Kril. I always will. More than anything else in this world."

"Help... Please... It's too much..."

"We'll always be happy together. It doesn't matter what happens to you, I'll be there to save you."

The hero, his dreams all but shattered, and his lover holding him in her arms.

"I...Buuh..."

"Minnalis, I don't know if you're doing this for revenge or what, but I won't let you come between me and Kril. He is my hero... And I won't let you have your way... What's mine is yours: *Song of Life*."

She kissed him, like the end of a fairy tale. It was just the kind of ending Lucia always loved.

"Gaaaaaaaaaagh!!"

A warm light spread through his body; the light of the Spirits' blessing. This was a highly classified Spirit Art, one that only a few practitioners were permitted to learn. It could bring back a victim on the brink of death, no matter their condition, all for the cost of a portion of the caster's life span. Plus, the target would receive a significant stat boost for a short period of time.

"Hmm," I said, watching on. "So this is the ultimate form of spirit magic."

The light forced its way inside the body, pushing everything else out that didn't belong.

The parasitic maggots, *the rusted iron stakes I used to ensure the cover held*, all of them vanished in a scattering of light.

"Tee-hee! ♪"

That's right, Lucia. This is how it all ends in your head, isn't it? I can't imagine it's easy giving up your own life like that. I don't know how it works, but I expect you'd need to spend half of it at the very least. But

I think I understand. For just as you have chosen the object of your obses-sion, so have I chosen mine.

Still, Lucia, there's something I haven't told you. That day is far, far in the past now, and I've had such a long time to think about it.

"Haah... Haah... Now you'll get what's coming to you. Once Kril is back on his feet, you'll see. With the Spirit's protection, he'll—"

"Lucia."

I'm afraid the story in your head bears very little relation to reality.

"When did I tell you that was Kril? I don't remember saying that, do you?"

"...What?"

I had been waiting so long for this moment. The moment every-thing was washed away, swallowed by the tears of a shattered world.

"It...it's not...?"

After forcing everything out of his insides, the magic set about purifying the exterior, dissolving away the facade I had made. His arms, his legs, his torso, and his face, all returned to normal.

"Listen to me, Lucia. There's something I want to ask you."

As she watched on in shock, I leaned over and whispered.

"How were you planning on bringing Kril back? *He's been dead for three days.*"

"NOOOOOOOOOOOOOO!!"

"That was just his skin! The rest was all eaten away! Oh, Lucia, how does it feel? Tell me, how does it feel?"

"Agghh... Aggghh. Th-this can't be happening... It can't..."

"Ugh...gh... Ah...ha-ha-ha... I'm back. Just as I was about to die. Ahhh... aaahhh..."

As Kril's skin slowly dissolved away, the true identity of the person beneath was revealed. It was none other than the man whom I'd once called my father.

"How does it feel to know that you just gave up half your life to save *him*? Tell me, tell me!! Tee-hee-hee-hee!! Ah-ha-ha-ha-ha-ha-ha! ♪"

"Minnalis!! Rgh! Aaaaaaaaagh!!"

Ah, how long I'd waited to see Lucia's face, looking up at me from the mud! How wonderful it felt!

"You're sooo stupid! Did you really think everything was about to turn around? Did you? Did you? Did you think Kril was going to get up all strong? That he was going to save the day? That he would hold you in his arms and tell you *it's all over now*? Well, I'm sorry, but he can't! I killed him! Whoopsie! ♪ Tee-hee-hee! ♪"

"Aaaaaarghhh! I'll fucking kill you, Minnalis! Rrraaaaagh!!"

She lay in the mud, kicking and shouting abuse as the dirt-caked snow melted into slush around her. She'd used up half her life and was completely out of energy, her face marred with unsightly tears.

"Die, die, diiiie!!" she screamed. "Get out of my sight! Wrraaaaaagh!!"

A pleasant tingle coursed through me. It was a whirlpool of sugar and salt, tinged with just a little bitterness, that made it feel like I was melting away.

"Why did you have to come back now, of all times?! I was just about to be happy! Go away! Disappear! Diiiie!"

She screamed wildly, as if to shred her throat, the air, and her very soul. This was what I wanted to see. All those years of waiting. This was what made them all worthwhile.

"Give him back!! Give him back! You thief! You home-wrecker! You— Ghk!"

"How dare you... How dare you bring me back to life!! I was

finally about to break… I was finally about to die!! Why did you have to bring me back here?! Now I have to start all over again!! No…no, no, no, nooo! Please no!!"

"Ghh…Khh…"

"Tee-hee-hee! ♪ Well, that's not nice. She gave up her life to save you, you know? What a shame. What a pity. What a wreck. I can't believe I get to see this!"

Tell me, Lucia. How did you feel that day, looking down on poor old me?

Tell me tell me tell me tell me tell me tell me tell me tell me tell me tell me.

Please. Please. I want to hear it all from your mouth.

"Ah-ha-ha! Ah-ha-ha-ha-ha!! Suffer!! Suffer through a hell of my making, far deeper than any I had to endure!! Cry until your eyes bleed!!"

And then, once it's over, you can finally die. Ah-ha-ha! Ah-ha-ha-ha-ha-ha!!

The sun set. And rose. And set, and rose, and set. Soon it would be precisely three days since it had all begun.

It was just before dawn. Snow fell from the clouded sky and blanketed the land.

On the first day, the village was filled with fear, confusion, and hate.

On the second day, it was only hate.

And on the third day, there was nothing at all. Just white.

White like the snow that started falling the previous day.

White like the maggots, squirming, seeking their next meal.

White like the bones, stripped of flesh, undying, while the villagers' souls were trapped within.

The only one who remained was Lucia, lying flat on her back, gazing up at the sky with empty, hollow eyes.

She had been thoroughly tortured. Her arms and legs were missing, and her belly was sliced open. In the cavity were irons, pots, things she had no doubt expected to use in her future life. Her eyes were gouged out, nothing now but vacant pits, and her skin had lost so much blood it was hard to see where it stopped and the snow began. Only the ruptured flesh where the maggots had bitten through still retained its color, but by now, the falling snow had covered those holes as well.

She was a living corpse, and it was only thanks to Master's barrier that she could voice anything resembling speech at all. The power of Sloth prevented certain changes from occurring in the targets while it was in effect. Within this workshop, even Death's scythe would not save these people from eternal torment.

"I'm…sorry…I'm…sorry…," she kept repeating in delirium. On rare occasions, she would lapse into screaming, and I would feel my heart flutter.

"…I suppose it's almost time to end this. It's been so long, yet it still feels so short."

I thought of my bedridden mother on the verge of death, repeating the same apology over and over again. They were the same words, but some of these felt so much different. Lucia's apologies were like thick logs on the dirty black flame of my heart. Each one exploded into a shower of crackling sparks, turning the color of the fire into a deep and calm blue.

"…Sorry…I'm…sorry…I'm…"

I had tasted much of the villagers' hardship over the last three days. I had seen long-time family members and spouses forcing their pain on one another. I had seen them suffer in pain, choke in agony, weep in sorrow, and be claimed by despair. I had seen them turn against me, only to be trampled; bargain with me, only to be chopped up; and beg for mercy, only to be eaten up from the inside out.

I had seen it all, and it washed over me like ocean waves.

"But it still isn't enough…"

It isn't enough. It isn't enough! It isn't anywhere near enough!!

Aaaaaaaaaaagh! Why must I be so incompetent?! Why couldn't I make them suffer more?!

"…We're out of time. And so I must etch this face into my memory. I will remember you until the day I die, and long afterward as well, Lucia. Wherever you end up, I pray it is a place of suffering. With my whole heart."

Far away, over distant trees, I heard the sky crack. Master's barrier was beginning to collapse. There was no time. I had to finish things with a bang.

"This life is hell with you in it, and I'm sure it will be hell without you as well. But as long as I have the memories of these past three days…I can go on living."

"Forgive…me… I…just…wanted…to…be…happy… I'm… sorry…"

"I know. Everyone just wants to be happy. I did, and I'm sure my mother did, too. You know, Lucia, I'm also in love. I'm bound to him more tightly than I ever thought possible. And I think now I can see why you did what you did that day."

"Please…so much pain…why…why…?"

"So please accept my heartfelt congratulations! I'm sorry you couldn't be with Kril! But you're such a beautiful, maggot-eaten bride! Ah-ha-ha-ha-ha-ha!!"

""*"Skreeeeee!!*"""

At my command, the swarm of maggots all descended on Lucia at once.

"No…no…help…help…I don't want…to die… I was finally…
ha…ppy…"

I watched her face, racked with despair, until it became nothing
but expressionless bone. That instant, the barrier fell, and a single ray
of light shone down through a crack in the clouds.

The falling snow glistened in the sun. The grubs, gorged on nutri-
ents, fell still as they prepared to grow their wings.

"Ahhh, I see. It's just like Master and Shuria said. The crying."

Tears streamed endlessly down my face. Exposed to the warmth
of the sun, the ice around my heart was melting.

But it wasn't over yet.

"Okay, it's time to go."

There were still people left. I had to return to Master and Shuria
and end this.

I wiped away the tears a few more times and set off walking, turning my back on the bleached-white village.

The next day, a group of people arrived in Quiquitto Village for their
friends' wedding. They had been waylaid by monsters, and ended up
taking the long way around, thus arriving spectacularly late. When
they got there, however, they suspected for a moment they had mis-
read the map.

There was not a single living person anywhere to be found; just a
bunch of ruined buildings and snow-covered skeletons, as if the place
had lain undisturbed for hundreds of years. The only creatures living
there were a swarm of white butterflies.

It was by all rights a beautiful sight, but the invitees couldn't help
feeling deeply disturbed.

Later, an investigation was launched into the sudden fall of Quiquitto Village, but no information was forthcoming. Given its out-of-the-way location and the eerie circumstances of its demise, very few people passed through the place, and soon it fell into obscurity. Even the hamlet's original name was lost to history, and the few who knew of its existence called it only by the name penned in the journals of those unfortunate discoverers: "The Bleached Village."

EPILOGUE

"Master, I'm back."

"Ah, welcome back, Minnalis." "Welcome back!"

When I returned to the cabin where the others were, I found that Kaito had used the power of his Lust sword to alter space. I could see Quiquitto Village below me, as though I was walking on air. It was very peculiar.

Master and Shuria both greeted me with a smile. Sloth was lying on the floor, and Lust was perched atop him, pulling playfully at the straps of his clothes. And in the center of the room lay Leone and her party, unconscious.

"All righty, that's done!" said Shuria. "Now our little latecomers should stumble upon the children in the woods quite nicely!"

"So this is what Lust's Toybox can do," I marveled. "It's quite impressive."

The scene I was looking at appeared to reflect reality perfectly, and Shuria was waving her finger, pushing groups of monsters around the forest, closing off routes by felling trees, making sure the group of people headed for the village took exactly the route we wanted.

Thanks to her, we had managed to spend these last three days without anyone finding out what we were up to.

Master's Lust sword allowed him to set up an area and enact certain rules within; for example, allowing me access to the powers of his soul blades. The cost of doing so was to provide as much blood as the girl's fickle whims demanded. According to Master, this was relatively light as far as the Swords of Sin went.

Sloth's power, on the other hand, was almost unfair. For the cost of a single cursed item, he could set up a "workshop," wherein the laws of nature could be turned on and off as he pleased. Unlike Lust's power, nothing could resist these effects; Master told me that even the evil dragon had been slave to its laws.

But the way I saw it, it seemed like Master's Swords of Sin simply broke the rules.

"Did you have fun, Minnalis?"

"Yes, I did. All that's left is to clean up."

I walked over to Leone. There was still one thing left to do.

"This is the end, Leone. Good-bye."

I drew my knife, but just as I brought it down toward Leone's neck, Master grabbed the blade to stop it.

"…Master? What is the meaning of this?"

"What are you talking about? I can't let my partner in crime do something stupid, can I?"

"What's stupid about this? Leone is our enemy. She skirted the contract and hid this village from us. If we hadn't uncovered her deception, we wouldn't have been able to do any of this. She tricked me!"

"You're right. I usually get what I want via threats, so I'm not used to honest negotiations. I should have been more careful and checked for loopholes. It's my fault."

A few drops of blood from Master's palm dribbled down the edge of the blade.

"Why are you trying to stop me?! Leone's our enemy! She interfered with our vengeance! She deserves to die!!"

"Then do it with a calm heart and a steady hand, Minnalis. Yours are shaking."

I gasped, and Master seized that opportunity to flick the knife away from me, sending it spinning across the floor. I fell to my knees in shambles.

"Wh-why…?"

Why were tears streaming down my face? It just didn't make sense.

"Listen to me, Minnalis. We've done what we came here to do. She can't stand in our way any longer, so there's no reason to kill her."

"But… But…!"

But she was our enemy. She had to die.

"Even when Leone sought to stay your hand, she did it without resorting to force. She might have been deceitful about it, but she cared about you."

"But… But!!"

Leone was my enemy. She needed to die. Even if I didn't want to do it. Even if my hands were quivering.

"She's our enemy… She…has to die…"

"She's too good for this world, that's for sure. A naive fool who can't bear to see me acting in anger. Even I can see that, and I'm not the one who's known her since childhood."

I know she only cared about me. But even so…!

"She's our enemy! I have no choice! She needs to die!!"

I shook my head madly from side to side, when suddenly Master grabbed my cheeks in his hands.

"Minnalis!! Listen to me. You always have a choice. Nobody's forcing you to kill. Don't be silly!"

I tried to wrest myself free of his grasp, but he didn't let me go.

"I made that mistake already," he said. "I didn't know what I wanted. I didn't know what I should do. And by the time I did, it was too late. You don't know how many times I've been forced to think back to that day, wondering how I could go on living after the mistake I made."

Master closed his eyes, his pain clear to see.

"You haven't made that mistake yet. If you kill, don't hesitate. And if you hesitate, don't kill."

He spoke, never breaking our gaze for a moment.

"Minnalis. It's okay for this to be the end. The people who upended your life are all gone now."

Those words were the finishing blow.

"...It's not fair," I said. "How am I supposed to kill her now?"

"If you can ask that, then you're in a much better position than I was."

Master sighed and shrugged his shoulders, giving a dry smile.

It just wasn't fair. In that moment, my strength left me.

"Hug me, *Kaito*. Please. So tightly I'll break. Stroke my hair, touch my cheeks. Tell me what a good job I did. Tell me how important I am to you."

"Of course. You're my irreplaceable partner in crime. You did so well. Your vengeance was sublime. Let it all out."

"*Sob...* Waaaaaaaaaaaahhh!! Aaaaaughhh!!"

It was like a dam spilling forth. My tears, my wails, I couldn't hold them back. My heart, my body, my emotions were completely out of my control. I was like a baby, crying in Master's arms.

"Oh, Minnalis. What am I going to do with—?"

"Finally showed me an opening, son."

"Hurgh! Gh?!"

"...Huh?"

At that moment, a figure had crept from the darkness like a shadow and planted two poisoned daggers in Master's back.

As painful as it was to admit, I had let my guard down. With my vengeance exacted, I thought that I could breathe easy, just for a moment. I felt the poison enter my system from the two blades lodged in my shoulders. It was like being crushed to death by a boa constrictor.

The poison first forced Lust and Sloth back inside me.

"Hwah?! No, no, I still wanted to play!" "Aargh, what a bother…"

Then the toybox I had created with Lust's power dissolved away, and the cabin returned.

This poison…it's the Wine of the Holy Grail! This is bad…very bad…

"Gordo… You— *Ack?!*"

As soon as the Swords of Sin were dismissed, the Curse of Saints hit me at full force. Blood sprayed out of me as if a hundred little blades had sliced me at once, and a paralyzing pain ran through my body. The Wine of the Holy Grail nullified intrinsic abilities, and there was also a second poison that made my arms and legs go numb. Since the drawback of using Lust was that my resistance to status conditions dropped, it was more effective against me now than ever.

"Ho, so you've heard of me, young lad? Still, I must confess, I didn't expect you to…fight…back…"

Gordo slipped to the floor, my Soul Blade of Beginnings stuck straight through his heart. But there was no time to waste. If he had access to the Wine of the Holy Grail, then there was only one person who could be responsible…

"Master!" "Kaito!"

"Stay alert! Draw your weapons!"

But it was of little use.

"Stream of Water: Avalanche. Prison of Water: Submergence."

"Wha— Ugh?!" "Eee—ah…gh…?"

A torrent of water flattened the walls of the cabin. Not a second later, a bubble appeared, encasing the two girls with no way out.

"Metelia!" I yelled, recognizing the spells. "What are you doing here?!"

In answer to my shout, an echoing voice rang throughout the forest, as pure and clean as a running stream.

"Tee-hee-hee. Oh, my dear Kaito. I've finally caught up with you," it said, as a figure stepped out of the trees.

Her hair was the color of the sea, as smooth as roiling waves. She was beautiful specimen of a woman, yet she was shrouded in such an aura of such incorruptible piety that any and all improper thoughts perished with a single glance. Her robes were flowing and white, and the head of her porcelain staff was trimmed with stars, like the night sky. It was the holy priestess, Metelia Laurelia, said by all to be the most gifted of her line.

"Oh, Kaito. It's been such a long journey. You don't know how far I've come."

Soft words fell like treacle from her lips, while on her face shone a smile that would charm the heart of even the most abstinent priest.

"Come, Kaito. Let's see this story restored to the proper path. The way it was always meant to be."

The Wine of the Holy Grail was a closely-guarded secret of the Church. Only a priestess like Metelia could create it, and aside from the fact that you couldn't store the poison for very long, it had no weaknesses or drawbacks to speak of.

Why is she here? Why?! I thought she was in the See, conquering the

Coffin of the Undying! She shouldn't even be allowed outside while that damn archbishop is still out and about!!

I knew that using the Swords of Sin transmitted my location to her, something I had been doing continuously for the past three days. So I had expected the Church to send somebody to investigate sooner or later, but not her, and not so soon.

And this power…it's like she's conquered the dungeon already! Dammit, and I'm in no condition to fight…

I had never been in a worse position. I was suffering the drawbacks of both Sloth and Lust, I had just been stabbed in the back twice, I was paralyzed, with no access to my soul blades, and I had used up the last of my mana maintaining the Blackwheel Workshop. To make matters worse, both Minnalis and Shuria were out of the picture. They clawed at the walls of their prison, but I knew that the technique Metelia was using wouldn't break down so easily. The walls were made of compressed water and were more solid than any cage of iron or steel. Not even sound could escape from inside it.

Metelia, however, showed no sympathy for my plight and continued talking.

"Ahhh, Kaito. You're hurt… I'm so sorry. It's all because of my own weakness. If I had only been stronger, then things wouldn't have had to end the way they did, and *my Lady would have had no need to restore this world.*"

"What?! You mean…you still have your memories?!"

"Why, yes, of course. Each memory of you is etched deeply into my heart, thanks to the blessing of Lady Lunaris. You and I are special, Kaito, as arbiters of Her will."

"…What? What do you mean?"

Ignoring my confusion, Metelia wiped the tears from her eyes and crossed her arms over her chest, as if holding something precious very close to her.

"I must apologize. I really, really, must, Kaito. For allowing you to be hurt again. You've suffered so, so much, and it's all been my fault...because I was too weak to stop it. It must have been so difficult...and I was powerless to even be by your side. I must seem so pathetic."

"Metelia..."

She wept openly, brushing aside the tears to no avail. I detected no trace of deception in her actions; it seemed she really did only care about me. Yet I couldn't suppress the smoldering flame of doubt that arose in my chest.

"Why...," I began. "Why did you betray me? Why did you kill me? What did you stand to gain?"

It was an answer I had long sought. Metelia wasn't like the others, who'd hounded me across the land in the year following their betrayal. After casting the Curse of Saints upon me, she had been content to leave me alone. Even at the very end, she didn't lay eyes on me. She just clasped her hands together, eyes closed, and prayed. All my other former party members were possessed by unbridled hatred, but not her. It didn't make any sense.

"...I do not think I have ever betrayed you," she replied.

"Wh-what?! How could you say that?! You sealed off my strongest weapons and declared me an enemy of your god! What do you call that if not a betrayal?!"

But Metelia shook her head.

"That was all to *save* you, my dear Kaito. You had been taken in by the demon lord. It was a necessary step toward capturing you and purifying your soul."

"Purifying...my soul?"

"Yes. And so I followed the guidance of my Lady Lunaris! The hero and the priestess are to be joined in holy matrimony; it is the way things must be!"

"What are you talking about…? Explain yourself!"

"That is what Lunaris wishes, and so that is the way it must go. There is no reason to doubt, no reason to fear! Tee-hee-hee!"

She spoke as if possessed. A deeply unsettling feeling rose from the pits of my stomach.

"Can I tell you a secret, Kaito? Sometimes, I don't like the things Lady Lunaris tells me."

A voice from the past rang in my ears. A pier at the edge of a silent lake, in the depths of a forest bathed in stars.

"When I talk to Her in my dreams…she scares me. It sometimes feels like she's forcing me along a path I don't want to go down. I don't want to stop thinking. I don't want to stop worrying. And sometimes that makes me feel like I'm not fit to be Her priestess…"

The Metelia I knew never used her revelations as an excuse. She never took them as oracles, even though they literally were. Whenever she would convince others to follow her Lady's will, she did so with her own words, using her own logic and her own emotions. She'd burdened herself with hardships she didn't need to take and was hurting because of it. She'd been in so much pain, for so very long.

"…You're not Metelia. Who are you?"

"Hmm? Who else would I be?"

"Metelia would never tell me there's no need to worry."

"…Huh?"

She seemed genuinely surprised by my words.

"Metelia never wanted people to offload their decisions to faith. Was that all a lie?"

"A lie? Uh…ah…no…I…that's not what I…"

Metelia suddenly got all panicked, but there was no time to press the initiative. I felt my hear straining to beat, and then everything went all blurry.

Shit...the poison...I can't resist it any longer.

"M-Master!!" "You'll pay for this!"

"What?! *Prison of Water: Swirling Tides!*"

Minnalis and Shuria had taken advantage of Metelia's lapse in concentration to push through the walls of their bubble, but there was another stage to the spell. The sphere of water changed into a serpent and wrapped its body tightly around the two, pinning them in place.

"...Please don't interrupt when my darling and I are talking."

"Urgh...gh..." "Hgh...ugh..."

The rope of water tightened around the pair's necks.

"No, stop!" I yelled.

"Don't worry, Kaito. I won't kill them. I know how they leech off your life force like the parasites they are. I'll keep them alive... for now."

Metelia's moment of disquiet swiftly passed, and Minnalis and Shuria both fainted. When she looked back at me, her smile was as firm as it had been just moments before.

"That's right. There's nothing to fear. I simply need to cleanse your wicked heart that has been seduced by evil."

When she said that, the scene of my death flashed in my mind.

"Krh...!!"

"Oh, don't worry," she said. "It won't require anything so...drastic as last time. That tragedy only needed to be performed once. It's time to start again, Kaito! Become the hero you were always meant to be and cleanse this world of evil!"

"...And what makes you think I'm going to do that again? What do you think got me into this mess?"

"Oh, Kaito. What a sad, lonely man you are. But it's okay, I'm here. I have already laid out everything you must do. This time, I will be able to support you. This time, we can find happiness together."

Metelia smiled broadly, as though she were in a dream. It was a look all the more terrifying given the vile things she was saying.

"Spit it out, Metelia! What are you trying to do?!"

"We're going to start over. You shall save the world from the demon lord, defeat the princess, and live happily ever after with me by your side. To that end, Kaito, I must ask that you return to your world for a time."

"Return...to my world?"

"Yes. And in your absence, I shall tidy up this world for your return. I shall rid it of all that wishes to prey on you. The princess shall become nothing more than a powerless puppet; the demon lord an incompetent pawn. Everything shall be made right for you. And then, and only then, will I call you back to this world. This time, we won't need that ragtag group of fools the princess arranged for us. It shall be just you and me against the world, as Lunaris intended."

"...You...you're insane! You're just going to send me back and forth like that?! How many lives are you willing to sacrifice?! Do you think I'm just going to sit still and let it happen?!"

"There's no need to worry. You have a kind heart, Kaito, and I would not do anything to cause it distress. Since you have not yet been tainted by the demon lord, you can return freely the way you came, and this jewel of mine will substitute for the offerings required to open the portal, for it contains the soul of the immortal Lichie, the dungeon boss of the Coffin of the Undying, as well as the hundreds of souls he imprisoned therein."

"Wh-what?!"

She produced an orb, glowing with a purple light so dark as to be almost completely black.

"This is fate. This is the will of Lunaris. Why else would you have used Sloth and Lust at this exact moment? The pain of Lust is that it makes you susceptible to all status conditions, and the pain of Sloth forbids you from enacting any and all magical influence. It pains me to say this, Kaito, but you no longer have the means to resist my sending ritual."

Metelia began channeling mana into the stone, and a seven-colored magic circle spread out beneath me.

"I'm so sorry, Kaito. It's all because of my weakness that you've been forced to endure so much misery. But upon returning to your world, all those painful memories will be washed away. I'm heartbroken that you won't remember me, but I swear to create so many more pleasant ones upon your return."

The patterns around the circle looked just like the ones in the royal summoning chamber. The light that enveloped me was the same light that first brought me to this world.

"W-wait…hold on… Stop this!!"

It was all too fast for me to keep up with, but I managed to pick out two points. She was sending me back to my world. And upon doing so, I would lose my memories.

"Parting is such sweet sorrow, my dear Kaito, but we shall exchange our vows upon your return. There are many things I must do in the meantime to ensure that our story reaches its proper ending."

"No…stop. I'm serious. Don't do it!"

Fear and anger gripped my heart.

"Don't do it! Don't do it! Don't do iiit!!"

How could I go back to my old world now? How could I forget it all now? What was there for me, now that everything was gone? How was I meant to live in a world without friends, without family, and not even know why?

It would be nothing but a joke. A sick joke!

"Stop it!! There's so much more I want to do here!! I can't go back like this!! I'm not finished!!"

Though I felt ready to blow a fuse, I couldn't move a single muscle because of the paralyzing poison.

"It's okay, Kaito. You can start all over again. Forget everything causing you pain and grief and return to this land as the hero you were always meant to be. This time, I will be by your side always, and you'll never have to feel lonely again. Instead, we will share in each other's happiness, for ever and ever."

"What are you trying to do?!" I yelled. "Why are you doing this?!"

"Why? Why, Kaito, that's obvious."

She extended an arm, stroked my cheek, and parted her crimson lips.

"Because I want you, Kaito. No matter what else happens, no matter what the Goddess has in store for us, that will never change. Even if I walk the path laid out for me, the love that spurs me on is real. Mmmh."

"Mmph?!"

Before I could act, she pressed those soft, moist lips against mine.

Then, I felt a sensation I had not felt since the first time I came to this world, and the connection between me, Minnalis, and Shuria was severed. The world twisted around me, and all the colors blended into one.

It was like I was swimming in mud, tumbling through space until I couldn't tell which way was up anymore. As I fell helplessly, a dark, shadowy hand reached out of the blackness.

"Stop it!" I shouted. "Go awaaaay!!"

It passed through my skin, clutching something inside me that I knew I couldn't afford to lose. Its nails scraped off the layers, tearing it all away, shred by shred.

"Gaaaaaaagh! Stop iiiiit!!"

With each missing layer, I sensed myself feeling less. Becoming less.

"Those are miiiiine!" I screamed into the void. "Give them baaaaaack!!"

No matter how painful, no matter how nauseating, those memories were mine and not for others to touch!!

"Aaaghhh! Ghaaaaah!!"

It felt like someone was rooting around in my brain. I clutched tightly to whatever I could, so that nobody could ever take it away from me. These were things I swore never to forget. That I *could* never forget!

"Gh…gah! Hah?!"

With that single purpose in my mind, I spent what felt like eternity falling through space, before experiencing the sensation of crashing through glass and landing hard on my back. The noise sounded so distant and faded.

"Eeeeek!!" Wh-what happened?!" "What's with his getup, is he a cosplayer?"

The oppressive warmth of my surroundings gave way to a crisp air I had missed. Yet I lacked the strength to even open my eyes.

"They're…mine…you can't…take them…from me…"

Still, I wrestled with the shadowy hand in the confines of my own mind. If I let my mind wander for an instant, I would forget everything. I would forget all about xxxx, and xxxx, too. I still remembered, even now, the names of all those who'd killed me, and the feelings of vengeance I cultivated.

"Grrraaaaaaaaaaaagh!!"

I would never forget what xxxx did to me.

I would never forget who killed my friends and family, and took everything away from me.

Let go! Let go, let go, let go!! It's mine and you'll never have it!!

"L-look, he's in pain and covered in blood! Somebody call an ambulance!" "Shouldn't we call the police? Who knows what he's up to!" "Calm down, I'll go get a teacher!"

I held onto that thought with all my strength. I couldn't let them take any more. And yet...

"B-brother...?"

At that moment, I heard a voice I'd wanted to hear for so long. To my hazy mind, it sounded little more than a whisper, but it struck through to my very core all the same. My mind completely empty, I raised my head and saw a familiar classroom filled with familiar school uniforms. Yet more than anything else, it was the sight of *her* that gripped my vision and refused to let go.

"...No... No, you can't."

Smooth and glossy black hair that fell to her knees, tied with a blue ribbon at the height of her thighs. She looked older than I remembered, and taller, too. I thought I'd never see her again. I had resigned myself to it. But I had seen her many times in dreams, each one a needle in my heart.

"You can't do this to me... You just can't..."

Everything I swore I wouldn't forget. Everything I'd carved into my heart.

It all fell like sand through my fingers and disappeared when I took one look at her face.

"It's just...not fair."

As I blacked out, the vision of my little sister Mai entered through my helpless eyes and took up residence in a dark, empty space.

I watched Kaito disappear through the gate, then closed the portal with a contented smile. He was safe. Back in his own world, where for now he would stay.

Ahhh, Kaito. Kaito, Kaito, Kaito.

Wait for me. I shall cleanse this rotten world and call you through once more. The demon lord, those parasites who follow you around, and everyone who ever tried to hurt you will be gone. Then, there will only be me left to welcome you back.

"Hee-hee-hee. I can't wait to go on a journey, just the two of us..."

Just imagining that day brought a smile to my face and put a spring in my step.

"But first things first, I have to take care of these two..."

"Sorry! I can't really let you do that!"

"Wh-what?! Who's there?!"

I spun around, searching for the source of the sudden unfamiliar voice. Behind me was a woman, standing as though she had been watching the whole time, floating in midair. Her shoulder-length hair curled tightly at the tips, and she wore a habit that looked *deceptively similar* to nuns of the Church. She chuckled, a mischievous smile on her lips.

"...A Demilich? Some old agent of the Church, turned to heresy? Or perhaps a wraith, the ghost of some poor fool who sought to impersonate our number. Return to the land of the dead, foul spirit. *Purify!*"

I unleashed my spell, and a white light enveloped the phantom. I couldn't let any wandering specter interrupt my mission. However...

"How rude. I'm not a ghost, thank you very much. Besides, you *stole this off me."*

"What?!"

My spell had no effect on the woman. She just stood there, grinning back at me.

"What manner of creature are you?!"

"You know, I sometimes wonder that myself. Anyway, I'd better be taking these four with me before something happens. Oh, and I'll take those two as well. Thank you!"

"Not so fast! Come back!!"

"Sorry, too slow!"

I fired off an Aqua Lance spell, but before it could connect, a large hole appeared in the ground, taking all six people in the cabin with it.

"Well then, buh-bye! ♪ I hope everything goes okay with your plan and all! ♪"

"Come back!!"

But the chuckling woman disappeared without a trace. The only ones left in the cabin were me and Gordo's corpse.

"Rrrrrrrrhhh!! I can't even trace the teleportation spell! Why is there always someone trying to get in my way?! I just want to be together with Kaito for ever and ever!"

I gave a long, deep sigh, as if exhaling my very soul. There was only one thing for it. For now, I would need to head back to town and come up with a plan. Kaito was in his own world, so no one could touch him. Even those parasites could no longer sustain their connection to him across the rift between worlds. I didn't care who that woman was, as long as she kept her foul hands off Kaito.

Thinking about it that way, I returned to town, only to receive a message so perfectly timed it had to be mocking me.

The See was under attack by demons.

STATUS

Kaito Ukei   Lv1

Age 18 • Male • Human

HP: 1,245/9,345   MP: 340/8,140 (8,569)

Strength: 4,264   Stamina: 5,364

Vitality: 6,545   Agility: 5,587

Magic: 2,137   Resistance: 4,547

Intrinsic Abilities: Soul Blade▽, Auto-Translate
Skills: Unarmed Lv 15, Track Lv 34, Stealth Lv 53, Enhanced
Senses Lv 22, Divine Swordsmanship Lv 29, Air Step Lv 65,
Godfoot Lv 31, React Lv 25, Control Body Lv 39, Control Mana
Lv 42, Meditate Lv 32, Imperial Intimidation Lv 12, Natural
Healing Speed Up Lv 33, Martial Arts Lv 22, Iai Strike Lv 45,
Notice Lv 72, Carve Lv 31, Fishing Lv 5

Status: Afflicted (Condition Resistances Nullified, Influence
Nullified, Memories Locked)

Soul Blades: 64 unlocked, 24 locked
Swords of Sin: Envy, Lust, Sloth: Unlocked
Pride: Locked - Required Experience Points: 300,000
Greed: Locked - Required Experience Points: 300,000
Wrath: Locked - Required Experience Points: 300,000
Gluttony: Locked - Required Experience Points: 300,000

Unallocated Experience Points: 318,554